Sing and Shout

A novel about the music industry

# SING AND SHOUT

# A NOVEL ABOUT THE MUSIC INDUSTRY

Jim Cozens

BELLEW PUBLISHING
London

First published in Great Britain in 1994 by
Bellew Publishing Company Limited
8 Balham Hill, London, SW12 9EA

Copyright © Jim Cozens 1994

The right of Jim Cozens to be identified as Author of the Work has been asserted by him in accordance with the Copyright, Designs and Patents Act 1988.

All rights reserved. No part of this publication may be reproduced, stored in a retrieval system or transmitted, in any form or by any means, electronic, mechanical, photocopying, recording or otherwise, without the prior permission of the publisher.

ISBN 1 85725 066 4

Phototypeset by Intype, London
Printed and Bound by Hartnolls, Cornwall

# Acknowledgements

In acknowledgement of those who have contributed to the making of this book, without which my expensive word processor would indeed have been a waste of money.

I would like to thank Julie Morgan for her help and encouragement; David Croft for three lifetimes of ridiculous gigs; Gill Croft for not murdering David, for reading the first draft and laughing for reasons other than spelling mistakes; Catherine Styron for guiding me around Nashville. Special thanks to Suzie Burt for rescuing the unsolicited first draft from the Bellew waste-paper basket, cajoling me into finishing it, editing it, and then cranking the production machine until the book finally came to life.

This book is dedicated to optimism and great songs.

P.S. The soundtrack album for the book will be available as soon as somebody returns my call.

# Up Front

Without doubt, getting a record deal is one of the most difficult things anybody can ever attempt. It is an epic struggle of desperate passion, an extra-long-distance, heavyweight, mud-wrestling, marathon race through a swamp full of armed crocodiles. It would be an Olympic event, but they don't allow blood sports.

But the music business is the door to fame and fortune for the rock-and-roll generation. Anyone who ever bought a chart record, anyone who played in a school band and drove them nuts at the sixth-form dance. Anyone who was at the dance going nuts. Rebels and weirdos, the beautiful, the brain-dead and the hopelessly romantic. Anyone who failed an exam, hated school and would rather saw their own leg off than play rugby.

This makes record companies very popular with every right-minded adolescent who left school wondering how to make lots of money without doing any actual work.

Some get record deals. But then some people win the football pools and that doesn't really count either.

Some get over it. Some grow up to lead normal lives, raise children and find their niche in one of life's sensible provinces like medicine, politics, banking, military service or major crime.

Some don't.

# 1

A car clanked its way slowly through the south-London traffic. It was old, rusty and suffering from chronic depreciation. It contained twenty-eight cubic feet of assorted musical equipment, two squashed people and just enough space left over to make it rattle. The windscreen wipers flapped forlornly, smearing drizzle and grease back and forth in a most unhelpful way.

The driver braked sharply to avoid the car in front and was hit on the back of the head by a microphone stand. He described his feelings with the usual monosyllable having to do with sexual reproduction and shoved the offending stand back into the exact position from which it would get him several more times before the journey was over.

'Do we really need all that gear to do these poxy gigs?' he complained, rubbing his head and gazing into the mirror at the mountain in the back.

'You always say that,' said his passenger, 'and then you bring out that three-ton bass rig that looks like a block of flats.'

'I'll have you know that bass rig has the best sound that money can buy.'

'You didn't buy it, you made it. You made it out of iron girders and reinforced concrete.'

There was an incriminating pause and the passenger turned his attention back to the A-Z, squinting at the pages in the strobing street light.

'Precisely,' said the wounded bass player. 'It is a total custom job with a sound you cannot buy.'

'And a weight you cannot lift.'

The car slithered dangerously up to a set of traffic lights and the mike stand punctuated another expletive.

'People come up to me after gigs and tell me what a brilliant sound it is, bearing in mind the unconventional appearance.'

'I notice they don't hang around to help you lift it into the back of the car.'

'They may be discerning, but they're not stupid.' He wound down the window and tried to spot a street name. 'Where, precisely, is St Paul's Club?'

'It's off this street somewhere; we'd better ask someone.'

They pulled into a petrol station, but the man behind the glass just shrugged so they drove another three times round the block before they found the club right behind his garage. The car bounced up a rutted track, splashing in and out of the puddles. A semi-dilapidated Victorian building showed a light in a fourth-floor window. They parked the car as near to the front door as possible, dashed in out of the rain and went to find someone in charge.

'We're the band,' said the band.

'You're late,' said a toothless old man as he showed them up four flights of stairs to the dancehall.

'You haven't got a lift or anything I suppose?' said the bass player, breathing hard.

'No, mate,' said the man.

'Shit!' said the band.

# 2

Jules Charlie sat as still as possible on the leather sofa, trying not to make embarrassing farty noises. He felt distinctly out of place.

The Artists and Repertoire department of a record company is a fortress with walls of steel and secretaries trained by the SAS, and CBA Records was particularly well defended. After years of constant bombardment by cassette-lobbing, would-be pop stars, they had developed a highly-refined siege mentality, together with some amazingly cunning ways of dealing with the problem.

Jules was familiar with most of them.

The first thing they try to do is ignore you to death.

In Jules's opinion there were only two ways to get an A&R man to return your calls: kidnap his family or become the managing director of his company.

Failing these, the best you can hope for is to develop a sympathetic relationship with his secretary, which is defined as one in which she does not actually laugh out loud when you give your name.

The second thing they do is try to persuade you that you really don't need to talk to the A&R man at all and that, if you send him a tape, he will listen to it and let you know what he thinks.

This one ranks right up there with 'the cheque is in the post', but it still works like new. Every week, some luckless employee gets to log each of the fifteen hundred or so cassettes that turn up and send the A&R man's carefully considered reply from a carefully considered heap of identical letters, all of which say 'Thank you for sending your tape, but we feel that the material does not suit today's market needs.' Very groovy. It's like being balled out by a speak-your-weight machine.

Jules had been sending tapes and talking to speak-your-weight machines for as long as he could remember, so this was a red-letter day.

He looked about him. The CBA fortress turned out to be a not very impressive bunch of offices in the West End with a distinctly pre-war feel about them. Definitely Dad's Army. The ceilings and walls were a shade of nicotine and there were crates littered about containing files and cassettes as though they were in the process of moving offices. Through a hole in the lino by his feet he read a faded newspaper which had the headline, 'Peace in Our Time' and a review of Cliff Richard's debut single.

He had no idea why he had been summoned. He didn't know anyone in the company and he didn't remember sending them a tape, at least in the recent past, let alone what songs might have been on it. 'A meeting,' the girl had said. 'What about?' he had asked. 'I dunno, I'm just a temp,' she had said. 'Can I have a word with him?' he had asked. 'He's in a meeting,' she had said. She had obviously had basic training.

An A&R man calling you to arrange a meeting was like a surprise tax rebate or snow on Christmas Day. It just did not happen. Not in Godalming anyway. But happen it had, and there he sat. Buttocks clenched.

Thirtyish, tallish, fairish and English, Jules was ill-disciplined in mind and body. Out of rational control, his hairstyle said it all. It would have been a sort of Billy Idol spiky look, but the various regions of his head refused to co-operate in the matter. The top part usually got it right but the sides took on their own direction and the back part was just not interested at all.

It was nearer Coco the Clown than Billy Idol most days.

His body was more of a loose alliance than a federation. He could never rely on any of that, either. His shoulders were too round, his bum too big. His nose had once tried to kill him by blocking up both nostrils while he was asleep. For years it went on. Waking up every morning with a mouth like the Sahara Desert. That was when he had developed an addiction to nasal spray and had to dry out under medical supervision.

He had blundered through his schooldays in a perpetual fog. Academia was obviously out of the question; nothing that had ever happened at school made the slightest sense to him except playtime, and the most that could be said for his achievements on the sports field was that they were consistent with the level of his enthusiasm. Which was zero.

With the onset of puberty, and having observed the pulling power of a guitar-playing acquaintance, he had decided to join a band. OK, he couldn't actually sing or play an instrument but, other than that, it was, he thought, a brilliant plan. Guaranteed homework-free popularity. This was a key decision in his life.

After much posing with a tennis racket miming to records, he had saved up just enough pocket money as to be so pathetic that his parents eventually gave in and bought him a Spanish guitar. Earlier in life he had had a genuine 'Beatles Guitar'. In reality, it was a genuine ukulele made of genuine red plastic with a photograph of the Fab Four on the front along with their simulated autographs, but his mother had sat on it and so that was no good.

So Jules, with more optimism than talent, began his quest in the mistaken belief that playing the guitar would make him attractive to girls. He wanted fame and wealth, of course, but most of all he wanted Rosemary Stacy to fancy him.

## 3

It was 11.45, or first thing in the morning, as it is known in the music business. Jules had been waiting for an hour and a half.

'Coffee?'

The question drifted across the room from the secretary, an attractive, jean-clad girl with a good deal of wild blonde hair, dark-brown eyes and defensive glasses, who seemed to spend the whole time answering the phone and saying, 'I'm sorry, he's not in yet, can I take your number and I'll get him to call you,' while not writing anything down.

'That'd be great. Black, no sugar please,' said Jules, glad of a break in the monotony. In fact Jules hated black coffee with no sugar, but he had an idea it made him more mysterious.

She took off her glasses and smiled at him. 'Have you come far?'

'Godalming.'

'Oh... Traffic bad?'

'I came on the train, actually.'

'Oh.'

The phone rang again and there was a brief pause in this sparkling conversation while she planted the glasses back on to her nose and delivered her line to another hopeful caller.

Jules tried a new tack. 'Is he always this late?'

'Who, James? Yeah.'

'Doesn't he work in the mornings?'

'No, he doesn't come in in the mornings, he doesn't work in the afternoons.'

He smiled.

A noise that started in the stairwell rumbled up the corridor and finally crashed into the office.

'Hi, James,' said the secretary.

James Deek breezed straight through without noticing Jules.
'Good morning Glenna, any messages?'
'Nope ... Oh yes, there was one, apparently your family has been kidnapped.'
'Likely story. Did they leave a number?'
'Yeah, here.' She followed him into his office.

James Deek wore a black leather jacket, a black t-shirt and black leather trousers with the words 'Kick Ass' stencilled on the back pocket in black. His dark hair was pulled back into a ponytail which rather exaggerated the size of his nose. A definite mistake. As a rule if a nose is taller than a person it should not be exaggerated.

Apart from his appearance, he was very similar in most respects to Jules. Roughly the same age, he too possessed a red plastic 'Beatles Guitar', although, not having encountered Jules's mother, his was still intact. He liked to think of it as an investment in the memorabilia market, but it revealed a murkier past. He too had mimed to records in front of the mirror, he too had wanted to be a star, he too had reached out for his dream, but bitter frustration had addled his brain and warped his values.

Working for CBA had begun as a ploy to get his own record deal. Get inside the company, he'd thought, make friends with all the right people and, at the right moment, reveal yourself to be a brilliant but undiscovered artistic talent. The company would be amazed, they would thrust him into the limelight and he would take his rightful place at centre stage.

On his first day on the job as a talent scout the managing director had asked him into his office and said, 'I hope you're not one of those glory-seeking bastards who only joined the company to get your own record deal.'

The gaff was, as they say, blown. Since then he had found that every single employee was trying to pull the same trick, including the managing director. Stalemate. He took it very badly. Frustration led to anger, which led, in the end, to a perverted desire to get rich and screw the world.

As it turned out, A&R work came quite naturally to him and he achieved great success in his career. Over ten years he'd never signed a band and had, therefore, never made any mistakes that lost the company any money and, consequently, he had never been fired. He was now widely regarded as one of the best in the business.

'And there's this guy here to see you, says you called him,' continued Glenna, pointing into the outer office.

'I did? What about?'

'I have no idea, James. I wasn't here yesterday; you got Francis to call him.'

'What's his name?'

'Jules Charlie.'

'Oh, I remember. He was the one that sent that tape to Mike Delta; he said it was brilliant and I had to get the guy in and sign him.'

'Just like that?'

'Just like that.'

'Outrageous.' Glenna peered at Jules through the crack in the office door. 'What's he like?'

'Who? Mike Delta? He's the managing director; you must remember him.'

'No, this guy.'

'I don't know, I haven't listened to it, but if Mike says sign him, I'll sign him. If there's any comeback, it'll be down to him. I have witnesses.' He walked back out of his office to where Jules was waiting.

It has been said that the first few seconds of meeting a person are the important ones, and that all of the billions of following seconds are used by people to convince themselves that the impression they got at the beginning is, in fact, true despite any actual evidence that might crop up later.

Jules was aware of this, and had prepared himself for this testing moment thoroughly. He had a brilliant opening line which had nothing to do with the weather or the traffic and it was at this moment that he rose to meet James Deek, speak his line and become his friend for life.

'Hi...'

'Listen Jules, I'm just going for a dump. I'll be back in twenty minutes. Glenna will make you some coffee.'

Jules's friend for life wandered off. The meeting was not going quite as well as he had hoped.

When James Deek returned half an hour later with the smug look of the recently relieved on his face, he beckoned Jules to follow him inside.

The office was a tip. It was large, with two Georgian sash windows, but any sense of space and light had been smothered by ten years' worth of accumulated junk. An ancient desk was piled high with cassettes and back issues of *Music Week*, three of the walls were covered in shelves crammed with more of the same and the fourth was decorated with the obligatory dozen or so gold discs, most of which were twenty years old. The only new thing in it was a stereo system with very large speakers which were standing on the floor and therefore covered in junk like everything else.

Jules attempted his entrance for the second time.

'Hi!'

'Hi, Jules. Come in, come in. Great to see you. Glad you could make it. I haven't seen you for bloody ages.'

'Er, no.'

Er, no? Great line. This still wasn't going quite right.

Deek's voice went up several decibels as he yelled out of the door. 'GLENNA, GET US SOME COFFEE, WOULD YOU! God, she is beautiful. I could give her a youth opportunity. Now, Jules, let me get right to the point. We've listened to that tape you sent us and I want to tell you, mate, we think it's bloody brilliant. It's got everything in it that sells units. It's got a groove a mile deep; is that a sample, by the way? Anyway, every hit has got to have like a real depth to it. When I was producing that stuff I did for Blam before they were really big, I always insisted that the track had to be at least foundation level if not lower. Anyway, you've stuffed more depth into one of those tracks than there is in this week's entire Top 100, so no worries there, but the words mate, the words. I'm speechless. Well, I mean, there are so many of them. You would not believe the crap that comes through this office. I tell them time and time again, I don't care what anyone says, a hit has got to have at least twenty-five words in it. Believe me, I know the business. I tell you, mate, your stuff is dynamite. It is wall-to-wall, floor-to-ceiling, surefire, total-scenario tax torture. We are talking Grammies, we are talking major dosh. It looks like a hit, it smells like a hit, it is a bloody hit and I want to sign it!'

Deek finished his machine-gun monologue with a flourish and slumped back into his chair.

Jules was confused. His mind reeled. This is simply not what A&R men do. Wondering if he'd missed a vital negative in the sentence, he rummaged round the back of his mind, but nothing in his experience had prepared him to cope with being offered a record deal by an illiterate megalomaniac on material he couldn't actually remember. In fact, now that he came to think about it, he realized that nothing in his experience had prepared him for being offered a deal on any pretext.

He rallied his thoughts and tried to decide how to play the situation. He half-remembered seeing an advert in which this guy got offered a record deal over the phone, went into the kitchen, opened a can of lager and when he came back to the phone, the deal was twice as big. He only half-remembered it because when he saw it he got so depressed he immediately went to the pub and had quite a lot of lager himself, although he was so pissed off he made sure it was some other kind of lager just to make a point. Anyway, since this was the only image he could bring to mind, he decided to be cool, go for broke and make his demands.

He looked James Deek straight in the eye, and there followed a short but meaningful silence. Then there was a five-minute burst of screaming and sobbing, which Jules later described as enthusiastic, but was in fact hysterical. The odd intelligible bits included sentences such as: 'Please, please give me a deal,' and 'Yo, baby! We're really gonna kick ass now,' and 'Yes, yes, I'm going to be famous.'

And finally, 'Where do I sign?'

So much for cool. It's a terrible thing when you can't trust your own mouth. The deal was signed before the screaming had died away, and so a star was born.

# 4

The Portsmouth-bound train rattled south through the Guildford tunnels and emerged once again into a deluge of rain. Jules gazed out of the windows as the shaggy, dark-grey clouds scraped over the North Downs and shared their watery wealth with Godalming.

Opinion is divided about Godalming, nestling as it does in the valley of the embryonic River Wey. People from south-east England think it's hilly. People from Scotland mutter about pimples and molehills and people from Norway think anything that flat isn't natural unless it's made of water.

Jules thought Godalming was hilly. He liked the view he got from his living-room window and he presumed that since the view looked downwards then his living room must be on top of something. He thought it was a hill.

Godalming is not really a town. It used to be a town, but the by-pass took away the passing trade and it sort of fell asleep. Now the by-pass has its own by-pass and it's almost comatose. Nevertheless, if you like sleepy places it has much to recommend it.

The disputed hills are fringed with tall trees, which stand against the sky behind the church in splendid silhouette on a summer's evening. The meadow has cows and the allotments have people. The streets are the usual muddle of ancient and modern architectural styles but the overall effect is so pleasing to the eye that you can tolerate having to pay close attention to avoid getting run over by traffic that wants to annexe the pavements.

The train was not crowded. It was only five o'clock, and the tidal wave of the Network South East lemmings had not yet begun in earnest. He stood up and pulled his jacket down from the rack as the train screeched and slithered into Godalming Station. It stopped and he jumped out.

He ran through the rain, out of the station and across the road with one hand over his head and the other on the large envelope safely lodged in his jacket pocket. He headed for the pub. The peculiar events of the day whirled around his head and he felt an urgent need to tell someone about them. That someone ought to be Frog.

Frog was not his real name. His real name was Neil Drinkwater, but Neil Drinkwater is simply not a good name for a rock star. He and Jules had debated it at some length. What with Sting, Fish, Edge and Slash they felt that monosyllables were definitely happening, but all the really good ones seemed to have been taken. Jules wanted 'Horse', but Frog took exception to that as he felt it reflected badly upon his voice.

Not having a better idea, they settled for 'Frog' because he'd once kept one as a pet. A pathetic reason. He meant to change it when he thought of a really good one, but he never did. So there it was.

Frog and Jules had been friends for a long time. They had first met at school but, while Jules was pining after Rosemary Stacy, Frog was developing a reputation for romantic achievement beyond his years.

He was unusually tall by the time he was thirteen, and his dark complexion and worldly eyes gave a totally false impression of wisdom and experience for which girls seemed to fall heavily. Usually going out with three or four of them at the same time, most of them older than him, he was occasionally implicated in rumours about some of the younger teachers. For a long time Jules hated him as a matter of principle.

Frog took up playing the guitar to keep out of trouble, but it wasn't until they had both left school that the two of them got together and started to experiment playing stuff together. They rehearsed in Jules's bedroom every day for two years, playing old Beatles songs and speaking with confidence about what they would put on their first album. Three sets of neighbours moved house.

They went on to play a lot of gigs together over the years, most of them appalling, all of them for no money, and so it seemed to Jules that Frog should be the first to know about his record deal.

He ran up the steps to the saloon bar of the Batsman. Frog was *in situ*.

'Hi, Frog, want a drink?'

Frog replied in the affirmative, as was the tradition.

'Now there's a revolution in entertainment thinking. I will have a drink, now you mention it, but I shall refuse to enjoy it until you tell me why you're being so smug.'

The Batsman used to be an 'old buggers' pub, in which two resident old buggers sat on their own rinsing their false teeth in two pints of bitter of an evening, all cosy at the formica-topped bar. New owners had converted it into a friendly, bustling sort of a place and Frog and Jules spent an evening there from time to time.

The two old buggers didn't seem to mind. It's quite possible they never noticed. They still sat at the bar rinsing their teeth and clearing up the glasses at closing time in exchange for a free pint.

Frog took a slurp from his pint and looked as though he was enjoying it despite his threat.

Jules slurped his own. 'Frog,' he said, 'how long have we known each other?'

'About fifteen years, I think, give or take. You're not going to ask me to marry you, are you?'

Jules held firm to his conversational plan. 'And in all that time what subject has occupied our most secret and drunken conversations? What prize have we sought? What goal? What, in other words, was the very point of our existence?'

They both raised their glasses, took a large gulp, raised a hand and chanted in unison, 'To be musicians.'

'Quite. Which, in its purest form,' Jules went on, 'means getting pissed, getting laid and getting so amazingly rich that we'd never have to do any real work again.'

'Tacky but true.'

'So what if I were to tell you that I had struck gold. Hit musical pay dirt. Made "The Big Gig"?'

Jules increased the power of the smug look to factor ten.

'Bloody hell, Jules, you haven't got us a residency at the Holiday Inn, have you?'

'Bigger.'

'Cruise gig on the QE2?'

'Small potatoes.'

A completely stupid expression lodged itself on Jules's face and refused to move on despite repeated application of the beer glass from the friendly end.

'Well, what then?'

'I . . .' – Jules paused for effect – 'have been offered . . .' – more effect – 'a . . .'

'What? A second-hand Volkswagen? What? I'm going to kill you, Charlie, if you don't stop pissing about and tell me immediately what the hell is going on.'

'A RECORD DEAL!'

The words burst forth with such gusto he threw his drink into the air and fell off the barstool.

'AAAAAAAAAAAAAAAAAAAAAAAAAAAAAAAAA AARGH!!!'

It had been a good day for screaming and Frog screamed a second-part harmony for good measure. They jumped about the bar.

Jules did his 'odd' dance in a victory celebration.

Jules's odd dance was his trademark. The trademark of a total non-dancer. It involved locking up every joint and stiffening every muscle until the body was one big plank of wood and then hopping earnestly from foot to foot approximately in time with the music. It was particularly effective when he was holding a guitar.

When the noise and the general back-slapping had died down and Jules had received elementary first aid and been allowed back on to the barstool, he said, 'I gather you approve then?'

'I am, without a shadow of a doubt, so surprised that I may well buy the next round.' Frog waved vigorously at the barman.

'Not that I don't think you richly deserve it, of course, Jules, but how the hell did you do that?'

Jules shrugged an 'it was inevitable' kind of a shrug.

'Bloody hell, Jules. This is, well, great. Immense wealth, massive house in Weybridge, yes, I think it is definitely a good career move, what can I say? Suckmuck-bloody-doo Jules, check it out and do the deal!'

'I've signed it.'

Frog looked concerned. 'This is not so good, Jules. What did you sign? You always said you wouldn't sign anything without checking with a lawyer.'

'Yes, I know but that was when no one was offering me a deal at all. This is different.'

'I'll say it's different, Jubaluba. You always maintained that you were not a prat, but now we know for a fact that you are!'

There was a moment or two of serious reflection on the perils of signing stuff without the benefit of legal advice, but eventually the idea of being a megastar reasserted itself and the conversation started up again along more comforting lines.

'Well, I'll be buggered,' said Frog. 'You've got a record deal after all this time. So what is it? What do you have to do? What do they have to do?'

'Tell you the truth, I'm not at all sure. You see, I got a phonecall last night from a guy called James Deek at CBA asking to see me this morning, and when he finally turned up, he gave me a long speech about how brilliant my songs were and then offered me a deal on the spot and I, er, signed it.'

'Outrageous. I should back a few horses if I were you; this seems to be your lucky day. Which songs were they?'

'Well – and this is going to sound really weird – I don't remember.'

'You don't remember which songs?'

'I don't remember sending any at all.'

'Don't be a pillock, you must have sent him something. Didn't he say?'

Jules frowned. 'No, actually, he didn't and it was impossible to tell from anything he said about them. As a matter of fact, I couldn't understand much of what he said at all. For a while I thought he was talking in Esperanto but it turns out everyone talks like that up there. Apparently, to him the stuff sounded like the San Andreas Fault with lyrics.'

'Didn't you ask?'

'I didn't like to.'

Frog paced up and down in front of the fireplace, stepping over the dog. 'Hang about, Jules, we must be able to work this out. When did you send the tape?'

'Well, about six months ago, I did a big mail-out of loads of stuff to loads of people. He must have got one of those.'

'There you go then, what was on that?'

Jules scratched his head. 'The thing is, I did lots of different versions, you know, one for the publishers, one for the record companies, one for management companies and a different one again for individual artists. I did at least fifty copies of one sort or another.'

'OK, OK. So you must have sent him the record-company version then.'

'Er, not necessarily. You see, when I'd finished all the tape copying, I couldn't remember which was which and I couldn't be bothered to listen to them all again, so I sent them out at random in the end.'

'Good grief!' Frog smacked the palm of his hand on to his forehead. 'Obviously "prat" is too limited a concept here. I shall have to move you up to full moron status. How could you be so dumb?'

'Well, I didn't think it was important. I imagined that anyone taking an interest would at least mention which one they'd had. Actually, I didn't really expect anyone would call me anyway.' Jules finished his drink. 'They never do.'

'So why do you send them to people?'

'Don't knock it, it worked.'

Frog cheered up. 'Hey, listen Jules, who gives a stuff? In any case, you got the deal, whatever it is, so let's stop worrying and celebrate. Tomorrow we'll go and see this lawyer friend of mine, "Brian the Brief", and see if he can unravel this contract and find out what you've signed. So... what do you think? Do you think we should... do you fancy a... have we got time for another...'

'Drink?'

'I thought you'd never ask!'

'Rock and roll.'

# 5

CBA was a highly respected record company with twenty-five years of musical history behind it, walls full of gold records, faded stars, jaded stars, frauds, awards and a Radio One documentary to boot. Its founder, Cagg Brown, had also been the founder member of the Purple Insect Revival, a band which was signed to Parlophone in the days when record deals were available at the Post Office.

Their second single had bombed completely, and they were subsequently dropped by the label but, after a particularly good party at the offices of the record company, Cagg woke up all rumply in the back seat of his Ford Consul somewhere in Leeds having half-inched several thousand copies of it and stashed them in the boot. Later that day he made a killing at the local market selling them off as placemats, and he developed a taste for retail trading.

After a year of flogging off the redundant stock of every record company in the UK, he made enough money to go legit. and moved his offices from the Ford Consul to a lock-up in a naff bit of Chelsea. His really big break came when he signed a local pub band called Pretty Millie and bought the publishing rights to all their songs for a thousand pounds. The band were hungry and Cagg was greedy. The perfect combination.

Their one and only hit, 'Winter Time', had been released forty-seven times in different countries and gone Top Five every time. Up until last year, it had sold fifteen million copies and grossed twenty-five million pounds in royalties and sales. The band, on the other hand, have now spent the thousand pounds and are still doing gigs at the pub.

All in all, Cagg and Co. had a pretty wild time for about ten years but, by the end of the 1970s, the good times were more or less over. A short revival in the mid-1980s had slowed their decline, but CBA got into financial difficulties and were bought up by an American record label who were in turn merged with and taken over by another, and then another. Now the whole lot had been bought by Lousengesmind Inc., a New York firm of accountants, and Cagg, having no interest in speedboats or hot-air balloons, had dedicated his life to finding out whatever happened to his old Ford Consul.

Meanwhile, the wheels had kept turning at CBA. They still had the name and one or two acts, but it had been several years since they'd had a significant hit and it was beginning to look as though they were going to have to release 'Winter Time' for the forty-eighth time if they were going to meet the financial targets set by the parent of the parent of the parent company and avoid any embarrassing questions about their activities.

James Deek was not particularly worried about targets. He knew that all you had to do was manage the back catalogue, avoid any costly signings, and life would go on.

He was, however, slightly worried that, having faxed him to sign this guy Jules Charlie, Mike Delta was not present for the following A&R meeting. The board room filled up with the usual collection of post-weekend debris, but no MD.

'Does anyone know where Mike is?' Deek looked around hopefully to see if anyone showed any signs of life. They did not.

'Mo?' Deek directed his attention to Mo Gordon, one of the three A&R executives.

'No idea at all. He was supposed to be back yesterday to meet those guys from the American company when they stepped off the plane at Heathrow. I had to go myself in the end and they were quite revolting.'

He wrinkled his nose. Mo had a perfect face. A perfect nose, a perfect mouth, dark, perfect eyes, a brow so noble you could die and long hair that tumbled beatifully down over broad shoulders. He was not given to spoiling the effect with unnecessary facial expressions, but he had been deeply offended. He aborted the wrinkle before it could cause permanent lines. Women adored his face, which was something they had in common.

'Right. Where are they now, by the way?'

'Well, they're over with the Obnoxious Brothers' tour, so they're in Liverpool tonight for the first date and then tomorrow they're due to call in here before they disappear back under the large New York rock from whence they came.'

'Hey, Mo, this is the 1990s, right, if you want to make it, you have to break a few hearts, sell your soul, you know, pawn your personality. They didn't get to be multi-millionaires by being nice to people.'

'So I noticed.'

'OK, well, if Mike's not here, he's not here. We'd better start the meeting without him. So everybody... what's new?'

Everybody spoke at once. For purely historical reasons the collective noun for A&R people is a Deafness. Babblings, shrieks and whines rose as if to prove the point.

Deek put his hands over his ears. 'Hold on, hold on, don't shout, it's like a heavy-metal gig in here. Sheena, what was that again?'

Sheena Pristien, head of promotions at CBA, was talking the loudest. 'I'd just like to know who the bloody hell this guy Jules Charlie is that you've just signed for so much money?'

There was general, vocal agreement around the table.

'It's just that no one told me anything about him,' she continued. 'We do need a bit of notice, you know. Contracts tell me that he's been guaranteed a single to be released in three weeks' time to coincide with our twenty-fifth birthday and then an album to follow three months after that, then three more albums over three years. I don't see how we can do the paperwork in three weeks, let alone shoot the video.'

Mo Gordon lobbed in to show solidarity with the general air of mutiny. 'Mike's gonna go crazy when he finds out. We haven't had a chance to discuss it. I haven't even heard the demos.'

James Deek began to feel distinctly uneasy. A&R meetings weren't usually like this. He went swiftly into his well-tested, sloped-shoulder posture. 'Hang about, it was Mike that told me to go ahead on this one. He said he was taking a personal interest because he really believed in it. You know how he pines for the good old days. Called me from wherever and raved about this Jules guy and then a fax arrived last Thursday telling me to get the bloke in and sign him up. Sandy will back me up, she heard him. I don't have anything to do with it. As a matter of fact, I haven't heard the demos either.'

Sandy nodded.

'Great!' said Mo. 'Bloody marvellous! Has anyone heard the demos? No? So, none of us has heard the demos, then. Hoo-fucking-ray!'

There was an interminable silence while this thought filtered through the confusion.

James Deek's uneasy feeling had worked its way down to his bladder. He was annoyed that he was taking the flak for Mike Delta, annoyed that he would probably have to cancel his lunch date to sort it out, and there was something else that was nagging him, but he couldn't quite put his finger on it. Something someone said. And then he remembered.

He looked at Francis from contracts. 'How much money, exactly?'

'I'm sorry?'

'How much money did we sign this guy for, exactly?'

Francis looked at the figures. 'Well, the contract was already drawn up when you sent him over, so it's not my responsibility to question the A&R policy. I don't care how much money you spend.'

'How much money, Francis?'

'Three hundred and fifty thousand quid.'

James wasn't sure how long he had been sitting under the table sucking his thumb, but he looked up suddenly to see everyone else peering down at him. Glenna was offering him the telephone handset.

'It's Mike for you, James.'

He crawled out from under the table, sat back in his chair and took the phone. He performed that peculiar bodily contortion that people occasionally do when they simultaneously stretch their neck while pulling their mouth into a sort of downward smile. He grasped the handset and tried to grasp the situation.

He took a deep breath. 'Mike! Hi, how are you? Good to hear your voice.'

'James! You sycophantic old paperweight, it's completely disgusting to hear yours! How's the meeting going?'

The call was obviously long-distance and there was an annoying delay on the line. He put the call on the speaker.

'Er, not too well actually, Mike. I was wondering, for example, where you were?'

There was a long pause.

'Hello, Mike?' said James just as Mike began to speak. He laughed a slightly hysterical laugh and stopped speaking. So did Mike. More silence.

'I was saying...' James began just as Mike's voice crackled up again. More apologies.

'SHUT UP, JAMES!' said Mike very loudly. 'Just shut up and listen for a minute. Have you signed Jules Charlie yet?... Over.'

Silence.

'Now, James. That means it's your turn.'

'Oh, right. As a matter of fact, I have, Mike, and that was another of my especially underlined points. We were wondering... er' – he surrendered to his mood and yelled impatiently at the telephone – 'WE WERE WONDERING WHAT THE HELL IS GOING ON, MIKE?!!'

Mike Delta ignored the panic. 'That's great, James. Listen, I want to tell you a bit about politics.'

'Mike, listen to me, we're in the middle of a major cock-up here. I have no budget and I suddenly find myself committed to a six-figure advance. I do not want a party political broadcast, you know what I'm saying?'

Mike carried on speaking. He spoke, James spoke. They stopped, they started. Silences and interruptions, and still no one understood a word of it. They carried on the conversational hiccups until James started shouting again and Mike hung up.

The phone rang again. This time the satellite was in the same time zone.

'That's better. You know, you should relax more, James, you're too tense. I'm relaxed, wouldn't you say? I've always tried to remain horizontal in what is basically a vertical world.'

'Mike, you are Mr Cool.'

'And I've tried to run the company along the same lines, you know, sign a few bands, make a few quid, go to a few parties, and generally hang out. One day, I'm in the office, next day, I'm here in Barbados catching a few rays. This is a good life, James. I like it. But you know what, it doesn't suit some people and those kinds of people worry me. Ask me who, James.'

'Er, who, Mike?'

'The kind of people I worry about are the guys who bury their heads in the in-tray, want to be out there squeezing cash out of the world morning, noon and party time. The kind of people that run other people's companies from their comfortable New York offices, are you catching my drift here, James? Because I can slow down if you want.'

'Perhaps if you got to the point.'

'Just listen faster. These are the kind of people that don't know shit about the music business. The kind of people that dump a guy after he's given it his best shot. These are the kind of people who brag about it in magazine interviews, James; these are the kind of people who really piss me off!'

'I can see that they might, Mike. Listen, is this leading somewhere, or is it, like, just for my information? Only I'm in the middle of this meeting.'

James glanced anxiously at his watch and around the room at the faint amusement on the faces of the team.

Mike carried on not listening at all. 'I would just like to read to you a small section from *Caribbean Billboard* magazine. Taken from an interview with our bigshot American parent chairman, Dwight B. Lousengesmind. Under the headline, "Judgement Day for CBA", it says this: "When I bought CBA, I knew that, although basically a sound company, there would have to be a severe shake-up in the top management. To that end, I have great pleasure in announcing that the highly respected accountant, Adam Upenshutup, will shortly be taking over as the managing director of the UK company." Are you getting all this, James?'

He was beginning to.

James put on his 'so what' voice. 'Hey, Mike, this is bad. I mean, I can see that you have had a seriously bad day businesswise, but what can I do? This is the 1990s, right? Companies gotta grow, chairmen gotta go. I think you should have seen the signs, Mike.'

'I'm touched by your sympathy, James, I knew you'd be upset. As for the signs, well, I see them now, James, I see them now. Or, to be more exact, I saw them last week when I bought this fuckwit magazine. You know, it's a strange thing reading your own obituary in the pop press under a jokey headline. It can make a guy really depressed, but I gotta tell you, man, I perked up no end when I called the office and realized that no one else knew, and you know what I did?'

A glimmer of light appeared on the eastern horizon of the dawn of realization.

'Call me sentimental, and I know I haven't signed a band in years, but I suddenly thought, this is it. My last chance to help the guys out, you know, before it's too late. So I thought I'd make a special effort before I go so that you would have something to remember me by, and that brings me back to where we came in. James, I want you to play to the meeting the demo tape labelled "Jules Charlie". It's on my desk. I'll hold.'

James looked at the others. 'I think Mike has lost a couple of deckchairs off his promenade. I'd better get the cassette.'

Mo said, 'It's not a bad idea, James, we need to know what we're dealing with in any case.'

James left the room and returned shortly with a cassette. He placed it in the player and pressed the play button. Everyone in the room was riveted. The tape played for several seconds but made no sound at all apart from a seemingly deafening hiss amplified at fifty watts per channel. The hiss continued for several seconds more and the audience began to get restless. James's patience ran out and he fast-forwarded a couple of yards and let it run again. Still the hiss. Another yard and more hiss. He picked up the phone once again. 'Mike, are you sure this is the right tape?'

Mike made a noise down the phone like someone trying to start a Skoda. 'Oh, yes, James, that's the tape all right.' Churn, cough, choke, splutter. 'The very tape sent to me six months ago just as it plopped through the letter box by some plonker who presumably meant to put some songs on it. I dare say he's still wondering why he didn't get a reply.'

Mike could no longer contain himself and he cracked up into hysterical laughter. 'Silly sod. We probably did reply. Not suitable for today's market or some such crap. Isn't that the best tape hiss you've ever heard? I'm really excited about this one, man. It's a hit, it's a fucking number one. I'm only sorry that I won't be there to take the glory, but you can have that, James, with my blessing. Hell, this is the 1990s, right? Sign the hits and split, that's what I always say. Give my love to Adam.'

More hysterical laughter pinged around the room from the tiny speaker in the telephone until it was silenced by a click.

James Deek tried a few more places on the dud demo and then gave in. 'Well, guys,' he said, 'it seems we have just signed some jerk who is the worst tape copier in the whole of the fucking universe!'

# 6

Jules's friend, Frog, is the kind of person who knows everybody. He gets on with everyone he meets. Takes a pride in getting to know all about them, all about their families, their hobbies, their pets and their problems, wives, mistresses, daughters. That kind of thing. People naturally seem to confide in him. If he hadn't been in the motor trade he would definitely have become a psychiatrist.

In truth, Frog and Jules made so little money at music that they clung to their day jobs if only to protect the sanity of their much beleaguered, occasionally understanding bank managers.

'You paid how much for a microphone? You two ought to take up bank robbery. We wouldn't lose so much money.'

As a matter of fact, bank managers were not the only people grateful for this consideration. The owner of the local music shop more or less depended on it for his summer holiday. People are often under a mistaken impression that sex and drugs are the only addictions associated with rock and roll. These days, kit-crazy, 'gotta havit' kids are far more likely to be offered a line of credit than a line of coke.

While parents worry about their kids getting into crack, the kids are down at the music shop mainlining on keyboards, getting heavily into drum machines and effects. On a Saturday afternoon, music shops everywhere are alive with the sound of teenagers test-driving well funky equipment and signing finance forms at a totally kickin' APR of 35 per cent. Both Frog and Jules were chronic gadget junkies and needed a lot of money to feed the habit. Jules worked at the local hospital as a porter but Frog couldn't stand the sight of blood.

Flogging motors was OK. He didn't much care for cars by now, but he did like the people. A combination of 'Come-to-bed' eyes and 'Let's-go-to-the-pub' feet and he seemed to know just about everybody in Surrey and Hampshire. Hence, within a day of the extraordinary meeting with James Deek, Jules and Frog were shown into the office of Brian (the Brief) Payedwell. A good mate of Frog's and a solicitor of no fixed moral values.

'So what do you think, Bri?' Frog perched eagerly on the edge of the settee.

Brian the Brief flipped through the pages of Jules's contract to give the impression that he'd already read it and was just checking for typos. 'First of all, you guys, I've gotta say that I'm not really into the music business, right, but, having said that, a contract is still a contract, right, and a deal is still a deal, and I know enough about both of them to be able to tell a dog from a box of chocolates.' He paused for a moment to slurp tea from a chipped mug and wipe his mouth on his sleeve. 'Now, you've said, right, that this Deek geezer has given you this contract and that you, blinded by temporary insanity, for the sake of argument, have signed it.'

'For, as you say, the sake of argument, yes, that's a rough stab in the general area of an approximation to the actual shape of things.'

'Julesey, you are a prat.'

Brian the Brief peered over the paperwork at Jules. He was a big man, not tall but very round. He had a round face and a round body which was around seventeen stones, which he liked to throw about. On this occasion at Jules.

'Ah,' said Jules. There isn't much you can say when you've been insulted by someone doing you a favour.

'But look, right, it's not as bleak as all that. I can see a few loopholes that we might be able to crawl through. I mean, we haven't given away all our ice creams. Have you read this contract through?'

'No. Well, not really. I got lost in the "heretofores" and the "thereinafters". I was rather hoping you would sort out the difficult bits, you being a legal man and all, but I got the impression that it wasn't all bad because of the bit about the three hundred and fifty thousand quid.'

'Three hundred and fifty thousand quid, are you sure?' Brian rustled the paperwork, hunting rapturously through the document for the relevant clause. After he'd found the bit about the money, made sure it was dated and signed, he put it back down and tried a new tack. 'Listen, Julesey, are you sorted out for management?'

'I was trying not to think about it at all, actually.'

Jules had had many experiences of management. They usually come in two categories: 'Groupies' and 'Greedies' and, after his brief acquaintance with Brian, he had a fair idea which category he fitted into.

Brian ignored the negative waves and went for broke. 'Well, there you go then. Problem solved. I can manage you, help you through the business side, stop you making any bad moves and you won't have to pay, right, for all this expensive legal advice on an "up front" basis.'

'I thought you said you weren't into the music business.' Jules cast a worried look in Frog's direction. Frog cast one right back. After all, he had seen himself in this role.

Brian plunged on. 'No, well, I'm not, you know, into it as such, right, and I don't want anything to do with all that creative malarkey. Your songs are your business, right, but it's a cesspit out there; you need someone to keep you clear of all the lumpy bits. Call it a favour, I don't want to see you get tucked up by some spotty-faced wally who calls himself an A&R man. What's that stand for again?'

'Artists and Repertoire.'

'Right.'

Frog took advantage of the interruption. 'I don't know, Brian, do you think you know enough about it? It's not like the legal profession, you know; "Thank you very much madam, you now have custody of the cat and visiting rights to the kids and, by the way, here's a bill for a million pounds." This is more like trying to win the pools. Years of filling in the coupon every week and finally going bananas when you win fifty pence.'

'Listen, Frog, have you read this contract?'

'A bit.'

'Well, I have and I think you should stop worrying about the fifty pence and start thinking more about the million quid. I buy records, right? I bought a CD by Dire Straits the other day.'

'Er, yeah?' Frog was confused. He only ever understood about 10 per cent of what Brian said, but then he always said it with such force that it was too difficult to disagree. This was, of course, how he had done so well in the legal profession.

'So, what's to know? All it is, right, is a bit of plastic that costs a quid to make and gets sold to the punters at £11.99. Do that a few times and you're rolling in it. It's a piece of cake. I don't know why I never thought of doing it before. I've got this mate who does a bit of the old DJ for hospital radio, right? All he's got to do is play it a couple of times and everyone'll want it. WHSmith will be drowning in pensioners trying to spend their Christmas bonus on it. The green-hair brigade will be desperate to get their hands on one to rescue their street cred. The Yuppies will take out a second mortgage so that they can get a signed copy for the coffee table and we'll be in the Isle of Man, right, drinking gin and tonic and counting the tax-free lettuce.' Brian laughed and slapped Jules playfully on the back. Jules fell playfully off the settee.

Jules clambered back up on to the settee and made one last attempt to get back to the point. 'I've lost track of this conversation. All I want to know is, do you think the contract is OK?'

'You leave all the worrying to me on that score, Julesey. I'll get all this stuff typed up, right, that we've been talking about, and I'll send it over to you tomorrow together with a contract for the management. I'll sort out the legal costs, so don't worry about that, and then we'll take this Deek bloke out for a fat lunch and sort him out too. They can't resist a curry at lunchtime, those music geezers. We're going to get our eight score draws here, I can feel it.'

'Great,' said Frog.

'Er . . .' said Jules.

# 7

The sun made a feeble effort to shine as Jules and Frog walked back to their car. It had been a very damp summer so far, with violent storms that had brought the traffic to a standstill and had everybody diving for cover in the shops, preferably the travel agent, who had long since run out of brochures about Australia.

Small dogs and little old ladies lived in fear of being washed away down the drains and Age Concern had recommended the wearing of life-jackets when shopping alone. The River Wey had broken its banks more often than a horse breaks wind and the local ducks had annexed the meadow and half of Waitrose's car park. The council had leapt into action and pencilled in a meeting to discuss lifting the hosepipe ban. It was that kind of summer.

The sun sailed out into a tiny bit of blue sky and a watery ray illuminated Frog's car as he applied the key to the door.

'Look, it's an omen,' said Frog, squinting in the bright sunlight.

'It's a con,' said Jules, looking skywards. 'It's going to piss down in a minute.'

'No it won't. Look, it's clearing up. I think it's going to be another scorcher.'

'Look, I'm not sure about all this, Frog,' said Jules, changing the subject.

'All what?'

'Well, since we left the house this morning, I have had seven offers of management. One from the milkman, one from the guy who sold you that packet of fags, the guy in the petrol station, the three blokes in that open-top car we pulled up next to at the traffic lights, and now Brian the Brief. I think it would be best if you stopped telling people about this record deal.'

'I am wounded, Jules.' Frog did his best wounded voice and gave a matching facial expression. 'People want to know this stuff; it's a good story, something to brighten a dull day, it's news. The public have a right to know. Can I help it if I feel a strong sense of duty to communicate with people?'

'I just think we should find out a bit more about it before we put the announcement in the *Godalming Bugle*.'

'Jules, if you want to succeed, you've got to think "media". I'll be honest, I think we should go national on this one.'

'Please don't phone your mate on the *Sun*. I know what you mean, but what if CBA change their minds or something, we'd look like a couple of total dork brains.'

'They can't change their minds. It's a deal. You've signed it and they've signed it, so what's the old suckmuckdoo?'

Frog had a vocabulary including many original words and phrases, which he scattered about his everyday conversation. Some said they had deep, mystical significance, some said they were simply the product of too much whisky, but by far the deepest and most mystical was 'suckmuckdoo'.

It could be used to replace any other word that he had temporarily forgotten, as in, 'Oy, mate, pass me the old suckmuckdoo.' It could be used as an expletive if you happened to drop the old suckmuckdoo on your foot. It could be used to disguise a word which might otherwise be too rude or embarrassing as in, 'How's all that business with your suckmuckdoo?' It could be used to clarify a tricky concept in a philosophical discussion as in, 'If a man does not come to terms with his, like, inner self well... suckmuckdoo, mate, that's what I say.'

But by far the finest example of its use, one which had definitely put it into the category of art, was its inclusion among the lyrics of one of Frog's rare songs, 'I Love You', the chorus of which went as follows:

> You love me, Babe,
> I love you.
> Suckmuck dooee dooee,
> Suckmuckdoo.

Frog pulled up outside Jules's flat. The two of them scuttled up the steps from the underground car park and jumped through the front door out of the inevitable rain.

It was a small, modern flat in a modern building which resembled a collection of tubes shoved into the hillside. It had huge windows in all directions, which gave it a Tardis-like quality, seeming bigger on the inside than the outside. It had a good feel, including the brilliant view from the living room. Jules loved it.

They fell inside and stood, dripping, in the hallway.

Jules glanced at the telephone. 'Oh look, I've got a message on the answerphone.'

'Hey. It might be a gig.'

'Yeah, one of Sherman Ritzy's luxury venues,' said Jules with heavy sarcasm.

Sherman was an agent specializing in dens of iniquity and tube stations all over London. He was also a twenty-five-stone annihilation drummer who did gigs for which volume and physical bulk were essential to avoid lynching. He occasionally offered them work, which they took if they were desperate, which was always.

He pressed the play button. It was not Sherman, but James Deek, who announced his presence in his best telephone-answering-machine style. 'Er . . . oh shit, er, hi Jules, this is James from CBA, could you give me a call when you have a minute? I have a few problems I need to go over with you. Talk to you later, man. 'Bye.'

'Well, what do you think, should we return this A&R man's call?' Jules gave Frog a mischievous grin.

'No, let's make the bastard wait,' said Frog, who made a certain gesture to the telephone and headed for the kettle.

While Frog clattered around in the kitchen, Jules rummaged through his collection of demo tapes. Years of effort were represented here in an untidy heap, all out of order, half of them unlabelled. When Frog appeared with the tea, Jules was completely surrounded by tapes. He held one up.

'Have a listen to this; I think I've found the tracks I must have sent him.'

He turned on the tape machine, loaded the cassette into the slot that swung out in that slow and sexy way beloved by Japanese marketing men, and belted it shut again in the unsexy and impatient way beloved by people who have better things to do with their lives than hang around all day getting turned on by marketing tricks.

A song leapt out of the speakers and happened all over them, all over the room, all over the flat and all over the flat above, which fortunately belonged to Frog. They both believed in the 'Engineer's Principle' which states that pleasure is in direct proportion to volume and that ultimate pleasure can be achieved only at the instant before the onset of profound deafness. The two of them bounced up and down from the seated position singing the odd line and waving their arms about, putting in the drum fills, until it was over.

'You know, Jules,' said Frog approvingly, 'I've always said "Perfect Dream" was a good song.'

'Thank you,' said Jules, without modesty. 'I know.'

'Are you sure you wrote it?'

'Of course I'm sure I wrote it.' Jules was indignant. 'I'm just not completely sure that I wrote it first.'

The whole of pop and rock music has descended from two or three good songs written by the end of the 1950s. So, thirty-odd years later, it's a virtual certainty that every new song is completely identical to at least half a dozen others, pretty similar to a hundred or so more, and roughly the same as all the rest. The best thing is not to worry about it and just make sure you have a good time.

'Another illusion shattered,' said Frog. 'I thought writers lived in attics crafting each note and spending a fortune on candles. Now you tell me that all you do is buy an old Chuck Berry record and nick the chords.'

'Does moon rhyme with June?'

'So much for originality.' Frog tried hard to look disillusioned but it didn't work. He'd been disillusioned years ago, so he just looked the same as ever.

Copyright battles do, however, serve the community by keeping lawyers off the streets. 'Where there's a hit, there's a writ,' as the saying goes. It conjures a bizarre mental picture of a well groovy judge sitting up there on the bench with his Sony Walkman on over his wig and singing out of tune in the specially loud voice people always have, bopping away trying to figure out whether 'Crash My Funky Motor' by the Prats is, in fact, the same song as 'White Christmas' by Irving Berlin. Or whether slipping a dominant fourth into the last chord and banging the lead singer's head against the drum kit has made all the difference.

'I am occasionally given to wonder whether your heart is really in this writing business, Jules,' continued Frog, in philosophical mode.

'I don't think you could call it a business, really,' said Jules. 'It's more like a cross between a nationalized industry and "Game for a Laugh".'

Frog suddenly looked at his watch in alarm. 'Hey, Jules! Look at the time. We'd better get on the case.'

Jules got up from his heap of cassettes. 'Right. I should call James Deek.'

'No mate. We're missing "Neighbours"!'

# 8

Show business in general is 95 per cent about coping with rejection. That's why people go nuts. You don't get into it in the first place unless you really like the idea of a load of complete strangers telling you how great you are. So it seems cruelly ironic that such an insecure breed should have to spend so much of their time getting dumped on by A&R men, producers, casting directors and the like, just in pursuit of a little reassurance.

By the time any would-be star reaches the desired celestial position, their ego is so shredded that they need at least an arena full of devoted fans every day just to stop them putting their head in the oven, and this is, of course, the true derivation of the hip and trendy muso expression 'bread head'.

Jules, for one, thought he had developed a pretty good attitude, by and large. He had survived his share of discouragement. In fact, he had so many rejection slips at home that he never needed to buy lavatory paper, but now he was just confused.

In the last couple of days, he had been offered a record deal, 350,000 pounds and seven different managers. This definitely represented a good week as far as he was concerned. On his personal scale of 1 to 10 for Relative Brilliance Quotient, it scored around the four million mark, but still there was something at the back of his mind telling him that all was not well.

Lying awake that night, staring at the ceiling he hadn't painted yet, he felt uneasy; something didn't quite add up. Jules turned over, closed his eyes and decided to tell the back of his mind to get stuffed. He fell asleep and dreamt he was swimming in chocolate that tasted faintly of Brussels sprouts.

# 9

The next day, at the offices of CBA, there was a thin film of calm tranquility floating on several thousand fathoms of deep panic. The day before, the Americans had called in to confirm the position about Mike Delta, to sack nearly half the staff and give a general kick up the donkey to those remaining.

James Deek had been promoted to acting MD, pending the arrival of Dwight B. and Adam U. in a few weeks' time. James was broadly pleased with the turn of events from a personal career point of view, but he was still very concerned. No one had yet owned up to the Jules Charlie situation and he therefore felt his grip on the situation was about as secure as the British Secret Service on open day.

For Glenna, it was business as usual. She was still telling phone callers all about James Deek being in a meeting and how, if they left their numbers, he would get back to them. The callers still believed her, except for the odd one who would make a noise like someone screaming into a bowl of porridge, and she would still say, 'OK, byeee', porridge or not, and move on to the next.

A trumpeting noise came from James's office as he yelled through the closed door in his best intercom voice, 'GLENNA, COULD YOU GET FRANCIS AND SHEENA DOWN HERE? I WANT TO TALK TO THEM ABOUT JULES CHARLIE, FOR FUCK'S SAKE.'

'RIGHT!' she shouted back in her efficient voice and then had to wipe bits of Chocolate Hobnob off her typing. She picked up the phone and dialled. 'Hi, Francis, James wants to see you about Jules Charlie, for fuck's sake!' she giggled. She redialled. 'Hey, Sheena, get down here right away. Tricky Deeky wants to see you about Jules Charlie. And bring your steel helmet. It sounds like a council of war.'

They arrived before she'd put the phone down. This was not

their usual, casual, anytime in the next half-hour style. The era of bunking off was now officially over.

James started talking before they'd quite finished arriving, something he always did when he wanted people to think he was on the case. 'Yeah, great, come in. Listen, I want to run this Jules Charlie thing by you again, see where we stand, what the options are, that kind of thing.'

'Where we stand is right in the farmyard, James. You'd better believe it,' said Francis, grinning the grin of one who has remembered his wellies.

James carried on. 'Look, I had a bike go out to Jules Charlie's place yesterday afternoon and pick up the real demo, you know, the one he meant to send in the first place, so we'd better give it a really good listen and see what we can do. You never know, it might be TFA.'

He banged the cassette impatiently into the deck and pressed go. He sat motionless for a few seconds while the first few bars of 'Perfect Dream' burst out of the speakers, then he jumped up, snatched it back out again and lobbed it over his shoulder on to a heap of similar cassettes in the 'not' corner.

'I knew it, it's crap!' he said, and slumped back into his chair.

'How can you tell from that?' said Sheena, who felt she must have missed something.

'Look Sheena,' said James, getting seriously grumpy, 'if you want to be in A&R you might as well learn how it's done. For a start, the cassette is black, OK? Boring! It's been done to death; everyone's doing black cassettes. You play the stuff, OK, it has its chance. If it works, it works right off the top. No second chances in this business, sweetie. This stuff really does not make me jump out of my seat, you know what I'm saying, it's shallow, it doesn't go anywhere and it has no lyrics. How many times must I say it? A hit has to have at least twenty-five words. Good grief, will anyone ever listen?'

Sheena slumped back in her chair as well in a gesture of sympathetic despondency. 'I doubt it, James,' she said, and made up her mind to keep her mouth shut and let James dig himself in.

James jumped up and paced around the office, legs on autopilot, staring at the ceiling. Back and forth, round and round he journeyed, stepping neatly over the piles of paperwork and cassettes without looking. 'OK,' he said eventually, to no one in particular. 'So now, at least, we know the situation. The artist is crap, the songs are even worse.' He paced a bit more. 'We'll have to dump him.'

'No can do, I'm afraid,' grinned Francis. 'If we drop the options the artist gets to keep the advance. High embarrassment factor, major losses. It's in the contract.'

James went into his Basil Fawlty impression with full sound effects. 'Oh, thank you, Mike, thank you so very bloody much! Why me? It's not my fault you lost your bloody meal ticket. I didn't do anything, I've been good. I bloody-well signed Blam for this company, doesn't that mean bloody anything?'

He got to the good bit, where he started to bang his head on the wall. The others watched him in amusement. He did this about twice a week, about something or another, and it was always regarded as a bit of light relief on a boring day to come and watch him.

'Well?' he said, turning to face them again. 'Come on, shit for brains, let's have some ideas, what the hell are we going to do? We can't use him, we can't dump him.'

'Hey, James, this is the 1990s, right; you'll get another job. That is if Dwight B. lets you live,' said Francis.

'What?'

James spun round mid-pace and flung his arms out in a mock crucifix. 'Oh, thank you very much, friend!' At this point the combined effect of shouting, pacing and arm-waving toppled his gyro. Continuing his left-hand turn he tried to do a complete 360 degrees and carry on in the original direction, but his brain, being preoccupied with rescuing his liver from the previous night's overindulgence, abandoned any attempt at co-ordination and the various bits of his body cut loose and set off on their own. The legs stumbled over a particularly large heap of papers, his head jerked round and his arms flailed as he lost his balance and put his other foot on to the mammoth pile of cassettes. The cassettes shot out from under his weight and hit the wall like bullets from a machine-gun, but still James refused to fall. Now completely out of control, he flew backwards across the office, hopping on one leg, passing his loyal staff on the way, crashed into the door, burst through it clutching at the air and landed on his back with a final thud at Glenna's feet. She leaned over her desk and looked at him in amazement.

'Get some bloody coffee,' said James from his recumbent position.

There was a five-minute break while the laughter and applause died down and James rescued his cool persona from the lavatory. Sheena tried another approach. 'Maybe we should just do what the contract says, you know, release the single and everything.'

'Are you crazy?' said James, getting back into his arm-waving but resisting the temptation to start pacing again. 'It's crap. Everyone will know that I signed it. I'll suffer total reputation failure. No one will like me any more.'

'That's OK; no one likes you now,' said Francis.

James tightened his lips and gave him a murderous look. 'If I go, you go too, Francis, remember that. No, we're missing something; there has to be a way out.'

The room fell back into total silence for a moment and then James suddenly started to look happy again. His face broke into his version of a smile and he thumped the desk and said, 'I've got it! I have the answer.' He stood up and risked a trip to the window. Arriving without mishap he turned to face them with renewed confidence and composure.

'We'll launch him, OK, launch him into deep space,' he said. 'Into the frozen wastelands. Lose him. Bury him. It's a brilliant plan.' He turned back and gazed out of the window as if in a trance. 'Comply with the terms of the contract, of course, release a single, certainly but, if we do it right, I guarantee he will not be back to trouble us for single number two. He will beg to be released.' He turned back to face them again. 'Boys and girls, I have a plan. A plan so cunning I may well get an award for it.' He put on another of his silly voices, ' "And now the winner of the award for 'Most Bastard Trick Played on an Unsuspecting Artist': James Deek, YEEEAAAAH!" ' He hopped from foot to foot in amusement while the others waited patiently to be let in on the joke. 'We'll bury him so deep he won't come up till he's fossilized.'

At that moment Glenna stuck her head round the door. 'Jules Charlie, Brian Payedwell and a guy called Frog to see you, James.'

James waved at her to indicate that she should show them through and the 'Godalming Three' shuffled in.

'Jules! Hi, great to see you.' James did the necessary introductions. 'This will be your manager. How do you do? Francis and Sheena. Yup, and this is Frog, yes? Hi Frog, I'm James and this is Francis and Sheena.'

James settled back into his big chair and prepared to have a good time. He really loved a theatrical moment and he was going to make the most of it. 'Jules, Jules, we were just discussing your career, you know, and how we should handle it and we were kicking around a few ideas and stuff and we think we've got a great angle, you know, a really positive direction in marketing terms. To get down to specifics, which, I think you'll agree, is, you know, why we're all here, we have decided that the best thing right now, to launch you, as it were, in the market, both here and internationally, would be to enter you for the Euromission Songfest.'

# 10

It is said that, after a long illness, live music is now, in fact, totally dead. This is not strictly true. In late-twentieth-century south-east England, there are still loads of places to play live music as long as you're cheap and don't mind paying for your own beer.

Over the years, Jules Charlie and Neil 'Frog' Drinkwater had managed to get a gig in just about every pub, club and wine bar within a radius of fifty miles several hundred times over. Indeed, they held the record for the greatest number of performances of 'The Wild Rover' on a single night while earning less than twenty-five quid.

The trouble was, they ran the whole thing less like a business and more like an ongoing accident. Consequently, at any moment in time, including the money they earned in their day jobs, they could only muster the price of the next round between them and only see about two gigs ahead.

Closer examination of their lifestyles showed fairly clearly what the problem was. Frog, being a randy bugger with the CTB eyes and the LGTTP feet, spent most of his money on beer or on his ridiculously complicated love life and could only be regarded, therefore, as normal, but Jules had a far more depraved habit. He gave money away to recording studios.

Studios are warm and wonderful places. They're full of the one feature most likely to attract the average male faster than Sharron Stone in a tight T-shirt on a wet day. Knobs and buttons.

What they don't have is people who talk loudly over your songs, fall over your gear when trying to get to the cigarette machine and drunks that lean on you and ask you to play 'Stairway to Heaven' or 'Bohemian Rhapsody'.

'You mush know it, mate. Lishun, lishun.' The eyes close, the left hand clutches the air by the left shoulder, the right hand arcs crotchward. 'Dang, dang, dang, dang, DANG,' sings the star, 'dang, dang, DANG, dang, dang, DANG. Come on, everybody knowsh that one. Whashat really good bit?' More squinting. 'She's been dry-y-ing her hair-air-air for e-vuhhhhaaaa! It's bloody briwyant 'at one, you should learn it.' And so on.

But studios are expensive. It is cheaper to hire an aeroplane. The exchange rate is about 20 pub gigs to one day in a 24-track studio and Jules could spend money in a studio faster than Imelda Marcos in a shoe shop and was, at the last count, committed to 375 world tours worth of credit.

In return for all these years of compulsive recording he had, it must be said, accumulated a fair collection of demo tapes which he would, periodically, copy up and send to record companies in case they felt like being good chaps and sending fame and wads of cash by return post so that he could pay the studio bill.

Now, world-class optimism like this takes a bit of denting. Nevertheless, Jules was depressed. Just when he felt that all his patience had been rewarded and it was finally safe to write 'I told you so' letters to anyone he had ever met in his life to whom he had hinted that he might be the next Phil Collins – which was everybody – several weird things had happened to take the shine off his moment of glory.

It was a month since the Songfest bombshell and no amount of protest had any effect. The more he whinged, the more James seemed to want it, and gradually the truth had emerged about his 'big break'.

He was fed up because his surprise signing to CBA Records had turned out not to be the final realization of hitherto undiscovered talent, pissed off to discover he was simply an innocent bystander in some lunatic act of revenge perpetrated by CBA's recently 'ex' managing director and bloody livid that the worst thing this person could think to do was to sign him to his former label.

Brian, on the other hand, thought it was a great idea. 'I don't know what you're worried about, Julesey, that's a brilliant show, that Songfest.'

# 11

The Euromission Songfest was in its enormously successful third year. Each year had attracted bigger audiences than the year before and last year they'd had a viewing figure of some one hundred and fifty million for the final.

Sponsored by the European Community Cultural Committee, it was run by MusikSat, a new, deregulated television company, and shown exclusively on satellite television. It was also a total rip-off.

Observing its phenomenal success, MusikSat had attempted to buy the rights to the evergreen Eurovision Song Contest, but the BBC had refused to budge and so they had gone into competition with it.

Twisting the arm of the EC for a bit of Eurocred was easy because the British were so firmly opposed to it, and the sponsors promised to deliver a bigger and better music festival in the name of European cultural unity.

Success was inevitable. With minimal tweeking of the formula, they produced the biggest game show on the planet.

In a televised 'song contest' it should be remembered that the significant word is 'contest'. 'Song' is a fine word. It's the word that catches the eye in the title, provides the theme, attracts the punters and the participants and so on, but songs and music by themselves only make good radio. Contests make good television.

Thrills and spills, confrontation, winners, losers, tears, laughter and cock-ups, this is good to see, in close-up if possible. This ghastly fascination with other people's lives makes soap operas and road accidents so popular.

This subtlety is not lost on the programme-makers, of course, but it is only subconsciously appreciated by the viewers – most people tune in only for the voting, after all – and it is wilfully ignored by the contestants. Which is why they tend to take them so seriously.

Some people have twigged it. They laugh into their beer and whine about it, but in all other respects, ignore such shows completely. This includes the entire British pop and rock industry.

But, of course, nobody makes television programmes for the people who don't watch them. TV companies might not be 'cred', but they're also not stupid. One hundred and fifty million viewers can't all be wrong. Mums, dads, grannies and grandads tuning in to enjoy the annual beano. Whereas, if a record company can get as many as two hundred thousand kids interested in their next hip single release, they think they're doing pretty well.

The problem is that grannies and grandads don't buy records and the kids don't watch the programme.

It's a stand-off. The record industry complains that the original show was frozen in time around 1965 and has no relevance to today's music scene, and so they ridicule it. The TV companies say that the show is very successful and won't change it. Stalemate.

They're both right, but it leaves writers and artists in the UK with something of a dilemma.

They stand to gain commercial success.

It is possible to achieve commercial success out of this kind of show. If you are lucky enough to win outright, you can ride the wave of publicity, mobilize the grannies and sell a few million records. But trial by some weird and wonderful international jury is not something that you could put much faith in, no matter how good you thought you were. Let's face it, it if hadn't been for Abba you'd have to say, on the evidence, that the chances were slim to bugger-all. On the other hand, you might just get on the telly.

What you risk is complete isolation from the commercial music industry, the very oasis from which you hope, one day, to drink.

Frog paced up and down the saloon bar of the Batsman as he and Jules practised the traditional musician's response to a bum deal and debated the relative merits of the Songfest and teeth extraction.

'Of course you'll do it,' said Frog as he passed by in the direction of the cigarette machine.

'I'm not convinced,' said Jules, who had finally realized that having teeth extracted wasn't as bad as he'd thought it was.

'You've got to do it, otherwise you don't get the three hundred and fifty thousand. James Deek is no fool. If you back out now it's deal off,' said Frog, passing by again towards the dartboard.

'But the bloody Songfest, Frog, I might die of embarrassment.'

'There speaks the "Wild Rover" Endurance Record-holder. Of course you won't die of embarrassment.' Frog came alongside his pint and drank most of it. 'How bad can it be? You probably won't even get selected.'

'What do you mean, won't get selected?' spluttered the champ. 'I'll have you know that's a great song, that is. It's got style, it's got integrity, it's got sincerity and loads of other long words in it as well.'

'Exactly.'

'Maybe we ought to enter something else.'

'Now you're talking.'

'Under somebody else's name.'

'Now come on, think positive.' Frog carried on pacing and doing his best to look as though he was thinking positively. He screwed up his face and headed back towards the cigarette machine. Some of the other people in the bar started to give him funny looks.

He stopped again and looked round. 'Have we got a song that, you know, is like a single line repeated over and over again?'

'Er, no.'

'Pity. Well, come on, let's write one. How long can it take?'

Jules gave up trying to ignore Frog and said, 'OK, OK, well, let's think of a title, then. Um... I know, I know: "Diddley Dang Dang, Zoing Zoing a Sputnik, Scrunge Bang Splat and a Smackety Dack Dack Dack!"'

Frog looked disgusted. 'Jules, you're not taking this seriously. Besides, it's too long. You only get three minutes.'

' "Diddley Smack?" '

Frog zeroed in on his pint again. 'No, look, less stupid noises and more, you know, actual words. Something that people can relate to, drawn from, like, a real-life experience.'

Jules took a quick mental survey of his life experiences. 'Right. Ummm... OK, how about "Shake Your Beaker, Baby"?'

'What's that supposed to mean?'

'I was playing Trivial Pursuit last night.'

'And that's it?' said Frog. 'Thirty-five years of life on the planet and the most profound thought in your head is a cheap sexual innuendo based on Trivial Pursuit?'

'Don't knock it,' said Jules, waving his empty glass at the barman. 'It might work, Triv's quite international, you know.'

'I dare you to write a lyric about love and the really hard question.'

' "No Dice?" '

'I hate you when you're being smug. Look, never mind the title, what we need is a really strong rhythm and bass part at 120 beats a minute. You know, Euro-pop.'

Frog started waving his pointed index fingers about and making noises like a steam train. 'Right, you do the bass,' he said and he wheeled off again en route to the dartboard making more noises and getting more and more enthusiastic. Jules decided that he'd had enough of being sensible and joined in. When they were particularly drunk, they used to do one of the Blues Brothers' songs with the dance and everything in their live set and they experimented with these two concepts for several minutes until they were completely out of breath.

The barman was not impressed. 'Oy! Do you mind?' he said, breaking the artistic spell and breaking wind simultaneously.

'Listen,' said Frog. 'My friend here is a world-famous songwriter and is composing a masterpiece.' He paused for effect. There was none.

'No, he's not, he's that daft bugger who keeps coming in here singing "The Wild Rover". Drives me barmy. Now drink up and piss off before I call the police and have you done for impersonating musicians.'

Jules and Frog drank up and pissed off.

'I don't think he realized the true magnitude of your talent, mate,' said Frog as they parted for their respective front doors. 'Who does he think he is?'

'I don't know,' said Jules. 'He looked like a Euromission Songfest viewer to me.'

# 12

In an office not a million miles away, the telephone rang. It was answered by a girl. She looked like the girl who answered the phone at the record company. In fact, she had once been that girl. She had been trained in unarmed combat with the rest of the A&R security forces, but now she had a different job. A good job but less well regarded, rating only 5 on the Industry Credibility Scale with a Call Return Quotient of about 3.5. That's just above managers of bands you can barely remember and just below artists whose second album hasn't sold very many copies.

The office wasn't really an office anyway. It was a thinly disguised horse box. A few bits of wood panelling and a couple of climbing plants but a horse box none the less. A bit sad and leaning slightly to one side. It had long ago sunk up to its axles in mud never to see its Thelwellian future, never again to cause traffic jams on the A25 on the way to the Bank Holiday gymkhana. Now it had finally come to rest outside the premises of Rock Green Studios. The love child of manager, entrepreneur and ex-hippy Darren Jenkins.

Rock Green was an stylish edifice reconstructed from the shell of a Victorian, brick-built lavatory block with some money that his accountant had told him to spend rather quickly, and for this reason, and much to Darren Jenkins's irritation, it was often referred to as the Shit Factory.

A lavatory block is not what you expect to find in the middle of the Surrey countryside, especially one that has been very tastefully converted into a recording studio. But a hundred years ago it had been a place of relief for the loyal workers of the Dorking Engineering Company Ltd. The owner, a New Zealander, had been plagued from childhood with piles and, therefore, placed a great deal of store in the provision of lavatorial comfort. So much so, that the rest of the building was extremely rickety and during the traditional half-hour break for Christmas Day lunch in 1923, the explosion of a particularly large Christmas cracker caused a corner of it to fall on to the revellers below, injuring several of them in the process.

The loyal workers decided that enough was enough and set fire to the rest of it as a protest. The next day, all that remained, standing proudly above the ruins of the factory, was the charred, but otherwise unscathed, lavvy.

And so it stayed, blocked and overgrown, with a peculiar aroma, until it was found by Darren Jenkins. Darren hadn't known the story about the Dorking uprising. He just saw it as cheap space and, although he was faintly amused by the irony of putting so much money into a lavatory, it never really crossed his mind to wonder where it came from. He wasn't known for a sense of history. In rock and roll, a sense of history means that you can remember where you left your pint.

He wasn't exactly a rock and roller, either. A qualified accountant, he had practised for a year or so until his enthusiasm for counting other people's money reached the point where he started putting it into his personal account so he could look after it while he was on holiday. His fascination for rock and roll didn't really go much further than an extensive record collection until he was standing next to a guy in a lift one day in 1968 who asked him if he could help decide what floor he really wanted to go to.

One short lift ride later and he was the personal manager of a rock legend. Darren wasn't exactly on the case. Not so much involved in the man's success as nearby, but if luck is what you need, he had just got lucky. Go with it, he thought, and to hell with the consequences. This particular legend died young, but not before Darren had made a reputation and a mattress full of undeclared, dodgy dosh.

Afterwards he got into this and that, becoming gradually more twitchy as the Inland Revenue closed in and no one could remember the artists he'd worked with, until eventually he ended up with the Shit Factory. Reputations may fade but the lavvy was there for good.

As the girl picked up the phone, he looked on in an agitated fashion, as well he might, since the last call had been from his bank manager requesting an urgent meeting.

'Rock Green Studios,' sang the girl.

Darren lit up a third simultaneous cigarette and tried to work out who was on the phone from the odd word that she uttered at her end of the conversation. He raised his eyebrows at her as she put the phone down.

'Another wanker,' she explained. 'He asked me if we made records and I said we did, in a manner of speaking. He said he wanted to do one for about three minutes and what would we charge for a quarter of an hour? I said that he should pop in and talk to you about it.'

'Great, great,' said Darren, putting his cigarette down in the ashtray together with the other two. 'You know we can't afford to turn any opportunity down. What did he say his name was?'

'Brian Payedwell. He's coming in later this morning.'

'Great, great.' Darren tidied his desk a bit. 'Um, perhaps you could phone round the record companies again and, er, you know, tell them we've had a cancellation, drum up some business, that kind of thing?'

She gave him a look.

Darren was given to making this particular remark when business was slack and the bank manager was requesting an urgent meeting. Studio owners everywhere are the same and studio managers everywhere have the same reaction when studio owners make it. Leaving out the rude words, it comes down to, 'Oh no! Not again!'

They know that the effect of this marketing ploy is twofold. It makes them about as popular with record companies as pension advisers, and lets the industry generally know that they haven't got a booking. Added to that, it has never been known to work in living memory because record companies don't choose the studios anyway, they only approve the budgets and book them on behalf of the people who do. The people who choose the studios are the producers and the more influential artists, but they don't put their telephone numbers in *Kemp's Directory*.

Darren didn't like it when his studio manager gave him that look. It reminded him of his wife when he came home late from the pub, and it made him nervous. He decided to make a strategic withdrawal. He crossed the yard and disappeared into his very expensive and currently very empty studio to wait for Brian Payedwell.

Brian Payedwell was not far away. He was sitting in the back of Frog's Montego with his feet up on the chair in front talking on his portable phone. Frog was driving and trying to look as though he wasn't the chauffeur, and Jules was waving his arms about trying to attract Brian's attention.

'Jules, what's all this windmill stuff about?' said Brian, putting down the phone. 'You're creating a draught.'

'Look, Brian, this session is going to take longer than fifteen minutes,' said Jules. 'I wish you would listen to what we've been saying. You sound like a total pranny going on about fifteen minutes. Please will you let us do the talking?'

'Look, right, I know it takes longer than fifteen minutes to cut a disc, I know that. An artist needs time to do the business, right? Although I have to say I don't know why. A three-minute track, right, a couple of practice runs and bang, it's all over and you've still got time for a cup of tea at the end. But this is what we call in the business game a "negotiating position".' Brian picked up the phone again. 'I'm not going in there giving away ice creams before we start, right, I'll talk a bit and listen a bit, let them talk it up a bit. They'll feel good and I'll have the deal I wanted in the first place.'

'I hear what you say, Brian,' said Jules, turning back to face the front, 'but you just don't know anything about it.'

'I've listened to you two going on about it for the last couple of days.' Brian started dialling. 'Nearly driven me bonkers. It's just business at the end of the day, right, and I'm good at that. Just trust me, I'll handle it. The way you go on about it, you'd think it was black magic. I've done a bit of homework, right, and I can tell you that if you don't do the business right, right, you get stuffed by them poofs in the companies. Why do you think you've been cocking it up all these years? I've got this mate who's done a bit of this music stuff and he's told me where to look for the shit, right, which is everywhere. So don't give me a hard time, I will do the right deal. I'll tell you this, though, I'm not going to let them talk me into more than half an hour... John, how are you mate, it's Brian, where's that bloody contract?'

Brian's monologue took a telephonic detour while he gave someone called John a hard time about a bloody contract. Frog peered about the lane for the secret entrance to the studio and, after a few abortive trips into other people's driveways, he turned into a farmyard with a caravan in one corner.

Brian unwrapped his legs from the furniture and they all clambered out.

'Hi,' said Jules, sticking his head round the office door. 'Shit Factory?'

The girl smiled.

'Great,' said Jules. 'I'm Jules Charlie. We called a few minutes ago.'

'Hi,' said the girl. 'Morgan Fairway. How do you do?'

The rest of the delegation squeezed into the horse box and introduced themselves.

'OK,' said Morgan. 'Darren's in the studio; I'll just let him know you're here. Would anyone like a cup of coffee?'

Everyone had just had one about ten minutes before in Brian's office, but they all said they would love one now and Morgan scurried across the yard and into the building.

It is a curious thing about tea and coffee, that it represents this dual carriageway of polite convention running through the countryside of life. If people drank it only when they actually wanted it, then nearly all the manufacturers would go bankrupt.

A few minutes later, suitably equipped with mugs of coffee, they were shown into the studio to meet Darren.

An hour after that, they re-emerged with Frog and Jules talking animatedly about effects, keyboards and who they would get to do the brass parts. Brian, white as a sheet, clutched the side of the building for support.

'Four days?' he said, to no one in particular. 'FOUR FUCK-ING DAYS?!'

# 13

James Deek sat in the restaurant nervously making dunes in the sugar bowl. He was waiting for Brian Payedwell. The Supreme Tandoori was an entirely standard Indian restaurant with dim lighting and outrageous decor and James loathed it. In fact, he loathed all Indian restaurants, but today he felt he could handle it because, for the first time in a month, he had a warm feeling about the Jules Charlie disaster.

Now that Mike Delta had gone from CBA Records, the story about Jules had done the rounds, echoing up and down the corridors of the music business. Now everybody knew. Everybody sniggered and James was totally miserable. The lawyers had investigated all manner of devious tricks to extricate him, including trying to classify Jules as An Act of God, but to no avail.

The scam about the Euromission Songfest was definitely a good wheeze, but it was months away yet, and anyway it depended on Jules being so appalled that he backed out voluntarily, and he hadn't shown any signs of that yet.

But that morning, he had had a call from Brian Payedwell asking to renegotiate Jules's contract and suggesting a lunch meeting to lay the cards on the table. James smiled to himself. 'Greed and stupidity,' he said out loud, 'I love it!'

A passing waiter, not long in the country, raised his eyebrows knowingly at James's unseeing gaze and scurried away to fetch the lime pickle and a bucket of water.

'James, you old bugger!' A large hand thumped James on the back mid-gloat and he nearly swallowed his tongue.

Brian landed on the opposite chair like a five-ton elephant. 'How do you like it here?'

'It's great,' said the lying Deek.

'I knew you'd like it. That's why I chose this place. You music people, right, you can't resist a curry.'

James was trying not to look disgusted when the dodgy waiter scurried back again with the lime pickle and some poppadoms. He looked dismayed and Brian looked impressed. Lime pickle is not the sort of thing you eat on a first date. Or at all if you can help it. It's not so much a food, more a toxic waste, and is believed to have been invented at the time of the Raj as an act of defiance.

The waiter scurried away again, glancing over his shoulder, like a man leaving the scene of a firework.

A different waiter scurried in to take their order, perspiring freely.

'Er, no thank you,' said James after peering at the menu and completely failing in his attempt not to look disgusted. 'I'll just have one of those big crisp things and a little of this pickle.'

'Well, I won't,' said Brian. 'I'll have a Chicken Tikka to start with, right, then Meat Vindaloo, Vegetable Curry, Onion Bagee, Pilau Rice, right, and a Nan Bread and some of that Raita.'

'Onion or cucumber, sir?' said the waiter, bracing himself.

'No mate, Paperback!' said Brian and nearly fell off his chair with mirth. 'I always say that, James; it cracks them up every time.' He chuckled to himself while the waiter wrote it all down, including a note to the chef to beef up the Vindaloo by several degrees centigrade. He bowed courteously and scuttled off back to the kitchen.

'Look, Brian, what exactly do you want to discuss?' James felt intimidated by the food and wanted to get it over with as soon as possible.

'Well, James my old mate, it's just that I think you can do me a better deal on Julesey.'

'What kind of better deal?'

'Look, this advance money has all got to be paid for out of the sales revenue, right, so where's the bonus? The money goes down the toilet as far as I can see. Studio bills and all that malarkey. We end up paying for the whole thing out of our bit. You get the hit record, right, you immediately get all the money back and then you get all the profit to boot.'

James started to smile his smug smile. 'I see what you mean. You feel that you should be able to use the money to set yourself up. Is that what you're saying?'

'Right.'

'Brian, I have an idea that might appeal to you.'

Unfortunately, James chose that moment to take a mouthful of poppadom dripping with lime pickle and the rest of the meeting had to be conducted in the casualty ward of the local hospital.

# 14

The dawning of the day of the great recording found Jules and Frog busily jumping up and down at Rock Green, busily drinking coffee and busily agreeing how great it was to be there.

'You know, Frog, this is a great studio, this.'

Frog nodded while taking a swig from the mug, causing a mild panic and sundry choking noises. The engineer looked up. He thought he might sample it as a snare-drum sound.

The engineer was repairing the studio from the excesses of the heavy-metal band that had been in for the two weeks since Jules and Frog had first visited. Most of the wreckage had been shovelled out by the cleaners, but there were still a few beer cans wedged behind the mixing desk and they had to be removed before preparation could begin.

Jules and Frog watched as he switched everything on, noticed that several things weren't working, swore a bit, hit a few things until they gave in and worked, disconnected and then reconnected about one million four hundred thousand leads, lined up the tape machine, found a tape, found out it was somebody else's, swore a bit, went out to whinge at Darren, brought the tape back, put the tape back on the multi-track, listened to the stuff that was already on it, had a chat about it, wiped it and generally did all those things engineers do that you always wish they had done before you arrived, especially at sixty-five pounds an hour.

They had been standing at the back of the mixing room for about an hour and their interest in the plug-wielding was beginning to wane, when he finally turned around and spoke to them. 'OK, Mr Han Man, so what do you want to do?'

Milo was a good engineer, which meant that he talked, walked, looked, moved and in every way behaved very strangely.

He was nineteen years old and had not been out in daylight for three years. He had what is usually referred to as a studio tan. His skin was a sallow yellow and his hair was lank and unwashed. He made his way round the mixing room by propelling himself on the chair castors, occasionally colliding with things that appeared to be very expensive and occasionally rendering himself unconscious.

He spoke in a series of rapidly changing accents which he culled from the different clients as they came through, together with selected quotes from his favourite films, mostly starring Bruce Lee. He knew the mixing desk so well that he was rumoured to be having an affair with it.

Jules and Frog hung over the desk and talked about the track and how they wanted it to turn out.

'Have you actually heard it?' asked Jules.

'Er, no man, what's it called?'

' "Don't Wanna Change the Perfect Dream." '

They put the cassette into the deck and listened to it at warp factor three.

Milo assumed a groovy listening pose and waited till it was finished. 'You putting this in for the Songfest?' (Scottish).

'Yeah, that's the deal.' Jules looked a bit doubtful.

'Get-the-fuck-outta-here!' (Eddie Murphy – *Beverley Hills Cop*).

'Never mind bloody Songfest, it's going to be magic,' said Frog, who was feeling positive.

'It'll never win, it's too good. They must be mad, naht I meean Harry!' (Frank Bruno).

'Stark staring!'

'I'll tell you who's mad. Everyone who's worked in an A&R department for more than six months, they're mad!' (Steve Wright in the Afternoon).

Milo propelled himself at fifty miles an hour towards the cassette machine. He collected the cassette and zapped back, colliding with the desk. Some of the little lights went out. He hit them. They came back on again.

'OK guys, let's wax a hotty!'

In technologically sophisticated, post-musician Britain the process of recording has become extraordinarily boring. It's like a game of cricket, only without the excitement of changing ends between overs. If you happen to be doing your bit, it's OK, but most of the time is filled with getting levels, getting sounds, wondering what the bass part should be in the second chorus, fixing things that have mysteriously stopped working or, as is more likely, started to hum very loudly just before a take, having a nervous breakdown. That kind of thing.

And then there's programming. Programming the gadgets that play all the keyboards and drum machines is the most amazingly boring thing of all. It's all very well if you're the programmer, but it takes three days to program a riff that takes a guitarist ten seconds actually to play. For the luckless individuals who have to listen to it for three days, sticking your head in the oven becomes a jolly appealing idea.

Programmers are, therefore, a pretty introverted bunch. Clever, but about as exciting as a slug. Fortunately for them, hit records are made on the radio and not on the stage, so charisma is optional. That's why there are so many of them in the charts. They're cheap to sign, they don't go on expensive tours and they don't trash the bedroom because their Mum would give them a clip round the ear.

Jules and Frog experimented with the track in a variety of different styles during the day. They laid it out this way and that, experimented with the accent on the hi-hat, the reverb on the snare and the spatial relationship of the sampled brass parts. They played it on the guitar, they programmed it up on the sequencer, they eased the track forward and back on the synchronizing code, went through Milo's library of completely brilliant drum sounds and chose the completely brilliantest. It all went very well and, although there wasn't actually anything on the tape at all at the end of the day, they felt they had achieved a lot by the time they headed off to the pub to meet Brian.

Brian Payedwell threw a total wobbler. He had been baffled by the very idea of needing four days to record a track, but one whole day to get the snare sound made his head spin so much it almost stopped his mouth working. Unfortunately for Jules and Frog, it didn't completely stop his mouth working.

'You lazy buggers!' he ranted 'That's six hundred and fifty quid you've blown away! What's tomorrow going to be? The bit of crackle at the beginning?'

'Look Bri, it's not that easy,' Frog whinged. 'You've got to get the foundation right or the track'll just fall down.'

'Bollocks!'

People in the pub smiled into their pints and kept listening.

'If the song works, right, it works whether you play it on a piano or my Auntie Mabel's ear trumpet. I know that.'

Jules chucked in his three penn'orth: 'We just want to get it right. You know, get the groove, make sure it's a hit.'

Brian was not pacified. 'In my day, they could have done a whole LP in less time than it takes you two plonkers to have lunch. No wonder they had more hits back then, they had more records!'

There seemed to be a kind of logic in there somewhere and Jules and Frog decided to give in gracefully and stick to drinking for the rest of the night.

# 15

Mike Delta woke up in a bed in Barbados. This was unusual. He had woken up on the beach a lot lately, so he was a little disorientated, but he worked it out just in time to stop himself taking a leak on the carpet.

He glanced at his watch and noticed it was almost half-past October. Time to go home.

## 16

On the second day of the great recording, music actually started to happen. Sometimes, when you make music, it comes out just like it does in the movies. Spontaneous, enchanting, magical and almost unbearably groovy. One of the cruellest lessons any musician learns is that making music is almost never like that.

It all looks so easy. Bing Crosby waves his pipe in the air or the Kids from Fame leap into the street and all of a sudden music and dancing burst forth from every passer-by. The banging and clanking, screeching and roaring of real life fades away and stagehands who have never sung a note in their lives start singing four-part harmony to a song that, not only have they never heard before, but the writer is apparently composing right before their very ears. And while we're all pooh-poohing the idea that anyone would ever burst into song in the middle of lunch in the first place, we're all taken in by the suggestion that if it did happen, then that's what it would be like.

When you get into pop music as a kid, you have all these images in your head, you've got all the records and you go down to the music shop to buy a guitar so you can be like your hero. You buy a 'teach yourself' book and the sheet music of your hero's latest album, sit down in your bedroom and prepare for musical bliss.

What you get is musical shit. The disappointment can be terminal. Parents and neighbours complain about the noise and you can't understand why it doesn't sound like it does on the records. Most people over the age of fifteen never get over it. Their expectations are too high, their tempers too short. They will never persevere, never go on to have days like this one. This was a good day for romance.

Behind the soundproof doors at Rock Green, music gushed from the enormous speakers. Louder and louder, more and more wonderful. Jules, Frog and Milo danced about, intoxicated by the sheer fun of it all. Huge chords, exquisite sounds, gut-wrenching rhythm. They shouted, laughed, danced and fell about, drowning themselves in acoustic ecstasy.

By the end, they had more or less completed the track and it sounded great. They played the results back for the umpteenth time at warp factor eleven to take a cassette copy. They had heard it over and over again, but they were under the spell and wanted it to go on for ever. Finally, they could take no more. At two o'clock in the morning they shut down the pleasure machine and stepped back on to planet Earth. Out into the cold night.

'What a day,' said Jules drunkenly as they walked back to the car. 'Was it really as good as I thought it was or did somebody put something illegal in the tea?'

'There must have been something,' agreed Frog.

'I don't think I can remember having such a good time without alcohol or nakedness coming into it somewhere.' Jules opened the car door and got in.

'That is one stunning song, Jules.'

'Thank you. The bass and guitar were stunning too, if I may say so.'

'You may, you may, Jules. Feel no embarrassment. What did you think of my stunning backing vocals?'

'Stunning!'

'Thank you, thank you and as for the lead vocal, well, what can I say?'

'Stunning?'

'Stunning!'

'I tell you, Frog, it's a sodding hit!'

'Europe?'

'Certainly.'

'Japan?'

'Probably.'

'America?'

'Definitely.'

'World tour, here we come.'

And so the two of them drove home in a mood of euphoria, telling each other how stunningly they had performed and how successful they were going to be but, interestingly, because they are in the music business and not the theatre, they refrained from calling each other 'darling'.

When they got back to Jules's flat, there was a message on the answerphone. Jules pressed the playback and listened. A gruff monotone spoke. 'Good evening, superstars. It's Sherman here from GG Entertainments. I don't know if you want to do it, but I need someone to do next Friday night at St Paul's Club, so if you want the gig, give me a call in the morning. 'Bye.'

They both groaned.

There were also two messages for Magimix, whose customer service department had a very similar number and occasionally gave rise to some entertaining conversations about whisk ejection problems or ill-fitting parts.

'So are we going to do a gig for Sherman?' asked Frog, coming back to reality with a bump.

'We could do with the money,' said Jules, shrugging his shoulders.

'May I ask a question?' said Frog. 'What has happened to all the loot from CBA? It's been months since you signed that deal; you're supposed to be rich, aren't you?'

'Good question,' said Jules. 'Brian tells me he's got it sorted out and working for me, but I have to say I still haven't seen any of it.'

'You should find out, for God's sake. We haven't heard a peep out of James Deek since this started,' said Frog. 'And I trust that bastard about as far as I could throw Sherman.'

'Brian says not to worry about that, either. Says he's got him taped as well.'

'Now I really am worried. I think we'd better call him in the morning.'

'OK, I'll do that,' said Jules. 'You call Sherman first thing, I'll call Brian and tell him not to worry about the track and try to find out what's going on with CBA.'

'Right-ho. I'll be off now, it's well past my bedtime. We're not in the studio tomorrow, are we?'

'No. Thank God for a day off, I'm knackered,' said Jules. 'Hey, Frog, I think I'm going to listen to the track again, you want to hear it?'

'Yeah,' said Frog. 'I haven't heard it for twenty minutes, I might have forgotten it.'

They listened to it three more times before Frog left and Jules listened to it twice more after that before going to bed and dreaming about it.

# 17

The final mix of 'Perfect Dream' was a scorcher. Even Brian liked it because you could hear the words. It was submitted to the Songfest organizers.

Jules pestered Brian about what had happened to all the money but he fobbed Jules off by giving him an American Express Gold Card and booking Rock Green for a further three months to record the album. They were not, however, given a producer. Jules wasn't entirely fobbed. One or two worrying thoughts remained, but he was, generally speaking, having a really good time and he felt he shouldn't have to deal with worrying thoughts. He decided he needed to take his mind off things.

'Frog, I'm going down to Campbell's to test-drive this gold card. Do you fancy a shopping trip?'

Frog did.

Campbell's is a music shop. They flinched as they walked inside and struck the mind-battering, ear-shattering racket. People picking up guitars and murdering their favourite riffs, keyboard players clattering, drummers beating uncertain rhythms, PA and microphone purchasers 'one, two, check' – ing.

'We should never have come here on a Saturday without ear-defenders. How the hell do these people stand it?'

'They get deafer and deafer until they get an A&R job.'

The noise subsided.

'HALLO. CAN I HELP YOU?' said the assistant.

'Yes I want to look at keyboards.'

'SEESAWS?'

'Key... boards.'

'OH, KEYBOARDS. YOU WANT TO SPEAK TO NATHAN.'

'Why are you shouting?'

'WHAT?'

'Why . . . are . . . you . . . shouting?'
'WHAT?'
'Never mind.'
Nathan was busy with a customer so Jules and Frog mooched. They were good at mooching in music shops but today there was too much of a sense of urgency for proper mooching. They paced up and down. Jules began to drool slightly. Frog gave him a handkerchief to clean himself up but then he saw the bass guitars and had to ask for it back. They were in Aladdin's cave and Jules had the gold plastic lamp.

'I think we can spend more if we split up,' said Frog, eyeing the amplifiers. He disappeared behind a Marshall stack.

Nathan sauntered over. 'Yeah?' he said moodily.

'I need to get some new gear,' said Jules.

'Yeah?' Nathan had met Jules before and refused to get enthusiastic. 'What?'

'What passes for amazing in the way of a keyboard these days?'

'Well we've got those,' yawned Nathan, nodding at a smiling collection of black and white keys. 'We sell a lot of those. Mostly because they're really cheap.'

Jules wrinkled his nose. 'Cheap isn't the magic word,' he said. 'I want spectacular sounds, I want power, I want hard disks, I want floppies, hardware, software, I want midi connections to orbiting space stations. Let's talk systems.'

Nathan's mouth froze mid-yawn.

Adrian Campbell burst from his office. 'Jules, mate,' he said. 'Would you like some coffee?'

'Love some, Adrian.'

Jules's shopping list grew and grew. He never had been able to control himself in these situations. The money only made it worse. 'I think a Sinclavier is a must for the serious musician,' said Adrian, pen poised optimistically over his pad.

'We . . . ll,' said Jules noncommittally.

Adrian's hand trembled.

'They are good . . .'

Adrian squeaked.

'Nah. I guess they're a bit long in the tooth these days.' Jules strode off towards the guitars again. 'So where does that leave us?'

Adrian turned back a couple of pages. 'Well, we have three keyboards, four-rack mounted modules, a drum machine, the

Mac, the sequencer software, digital editing, the sampler . . .' He turned a page. 'Then we have the recording equipment. That's the three digital tape machines, the desk, compressors, effects, amplifier, monitors, microphones, headphones,' – page three – 'then there's the guitars and the guitar effects.'

Jules giggled and wobbled punch-drunkenly into a stand full of twin-necked guitars. They rocked back and forth.

'OOH!' said Jules, 'they look nice, I'll have one of those.'

Adrian scribbled it down and hurried after him.

It occurred to Jules that he hadn't seen Frog lately, so he hunted around. A piercing scream rent the air. It was Frog. Some of the scream had come out of his mouth and some hadn't. When Jules followed the noise he discovered Frog in the guitar demo room, standing in the *Back to the Future* position facing a tower of amplifiers and speakers. Round his neck was a glittering red, white and blue guitar carved in the shape of the word METAL. His feet were planted on the ground, about a yard and a half apart, knees slightly bent as he leaned back from the shock wave. The sound reverberated round the room. The strings fizzed and vibrated as Frog gripped a fistful and held them down, slurred into a bunch against the high end of the fretboard. The scream screamed on and on as Frog hung there with it, eyes closed, mouth open, suspended in ecstasy.

As it gradually faded away he sunk on to his knees.

'Hi, Frog,' said Jules.

'Hi,' he said. 'Can I have this entire room?'

Adrian scribbled some more.

In three hours they managed to spend £47,677.14p, but Frog suggested they might like to round it down a bit and it ended up a nicely spherical forty grand. Adrian agreed with practised reluctance. Just slowly enough to make the punter feel he was getting the best possible deal and quickly enough not to lose it.

'Not bad for a first attempt,' said Jules as they walked back to Guildford Station.

'I've just saved you eight grand,' said Frog cheerfully. 'Do you fancy a drink?'

'Yeah, you got any money on you?'

'Er, no.'

'Oh, well, give 'em some of the eight grand then.'

'Hey, do these gold cards work in car showrooms?'

'I believe they do, Jules.'

'Maybe we can try it out tomorrow.'

Adrian Campbell called his travel agent and cancelled his holiday in Marbella in favour of one in Bermuda.

## 18

Brian demanded the gold card back again when he heard about the shopping spree.

'Jules, you are a total pillock. At this rate, right, you will have spent your entire wad in ten days. Just leave the money side to me and get on and make a bloody brilliant album.'

Thus it was in Jules's good old dogmobile and not the Ferrari that he set forth for the studio a week later to make the bloody brilliant album.

He sat at the Farncombe level crossing. He was late, but then, the level crossing knew that. That's why it was shut. The Farncombe level crossing works on the principle of telepathikinesis, which means that it knows when you are about to use it and immediately puts a train in the way. The principle, prototyped in Farncombe, was originally intended for use on the platform and was heralded as a new era in dynamic timetable management, but it had gone badly wrong.

Jules waited, trying to empty his mind of all thoughts of a trainy nature, when there was a tap on the window. It was Norman Jarvis.

Norman was a nice enough bloke, a hairball in an ancient leather suit, but Jules would really rather not have had to talk to him right that minute. Actually he'd really rather not have had to talk to him any minute. Some people are blessed with a blindness to their own shortcomings and Norman had a definite white stick in that department. Norman was Norman's favourite rock guitarist.

'Hi, man. Did you get my message?'

Jules contemplated an emergency three-point turn but gave in and wound the window down.

'Hi, Norm.'

'I tried to get you last week but you weren't in so I left

a message on the answerphone, man. Say, that's one kickin' answerphone message by the way.'

Norm's style of speach was a sad mixture of a plummy public-school accent, a nerdy attitude and two-year-old street dialect.

'Yeah, Norm, I've been meaning to call you but what with one thing and another . . .'

'That's cool, dude, hey, now is, like, a happening time. We can rap right here.'

To Jules's alarm, he opened the passenger door and got in. That's to say he got mostly in, because he left the door open and a pudgy, leather-clad leg flopped out on the pavement of its own accord.

The level crossing seized its chance, scorched the train through and opened the gates.

Jules was trapped. 'Listen, I've got to be going,' he said as the traffic started to move and Norm relaxed in his half-in, half-out position.

'This won't take a minute, man.'

Jules gave in. 'Close the door, Norm,' he said.

'Cool,' said Norm. 'I need a ride into town. Where we going?'

'I'm going to the studio.'

'Oh, what? Total rave. I love studios. Which one?'

'I'm busy, Norm, what's the problem?'

The problem was that Norm had once had a record deal. It was only for three months, after which the guy that signed them got fired for it and they were dropped but, just for a moment, Norm had made it. That moment had been in 1978, but he was still living in it.

'Did I send you a copy of our album, man?'

'Is the Pope a Catholic?'

'Only I've got some serious shit interest from Kiss-O-Gram publishing and they want to put some money up to get the band back on the road, do some kick-arse gigs and, you know, like, shake up the suits.'

'Sounds great. What's the problem?'

'Well, I know you've always been into my music, like, the majesty of the riff, the grandeur of the groove.'

'Hmmm . . .'

'Well, this publisher chick is coming down to see us next week and I've sacked the vocalist.'

'That was a bit previous, wasn't it?'

'We weren't on the same vibelength, man. He was always

criticizing my songs. I don't need that kind of negativity in the white heat of the creative whirlpool of my life. He said the songs were dated, man.'

Norm nodded, man to man at Jules as though they were the last two true musicians.

'When did you write those songs?'

'Which ones, man? I write so many arse-kicking numbers I lose track.'

'The ones you sent to Kiss-O-Gram.'

'It is not the date of a song that matters, man, it's the size of the arse that gets kicked. The best songs were written in the 1970s.'

'As you say.'

'So, anyway, I knew you wouldn't let me down. Thanks, man.'

'Thanks for what?'

'It won't take you long to learn the stuff; we rehearse every afternoon up at Drongo's dad's farm.'

Jules twigged. 'Norm, I can't be your vocalist.'

'Course you can, Jules. I know your voice is a bit dodgy up the top end but we can work round that.'

'I mean I'm doing my own stuff. I haven't got time.'

'You can't pass this up, man, this is serious. This chick is coming down with a bag full of money to sign us up. She speaks my language. We rapped for an hour and a half on the phone last night and I know a chick's mind when she's, like, ready to tumble. You just don't understand the music-business mentality. Hey, I've been there, man.'

Jules stopped the car in an end-of-conversational sort of way. 'This do?'

'You're not the dude I thought you were, Jules.'

'Never mind. Go back to the level crossing and wait. Another vocalist is bound to drive by eventually.'

Norm got out. 'So, what are you doing these days?'

'This and that. Recording mostly,' said Jules as vaguely as he could.

'Radical, man. Do you need any session guitar? I can do that.'

'I'll call you,' said Jules over his shoulder as he gathered speed.

The studio was in turmoil when Jules finally arrived. Frog was surrounded by cardboard boxes and polystyrene shapes.

'The stuff's arrived,' he said.

Milo was busy wiring up the plugs and plumbing in the bits of equipment as they emerged from the heap.

'Where have you been, by the way?'

'I was cornered by Norm the Gorm. He wants me to sing in his bloody awful band.'

'Yeah, he asked me to do that,' said Frog.

'Me too,' said Milo through the screwdriver in his mouth.

'I told him to sod off,' said Frog. 'He's still trying to get someone to release that album he made in 1978.'

'He said he's got some "foxy chick" from Kiss-O-Gram coming down to sign him up.'

'It's probably just some temp who did two weeks on reception. Everyone in the business over the age of seventeen knows who he is.'

'I wish someone would just release it and get it over with. Then he might leave everyone alone.'

'Nah. The shock would kill him. He'd be lost without it. It's a mission of deep emotional significance the practical point of which he can't quite remember.'

They finished the unpacking and stood back. The new gear sat quietly in the middle of the mixing room, blinking its little lights and exuding the female pheromones that were impregnated into the casing by the marketing department. Jules, Frog and Milo looked at it with lumps in their throats and love in their hearts. Milo caressed the mat surface of the multi-effects system, brushing a speck of dust from its tiny head.

'Can I take this home with me?'

'No, you pervert, it's not eighteen.'

Milo slid the effects into the rack. The computer sat on a table next to the mother keyboard. A string of devices dangled from the midi leads that trailed round the room and ended up in the synchronizer. Fifteen keyboards, a sampler and a drum machine looking like something out of *Alien*.

Jules approached it. He selected a sound and placed his hands on the keys. Not being a keyboard player, this was always a bit hit-or-miss. He could play 'Lean on Me', 'Let It Be' and the opening chords to 'You're My Best Friend'. He opted for 'Lean on Me'.

Down went his hands. Silence, went the keyboard. They looked disappointedly around the various chunks of silent gear. The silence gathered for a moment and then a low sound rumbled from the speakers followed by a whistling, rushing sound. The sound grew until it was at the same time so deep and so shrill that Milo's hundred-times-used-never-washed-up coffee cup vibrated off the desk and fell on to some power leads. The cold dregs sloshed over the hot power and flashed their approval. The three of them rushed round the desk trying to disconnect the system and smother the flames. The steam and smoke finally set off the alarm and the main power was cut.

'That's not supposed to happen, is it?' said Frog, who was always a bit uncertain where technology was concerned.

'It's hard to say,' said Jules. 'The sample's called Earthquake.'

'Well, when we get the power back on, see if you can't edit out a bit of the low end from the seismic shock wave.'

They worked for the rest of the day to clean up the mess and reconnect the studio equipment before Darren showed up. They took care to gaffer things on to the stands and screw things into the racks properly in case of an aftershock. By eight that evening it was all working again and Jules sat down in front of the computer. He opened the instruction manual on his knee.

'This should be a piece of cake,' he said. 'I've always fancied myself as a bit of a programmer.'

Milo and Frog went to the pub instead. Three hours later they looked back in to find Jules hanging upside down from the beamwork, gibbering.

# 19

Nobody at CBA ever talked openly about Jules and the dodgy deal, but there was growing tension about the health of the company and the dumping of Jules Charlie was regarded as a key issue, so he didn't have too many friends. James Deek's secretary, Glenna, was about the only person with a sympathetic ear. Unfortunately, although she would always tell him what she knew, she didn't really know a great deal so he remained largely in the dark.

The album more or less carried itself along on the enthusiasm but all the effort was in the engine room, with no one at the helm. It went round and round in circles with all the artistic direction of a dog surrounded by lamp posts.

It sniffed about here and there, responding to the preferences of whoever was standing nearest the mixing desk at the time. Artistic differences were resolved by an adult discussion followed by a fist fight, followed by a trip to the pub, followed by drunken apologies and claims of lifelong friendship.

Production by committee, or Tugg's Technique as it has become known, is not, of course, confined to making records, but has wider applications as a management tool and has come to be regarded as required learning for most executives in the music business. It has therefore been added to the curriculum of the new, government-sponsored, University of Pop as a course in its own right.

Anyone wanting to study the technique and understand its full potential should apply and take the course entitled Decision-Making in British Studios, paying particular attention to Unit 7 with its practical demonstration by the celebrated Dr Tugg in which he and his associates show how to simulate the technique by role play, taking as their example a group of children with a television channel-selector on a Saturday morning.

After four weeks they had three half-finished tracks.

## 20

At CBA, outside James Deek's office, there was a very unusual view. The view was of Glenna's attractive, jean-clad posterior as she bent double listening at the keyhole and balancing in such a way as she hoped would convey to a passer-by that she was just picking up the pencil she had dropped there fifteen minutes earlier. There had been several passers-by, as it happened, and they had each assumed she was listening at the keyhole, except the postboy, who had seen her in a new light and fallen in love with her.

She took no notice and jammed her ear further into the woodwork and her bum further into the air, trying to make out what was going on. She was suspicious that James had sneaked Brian Payedwell into the office under cover of her pre-first-cup-of-coffee-of-the-day confusion and even more suspicious that he had shut the door. Normally he left it open so that he could shout at her for stuff and make himself look important to whoever it was. All she could hear was James doing a lot of smooth talking and Brian saying 'right' after every third word.

She stood up and walked back to her desk. She was absolutely certain that a massive stitch-up was on the cards and, although she had no idea what it was, she was pretty certain who was going to get the needlework.

She called Jules's number, but there was no answer.

# 21

It doesn't matter what you say about competitions; if you win something, it's great.

Brian got a call from MusikSat advising him that Jules's song had got a place in the first round and that they would be going on the telly. If they got through that, the final was, as usual, in Brussels.

Jules was euphoric. He began to grin in a most irritating fashion all the time, telling everyone in the pub he didn't really care one way or the other and then spilling a lot of beer as he tried to drink and grin at the same time.

The forms came, in all their official glory, giving the details. Work was suspended on the album and he and Frog chose a suitably anonymous name for the fictitious band and started talking about stage costumes and dance routines.

'Please, please don't make me dance, Jules,' said Frog from inside a locked cupboard.

'Well, not so much dancing as moving about so it doesn't look like we're wearing ski boots. It's no big deal,' said Jules through the keyhole.

'I'm not coming out until you promise me I won't have to dance.'

They began to rehearse under the direction of Ms Caroline Yesh from the local acting school. Small of stature but large of presence, she put together a series of moves that a child of five could follow. She then cajoled, ridiculed, praised and pummelled their efforts until they began to look as though they had managed to get out of the ski boots and into light infantry wear. Jules kept trying to do his odd dance, for which he was severely reprimanded.

It was agreed that they should get a couple of extras in the band, basically to decorate the stage and to fill it up so Jules and Frog didn't have to walk too far to meet each other. Brian said he'd got just the people, and turned up three days later with two extremely dodgy-looking boilers dressed in micro-skirts and fishnet stockings. 'They're bloody brilliant,' he said proudly as they stepped through the choreography tastefully chewing gum and filing their nails.

They had perfected the bored and beautiful look and ignored the proceedings in every way, except during the number itself and then while making a dash for the lavatory every time the music stopped to fix their make-up, but they definitely took the audience's mind off Jules and Frog.

There were only a few weeks before the shooting of the promotional clips and they were going to need all the time they could get.

Jules and Frog plodded and the Dodgy Boilers slinked their way through the choreography, over and over, all day, day after day until the embarrassment factor reached tolerable levels. Jules and Frog even got used to watching themselves in the wall mirrors without wincing, although the DBs didn't have any such trouble. As a matter of fact, the DBs could rotate their heads through 360 degrees when it came to checking out the wonderful factor in any mirror within 500 yards.

At half-past midnight at the end of the umpteenth rehearsal, Jules staggered into his flat and closed the door behind him. He was exhausted. He wandered into the living room and crashed out on the settee without turning the light on. He glanced over at the telephone answer machine and noticed the red light flashing, indicating that he had a message on it. He made a mental note to deal with it tomorrow and fell into a deep, cramp-inducing sleep where he was.

## 22

When Jules woke up, he felt very rough. His body ached because of the strange position he had slept in and he had that vague feeling of doom that always follows a bad dream you can't quite remember. But the sun was shining through the window on to his rumpled form and the sky was a deep-blue colour, so he decided to have a crack at getting up.

He steered what seemed to him to be somebody else's feet off the arm of the settee and lowered them cautiously to the floor. They weren't working properly, so he sat there blinking at them and trying out bits of the rest of his body to see what the full picture was. His bladder seemed to be working really well, so he took a chance on the feet and went to the bathroom before the bladder stole the initiative.

Shortly afterwards, he emerged feeling a lot better and, preparing a sumptuous breakfast from the cornflakes packet, he remembered the answerphone and switched it to replay as he passed it in the hall on the way back to the sunny bit of the living room. Jules was so surprised to hear Glenna's voice that he missed his mouth with a spoonful of cornflakes and dropped them in his lap.

'Jules, this is Glenna. We've got to talk, don't call me here, meet me at Guildford Station at 12.30 tomorrow,' she had said, and left it at that.

Jules hoped that he had remembered to check the answerphone the day before and that he wasn't twenty-four hours late. Never mind. He really liked Glenna and, besides, she was the only one in the record company who ever spoke to him. Whatever she wanted, it sounded important, and helping maidens in distress was one of Jules's favourite pastimes. Being an eternal optimist, he shoved all the bedclothes in the washing machine just in case.

He took off his soggy jeans and shoved them into the washing machine as well and wandered off to find a clean pair, feeling cool and doing his best to look like that guy in the jeans commercial. He wondered what the time was and glanced at his wrist. He glanced at his other wrist and wondered what he had done with his watch. He then ran back into the kitchen in a very uncool way and rescued it from the pocket of his now sodden jeans along with his car keys and a ten-pound note.

He dived back into the bathroom, showered and carefully blow-dried his hair; he was careful to keep it on the Billy Idol side of Coco the Clown and careful not to fart.

One of the major benefits of living on your own is that it gives you the freedom to break wind as often and as loudly as you want, but it is very important not to do it while using a hairdryer, because it will suck up the noxious gases, raise them to a nice, smelly temperature and blow them in your face.

Twenty minutes later, Jules, complete with wristwatch and clean jeans from the wardrobe, left the flat for the third and final time, having had to go back only twice for things he had forgotten to take with him. It was eleven o'clock.

Weird things aside, he felt good. The sun was shining and he hadn't had to get up at 5.30 in the morning to collect foul laundry from incontinent people since he had resigned from his former career.

He walked down the hill into Godalming to catch the train. He hadn't really thought much about it before, but he definitely liked Glenna. He walked and wondered, experimenting with the idea of a romantic experience.

He had never been much good at experiments at school. His straight-line graphs were always bent and the chemistry lab crunched underfoot with broken glassware, but this one was a pretty wild success. His imagination leapt out of control. He imagined opening nights, posh frocks and world travel. A mansion in the country, a rose in the field and horses round the door. A whole series of semi-pornographic scenes that had to do with mirrors, black satin sheets and lacy underwear. All this before he even got to the post office.

By the time he arrived on the platform, they had been married, had several children, one of which had become a record-breaking long-distance runner, divorced and then remarried in Acapulco.

He didn't mind that he had missed the eleven-fifteen and

would have to wait half an hour for the next train. Now he would be only forty minutes early.

Warning bells at the back of his mind clanged away about rushing the situation, but it was too late. The front of his mind had already planned out the whole of his life with her and she would just have to accept it. The back of his mind hit the pause button but went off to find the 'I told you so' tape just in case.

Glenna Washington, in blissful ignorance of the fact that her problems were over, rather felt that her problems were just beginning. Deciding to warn Jules about the dirty deal that James and Brian seemed to be doing on his behalf was putting her job on the line with a train due in thirty seconds.

She felt very strongly, however, that it was the right thing to do. Jules, after all, was a completely innocent victim of foul play. It wasn't his fault he was a prat. He needed protecting and Glenna needed to protect him. She cursed her mother for feeding her all this maternal crap along with her Farley's rusks, but there it was.

In all the relationships she had had with various members of the male gender, she had always ended up working like a one-armed paper-hanger to protect her man. To protect him from the things that might harm him, like working for a living, for example, or from realizing that he was a lazy, egotistical bastard. That kind of thing.

Her previous boyfriend had been a piano player. That is to say he would have been a piano player but for his emotional problems. He studied piano from the age of five and reached grade eight in two years. His parents moved house so that they could fit a nine-foot grand in the sitting room and Amadeus II thumped away with gusto until he was thirteen.

In a godlike existence, everything he wanted just sort of happened. A wave of his tiny hand and food appeared, toys, games, piano-teachers came and went as he got fed up with them. Not particularly wealthy, his parents spent all of their money, and a good deal of the bank's to boot, but they knew it was for the best, because their little boy would one day be a maestro.

Unfortunately, the little mite never recovered from not winning the Young Musician of the Year competition. He stamped his foot, stormed out of the studio and sobbed at his piano, blaming his teachers for not being good enough teachers, his parents for not being good enough parents and the biased judges and their stone-deaf, unwedded parents. Thereafter he refused to play as punishment for them all, and it turned into a lifelong grump.

Actually, he just wasn't that good.

The whole of Glenna's time with him had been spent with him anguishing over whether he would ever play again and her wondering whether it would ever occur to him how the rent got paid.

She told herself it would not happen again, that this was not a relationship. Jules was a nice guy, strange but basically OK. But this was just a favour. One human being to another. 'I think you're being stitched up, mate. Cheers, see you around.'

She gazed out of the grubby window at the countryside rushing by in the sunlight, and then she realized that the countryside was not, in fact, rushing anywhere. It was just hanging out enjoying the good weather. She was the one doing all the rushing. She decided she liked countryside and she wanted to spend more time in it.

The train pulled into Guildford Station and she stood up and fumbled with the door handle. Being one of those old ones that can be opened only by a left-handed, double-jointed gorilla, it took her some time. Luckily for her, a man came up to the door on the outside wanting to get in.

Having narrowly escaped involuntary passage to Portsmouth, she stood on the platform and looked around for Jules. She suddenly felt that this was all a big mistake and that Jules wouldn't be there or worse, that he'd phoned CBA and told someone else that he wouldn't be there. Then she would have to explain what she was doing. Fortunately, Jules appeared at that moment from the back of the Quick Snack and stopped this line of thinking before it could do any real damage.

He shouted and waved and trotted over, trying not to look too keen. 'Glenna, hi. I thought you weren't on the train,' he said. 'I watched everyone get off and there you were, absent.'

'I couldn't open the door.'

'Ah.'

They looked at each other awkwardly.

'So, what can I do for you?'

Glenna tried out the one-sentence answer in her head and it seemed a bit too unpleasant for a railway station. She decided on a softer landing.

'I think you should buy me lunch and I'll tell you a story.'

\*

Of all the fuel stops of the day that you might choose to be the launchpad of a new relationship, lunch is the safest. It is sexually unambiguous. Other meals have definite overtones that you might not want to emphasize on a first date. 'Will you go out to dinner with me?' is just phase one of a question that goes on through 'Would you like to stop for a cup of coffee?' and then, by extension, to 'Which side of the bed do you usually sleep on?'

Meetings for breakfast are not popular except with hyperactive, heart-attack candidates who are trying to impress the boss on a business deal. 'Would you like to have breakfast with me?' still doesn't sound quite right in a boy/girl situation. There is a definite hint of rumpled bedclothes about it. Tea and coffee breaks are just too short, but lunch is great. People wishing to get to know one another should go out to lunch. Time enough to talk, but with built-in escape routes all along the way. It can be as long or as short as you want, depending on how things work out. If the salad doesn't go well, you can skip the Danish and coffee by claiming to be on a diet and go back to work. In any case, the end of the deal has absolutely nothing whatever to do with which side of the bed you usually sleep on. So communication is achieved and difficult questions are avoided. Perfect.

Jules and Glenna had a perfect lunch. They sat in the Castle Gardens and ate sandwiches from the Boulangerie. The sun shone upon the perfect lunch. The perfect lunch evolved into the perfect afternoon tea, which developed into a perfect bottle of wine at around seven o'clock which expanded into perfect dinner for two. It was a perfect day. Which all goes to show that you can't avoid the difficult question about whether to go in for coffee for long, no matter what meal you start with.

The conversation was huge and magical. It started out with the bit about James Deek and the dodgy deal and then set off on a wide arc, taking in every subject in the universe on its way around. Stuff about music, stuff about childhood, stuff about nuclear issues, stuff about green issues, stuff about life, about death, stuff they loved, stuff they hated, stuff about everything. Everything they said to each other was right. They positively vibrated in sympathy, one with the other. Jules even told her about Acapulco.

By the time they stopped talking, it was very late and there were two cold cups of coffee in the living room of Jules's flat.

All day, while they had been talking, they avoided touching each other. An invisible barrier surrounded them and the delicious tension was driving them crazy as they got closer and closer. When they finally touched it was like a lightning strike. Sparks and debris were scattered in every direction as they shared the white light of passion and the red heat of friction. They collided in an intense exchange of emotions, wrapping themselves around each other and travelling back and forth between Earth and various neighbouring planets. They ate and drank each other, they breathed each other, they laughed and shouted and in every way shagged each other stupid.

They lay in a sweaty tangle.

'Would you like a cup of tea?'

'I'm sorry?'

'Tea?' Jules propped himself up on one elbow and smiled at Glenna in the moonlight.

'In the absence of champagne, I suppose I'll have to say yes. Although a tartan flask does not have quite the same romantic appeal as an ice bucket.'

Jules got out of bed and walked into the kitchen. Glenna looked up and down at his receding silhouette with renewed interest. She pulled the duvet back on to the bed, covered herself up and straightened her hair a bit.

'What are you going to do about CBA?' she asked a minute or two later when he returned with the tea.

'I haven't a clue and I'm certainly not going to worry about it now,' he said, slipping back into bed beside her.

'Oy, you crafty bugger, what are you doing? I haven't finished my tea.'

'I'll make you another one in a minute.'

'As long as that?'

'If you're really lucky.'

Next day it took them half an hour to wash the cups up.

## 23

On 18 March, four and a half months after leaving for a three-week holiday, Mike Delta stepped off the plane from New York and back on to Angleterra firma wearing matching shorts and t-shirt, tennis shoes, sunglasses and a see-through plastic mac. It was cold, wet and, in all other ways, completely unlike the Caribbean. It was the kind of March that you had in the good old days before talk of global warming screwed up people's meteorological expectations.

His one-night stop-over in New York on his way home had been extended a bit on account of a few really good parties, but he had at least caught up on all the gossip about James Deek and Jules Charlie.

The music press had tired fairly quickly of the 'Delta Dorks Deek!' type of story. Ridiculous behaviour by record-company executives is hardly news, but it ran for a few weeks all the same. Mike smiled to himself at all the stories of James Deek blustering about trying to rescue a bit of credibility by being seen at clubs with new, young bands who, to judge from the photos which occasionally found their way into print, did not really know who he was. But now it had all blown over and things had apparently got back to normal at CBA.

His luggage passed him several times on the carousel before he recognized it and pulled it on to the trolley. It was a bit tattier than he remembered it, but then it had been through a lot since it had left London the previous August.

He went through the green channel, but it didn't matter because he always got stopped in Customs.

'May I ask from whence you 'ave just arrived from, sir?' said a bored Customs official in that 'what have we here?' tone of voice beloved by the uniformed type.

'Er, I can't remember,' said Mike over his sunglasses. 'Just think of me as happy to be here.'

Fortunately it doesn't take long to strip-search anyone only wearing shorts and a t-shirt.

An hour later, Mike stepped painfully off the tube at Chiswick Park. The English rain ran down his neck and inside the pointless mac as he dragged his battered bag across the High Road, the park and finally his own front doorstep.

The front doorstep was particularly tricky on account of eight months of accumulated junk mail blocking the hallway to such a depth that it was spewing back out of the letter box and on to the pavement.

He waded through the heap and stumbled up the hallway into the bedroom, dropped his bag and fell headlong towards the bed. He was asleep before he arrived.

Tall and fair with a fading tan, he folded his long legs into a deckchair shape with his head dangling over the side of the bed. He looked like collapsed giraffe.

The music industry occasionally makes a corporate mistake and allows someone like Mike Delta to slip under the boardroom door. He'd enjoyed six profitable years at CBA, but his success was resented by most people in the business and his demise largely welcomed because it was widely believed that he had cheated his way to the top by the flagrant use of business skill and good creative judgement.

He'd been an unlikely candidate. He did not play an instrument, had never been in a band, hadn't known anyone and was indifferent to stardom. He simply believed he was a star. A star student, a star college entertainments secretary and subsequently a star pizza-delivery executive. An opportunist, his opportunity came when the legendary Cagg Brown accidentally offered him the managing director's job when he came to the office delivering a pizza.

Being a star record-company executive therefore came naturally to him. He made a complete success of his first year, signing three bands, each of which sold large numbers of inexpensive, enthusiastically produced albums. When Cagg popped in the following year he realized, not for the first time, that his accidental decisions were a good deal better than the ones he thought about, so he accidentally went to another party and left Mike to get on with it.

Eventually, following a large tax bill and a losing fight against years of bodily abuse, Cagg sold the whole show to the Dwight B. Lousengesmind Corporation who, in turn, were owned by

Nagramiwa of Japan. Between them, Dwight and the Japanese managed to lose sight of all the music and dreams stuff and decided instead to peddle 'entertainment'. They toyed with fads as they came along, but it takes a big company at least six months to copy a five-minute fad and so they got caught in the tail-chasing trap.

Mike got pissed off and finally stopped making the effort until, one day, he got sacked to make way for a proper businessman.

When he woke up, it was seven o'clock in the evening and he felt like shit. Actually he felt like jet-lagged shit, which is worse.

His body told him it was lunchtime, while his head told him it was half-past Armageddon. He scratched his head, rubbed his eyes and tried to make his mouth work without dribbling. He squinted at the television at the end of the bed and switched on MTV, just in time to see Jules and Frog.

He picked up the phone, but it had been cut off.

# 24

MTV didn't exactly rave about the Songfest, but a few prime-time advertisement slots with clips of the songs bought their co-operation.

Glenna was also watching the MTV Songfest preview at Jules's flat, but Jules was not.

'It's finished,' she said over her shoulder.

Jules came out from behind the settee.

'I'm never going to lick my lips on television again,' he moaned. 'I looked like a pervert.'

'No you didn't, it was fine.' Glenna tried to sound reassuring.

'I did. And my head wobbles. I looked like a demented Thunderbirds puppet with a couple of loose wires.'

The phone rang and Jules spoke briefly to Frog about perverts and Thunderbirds while Glenna made some coffee.

'Frog agrees with me,' said Jules on his return.

'What does he know? I bet he was hiding behind the settee too.'

Luckily various of Jules's friends and relations who had seen it called to say they thought Jules looked great and finally his ego was coaxed out from behind the settee to join them.

'I've got to go through the whole thing again in two weeks,' said Jules thoughtfully. 'I wonder if Caroline can teach me how to stop my head wobbling.'

'If I were you I'd stop worrying about the show and start thinking about what's going to happen afterwards. Win or lose, life goes on and you have a career to rescue.' Glenna sounded genuinely concerned. 'You've been completely preoccupied with the bloody Songfest. Your album is lost in the Bermuda Triangle and you still have no idea what Brian has done with all the money.'

'I've got my gold card,' said Jules lamely and not entirely

accurately, but he had to accept that things were not going entirely as he had hoped.

Brian Payedwell was most certainly a successful businessman. He had a vintage Jaguar, a big house, a beautiful wife, three French tarts, two sets of books and a partner in a pear tree. Unfortunately, he suffered from a common delusion that the music business follows the same principles as 'business' business.

All business is a gamble, but if 'business' business is like horseracing – study the form, play the odds, back the favourites and you could stay ahead – then the music business is like the three-card trick.

From outside, it looks a doddle. From outside the music business you see only success. Failure equals invisibility. Struggling is only a phase before the big time and the big bucks. Just watch the cards closely mate, go on, pick one, you got a one-in-three chance ain't ya? Brian wasn't fooled for an instant, though; he knew he was on a dead cert.

'So what are we going to do about it?' asked Glenna.

'It's time to confront Brian and find out what's been going on, but let's get this bloody show out of the way first.' Jules stood up and looked at the brilliant view. 'I'm hungry, do you fancy a curry?'

Glenna thought she did fancy a curry and Jules went to put on the same shirt he'd worn on television just in case somebody recognized him.

## 25

Somebody did recognize Jules. A young woman with a notepad and a young man with a camera recognized him outside his flat a few hours later, as he and Glenna emerged from the dogmobile. They stood up to greet them. Publicity is a double-edged sword. It's all very well being noticed, but you never know what people will do.

'So, how does it feel to be a pop star?' said the young woman.

'Excuse me?' said Jules.

The camera flashed, causing temporary blindness all round and much manic blinking.

'Listen, I'm from the *Godalming Bugle*; can we get an interview?'

Glenna started to say no, but Jules didn't want to waste the shirt, so he agreed and Glenna went upstairs to see whether Frog was at home. He was. She brought him down.

Jules shuffled on a chair a few minutes later as the earnest young reporter sat on his settee, tugging down the hem of a short skirt. She fished out a pad, pushed her long, extremely blonde hair off her face and looked him disconcertingly in the eye.

'So how does it feel to be a pop star?' she repeated.

'Well, um, I don't know whether the Songfest really counts as stardom. Does it?'

It did to the reporter. She scribbled away.

'So, how did it all begin?'

Jules was just getting into his stride about Rosemary Stacy and his plastic guitar when she cut him off.

'Yes, OK, right, who were your musical influences?'

Frog watched quietly as Jules spoke of the Beatles and the reporter looked blank. She jumped in again.

'That's fine, great. Tell me, do you ever eat out in the town?'

'I'm sorry?' Jules's brain skidded round the conversational hairpin bend.
'You know. Local restaurants. That kind of thing.'
'Yeah, sometimes.'
'OK, so what's your favourite food?'
'Anything with poppadoms.'
He smiled; she didn't.
More furious scribblings.
Glenna and Frog could see the way the interview was going and retreated to the kitchen to make some coffee.
'And were you actually born here in Godalming?'
'No, actually I was born in Guildford.'
'Close enough.'
The reporter was doing her best to get the definitive interview for the local freebie, the *Godalming Bugle*. She was struggling a bit. She had the headline, 'Local Singer-Songwriter Rises to Stardom', but the facts didn't really sit too well underneath it. She thought if she stressed the local element, people might forgive a loose interpretation of the word stardom. They wouldn't, of course. 'I've never heard of him!' they would say as the paper made its short journey from the letter box to the wastepaper basket.

Bernadette MacAlister was young, keen and cheap, just the thing for a local newspaper. Journalism isn't everyone's cup of tea, but she'd won a couple of school prizes for English essays and went on to contribute occasional stuff for local magazines and by the time she reached the sixth form she had written two plays and a novel. A strikingly beautiful sixteen-year-old, she went off the rails a bit after an ugly incident outside a local club involving several drunken soldiers. That was when she developed a passion for sex, more particularly, exposing sexual hypocrisy. She was nearly expelled in her final year for an obscene article about the headmaster and the games mistress that she sneaked into the school magazine, and the writing was on the lavatory wall, so to speak. The *Godalming Bugle* wasn't exactly the *News of the World*, but it was a start.

Happily unaware of the fate of her work, she pushed earnestly onward with her local angle. 'So what is your view about the new by-pass?'

Frog reappeared with several pointedly small cups of coffee and disappeared once again.

Jules was waffling about the nice buildings in the High Street and the increasing incidence of 'squashed off-side foot' among pedestrians as the cars occasionally borrowed the pavements and ran over them.

'Right, ho. Um...' She searched her notes for the next blockbuster.

'Yes, right. So tell me, Mr Charlie, do you actually know Phil Collins?'

'No.'

She made a note to included a phrase along the lines of 'Phil Collins hasn't yet had the chance to meet Jules...' so that she could justify including a photograph of Phil Collins.

A thought flashed into her mind. 'You know he's opening the Godalming Festival.'

'No,' said Jules.

'Yes,' said Frog from the kitchen. He stuck his head round the door.

'Perhaps you'd like to appear as part of the local music performance on the Pepper Pot Stage.'

'Brilliant!' said Frog. 'You mean sing a few songs, that kind of thing.'

'Yes, why not? You could go on at the end after the massed school choir and recorder recitals.'

'Er...' said Jules.

'Great!' said Frog. 'We could meet Phil Collins and you could get a picture of the two of them. Maybe he'd like to sing with us. This is truly a brilliant idea.' He gave her his most worldly smile.

She blushed and tugged down the hem of her skirt again. 'Well, I'll see what I can do.'

'I'll call you,' said Frog to her retreating figure a few moments later as he ushered her out of Jules's flat.

Glenna emerged from the kitchen. 'What on earth did you want to let them in for?' she complained. 'I'm not even supposed to be here, remember.'

'Scrutiny is one of the burdens of greatness, Glenna,' said Frog. 'The public has a right to know where Jules eats lunch.'

'Possibly, but do they read the *Godalming Bugle*?'

'Does anybody?'

As it happened, James Deek's mother did.

## 26

The penultimate meeting of the Musical Events Co-ordination Group of the Festival Organizing Committee of the Godalming Branch of the National Golfing Widows Support Fund was in some chaos.

The Godalming Festival was in only ten days' time. Jules had been preoccupied of late, but preparations were all over the place. Banners, bunting, special editions of the *Bugle*, marquees and fairgrounds had sprouted in profusion.

The *Bugle* were co-sponsors of the event, which was designed to raise the profile of Godalming as a cultural centre. As a matter of fact, it wasn't particularly interested in culture, but it seemed a good way of generating local news and hauling in advertisers. The other sponsors were Nabbit and Waite, a local firm of estate agents who were interested in culture only as long as it stimulated the property market, but the organization of the event was being handled by neither sponsor. When you have generously committed your company to a charity project that seems to be eating your lunch, the standard ploy is to pass the buck.

The meeting comprised of ten t-shirt-wearing enthusiasts of assorted ages and professions all talking in random groups.

'People, people, PEOPLE!' shouted the chairman.

The crowd was subdued.

'If I can turn your collective attention back to the agenda.'

They all looked at the carefully word-processed page.

Graham Stickleback, the owner of a local sports shop, frowned the frown of one who feels he is the only sane person in a room full of idiots. 'So, people, where are we?' He looked down the table at David Trouser-Legg, a Godalming 'Brat-Packer' and former student at Charterhouse school. 'David. Have you got Phil Collins confirmed for the opening ceremony?'

'Yup! No problem. He'll be there. I have a note in my diary to call him tomorrow.'

'But is it confirmed?'

'Yup, no problem. Look, there it is in capital letters: CALL PHIL COLLINS RE OPENING CEREMONY.' He showed everyone the page in his diary triumphantly.

'Not the phonecall, David, his appearance. Is he definitely coming?'

'Yup, no problem. I've already spoken to his housekeeper.'

'Call me tomorrow when you've spoken to *him* and let me know what's going on.'

'Yup, no problem.'

'Is the stage organized, Mrs P?'

Mrs P looked over her headmistress half-rims. 'Well, I should jolly well hope so,' she clucked. 'The trouble I've had. Honestly, those bally workmen! I don't believe workmen today know the meaning of an honest day's toil.' Mrs P smote her brow with the back of her hand as evidence of her long suffering.

'Yes, thank you, Mrs P; and are all the banners finished for round the tower?'

'Oh, yes,' she cooed. 'The girls did them in their needlework classes.'

'Splendid.'

Jules and Frog sat at the back in silence with Bernadette.

Graham picked up a second, neatly word-processed page. 'If I can draw your attention to it, I should like to table a motion to accept Annex M as the new programme of the day's musical events.' He glanced up sharply as someone giggled.

'If you mean, "how about this as an idea", why don't you just say so?' said an irritated, but less committed voice from the back.

After a few moments, Mrs P waved Annex M at the chair. 'Graham?'

'Yes, Mrs P.'

'Only we did agree that the girls' recorder ensemble would carry the finale.'

'Yes, Mrs P, but as you can see there have been some last-minute additions to the programme and we felt that it might have more impact if it were changed.'

'When you say "we" Graham, I don't remember a motion being passed.'

'Precisely what I'm trying to do now, Mrs P,' said Graham, glancing at his watch.

Mrs P looked thunderous.

Graham gestured to Bernadette. 'Perhaps you would like to introduce our guests, Bernadette, and we can shed some more light on the issue.'

The meeting turned to face the back. Several of the less committed t-shirt-wearing enthusiasts lunged for the drinks cabinet, which woke up several of the even less committed.

'Good evening, ladies and gentlemen,' said Bernadette. 'In turn I would like to introduce our guest celebrities Jules Charlie and Frog.'

There was a polite 'how do you do' while the less committed committee members agreed with the even less committed committee members that they'd never heard of them. The minutes recorded their warm welcome.

'You may have read my article in this week's *Bugle*' – much shaking of heads – '... about the remarkable success of Mr Jules Charlie, who has risen from obscurity to success in the world of pop music over the last few months.'

The blank looks grew slightly blanker as she prattled on about their gracious generosity and demanding schedule.

'... and so we are very lucky to be able to include them in the finale of our day's events,' she concluded and sat back down.

Graham picked up Annex M again. 'I'm sure you will agree, Mrs P, that we are lucky to have this opportunity.'

'Surely they could go on in an interval or something,' said Mrs P desperately.

'If we could just put it to the vote.'

The neatness of the word-processing and the absence of any more beer in the drinks cabinet carried the day.

Committees come in many styles, from the heavily formal to the hilariously chaotic. It's an age thing. They start out with a new idea like babbling brooks gushing through the valleys, tumbling over the rocks finding a way round everything as they go. As they get older, they slow down, like the mighty rivers, they take time, deliberate and come to mighty decisions about how much more time they need to come to other mighty decisions and, ultimately, come to a dead stop in the sea of indecision. In general, if a committee is old enough to have had a change of chairperson, it's probably too old to do any good. Nevertheless, committees are a fact of life and, if you get into one for any reason, you have to learn how to make it work, depending upon your level of commitment.

You can be a 'committed committee member', a 'less committed committee member' or an 'even less committed committee member'.

Being an 'even less committed committee member' is the easiest. All you have to do is remember to turn up once in a while and then nod off. This category comprises about 75 per cent of all committee members. It is important only that you should remain awake during any voting to do with electing committee officers, or you will get lumbered with all the really disgusting jobs.

'Less committed committee members', comprising about 24 per cent of the whole, have a harder time. They have to remember to turn up, stay awake during the endless ramblings of the 'committed committee members' and generally help out in all the daft things they get set up for. They usually volunteer for at least one disgusting job every year.

The remaining 1 per cent are the 'committed committee members'. They would argue that the joy of serving is compensation enough for the long hours they put in. These people actually want to be committee officers. If there isn't a committee around, they create one so that they can become its chairperson. The only problem they have is motivating the 'less committed' and the 'even less committed' so they can accomplish whatever worthy thing they happen to be into. Such people generally realize pretty quickly that this is not too difficult. A bit of preparation, and heavy emphasis on procedure and human frailty does the rest. The only crisis they might face arises if there is more than one of them in the committee, which usually results in bloodshed at the Annual General Meeting.

Competence does not enter the argument. If you get very lucky, a 'committed committee member' will have more than one brain cell. The National Golfing Widows Support Group were not that lucky.

Graham Stickleback operated the Thatcher system, or 'rubber-stamp' philosophy. As far as he was concerned, whatever ideas came to him in the bath or on the lavatory were as good as carved on tablets of stone and it irritated him that he had to go through the meetings to 'agree' to what he was probably already doing anyway.

Annex M read as follows:

| | |
|---|---|
| 10.30am | Opening Ceremony. Phil Collins. George Nabbit. Self. |
| 11.00am | The Godalming Opera Company perform selections from Gilbert and Sullivan. |
| 12.00noon | The Guildford School of Acting sing Sondheim. |
| 1.00pm | Massed Junior School Choirs. |
| 2.00pm | Surrey Constabulary Brass Band. |
| 3.00pm | The Old Buggers Jazz Band. |
| 4.00pm | Barber Shop Surprise. |
| 5.00pm | The Barclay's Bank String Quartet. |
| 6.00pm | Recorder Magic from the Binscombe Junior School Class 5 |
| 6.30pm | The Guildford Opera Company sing *Carmen*. |
| 8.00pm | Nabbit and Waite's 'Rock Goes to Godalming'. A Star Search talent competition to find the next Phil Collins. With Special guest appearance by Jules Charlie. |
| 10.30pm | Awards and closing ceremony. |

Graham's lonely brain cell sparked in satisfaction as he tucked it neatly back into his Musical Events Committee file. Now that he had forced it through without any real debate he would have to wait until the big day to discover its fundamental flaw.

## 27

The Pepper Pot is an ornamental building standing on an island in the middle of the road in the middle of Godalming. The High Street passes in front of it and Church Street slopes gently away behind. A small upper room is supported by several arches above an open, paved area, the whole thing topped off by a cruet-shaped clocktower. In a moment of rare illumination, Graham had decided it would make a grand stage for the festival's musical events.

The day dawned bright and cheerful. The sun rose on the Pepper Pot. It rose on the neatly embroidered banners around the tower, it rose on the diversion signs and the police constables on point duty and it rose on Graham Stickleback putting the finishing touches to the stage.

Graham was giving thanks for the fact that the sun was shining at all. He was always nervous about the weather because God refused to comply with committee procedure. But shine it did, in a clear blue sky, as stallholders and shopkeepers began to arrive for what they hoped would be a culturally profitable day.

Still Graham had not spotted the problem with his masterplan.

David Trouser-Legg wandered up looking flustered.

'You know, Graham, I just don't understand it.'

Graham looked up from stapling the crêpe paper round the staging at the back. 'Understand what, David?'

'I still haven't heard back from Phil Collins. His housekeeper promised me he would be back from his tour yesterday and she assured me that he would call me right away. I just don't understand it.'

'Did you or did you not say that he was confirmed?' growled Graham, reaching for his file so that he could check the minutes.

'Well, I did say that he was a definite possibility.'

'Confirmed. You said confirmed.'

'Confirmed . . . ish.'

'My arse . . . ish! Excuse my language.'

'There's still time. He might call me on my mobile.' David pointed at the three-hundredweight portable phone he had borrowed for the day.

'Is that the portable phone?'

'Yes.'

'We might as well have borrowed a phonebox. Give it to me.' He dialled, and a very sleepy Bernadette answered on autopilot with a tirade of abuse. He held the phone away from his ear.

'Good grief, Bernadette, you don't have to take that tone. It's a quarter to eight, for heaven's sake. No, no, nothing major, it's just that our excuse for a celebrity co-ordinator, David, has fluffed it and we are no longer to enjoy the presence of Mr Collins at our gathering today.'

He listened for a moment and then groped around the handset until he found a way to hang up.

'She's going to talk to Mr Frog and see if Mr Charlie will stand in.' He looked at David as a dentist might at a particularly nasty cavity. 'Well, don't just stand there, you great pudding, come and give me a hand with these.'

Bernadette rolled over and prodded Frog. 'Fart face has fucked up,' she said.

# 28

Jules also rolled over when his own telephone rang a few moments later, but he found only the wall. He nursed his pulsating forehead as he spoke in bleary tones to Frog.

Rehearsals for the Songfest were wearing out his legs and his patience in equal proportions. Caroline was working them hard, and what with the endless walking around and standing around and the bickering that went on between the two brain-dead, dodgy boilers about who was nearer the front, nearer to Jules, in the camera line and so on, he was pissed off in a 'first thing in the morning' kind of way.

Glenna was staying up at her own flat, but he made enough coffee for two people anyway and drank it slowly from a swimming pool-sized cup as he sat looking at the brilliant view and life as we know it seeped back into his body.

He was disappointed, though not exactly surprised, that he wasn't going to meet Phil Collins after all, but he wasn't really concentrating.

He looked across the room at his acoustic guitar. Dust had gathered on the white, maple shoulders as it stood, untouched, against the wall. It was a curious irony that, now he was a full-time musician, he seemed to have stopped playing altogether. The record seemed to be mostly about programming, and the Songfest mostly about dancing. He hadn't written anything at all for months and he spent all of his time in meetings, prancing up and down in front of a rehearsal mirror or miming with a disconnected electric guitar borrowed from the local music shop because it was colour-co-ordinated with the costumes.

He picked up the little guitar and tuned it. Placing his fingers on the strings, he played a chord and then another as he enjoyed the quiet, silvery sound that it made. Like ripples on a pond

as the notes fell like pebbles into the stillness of the room.
Then the telephone rang again like a crashing boulder dropped into the water by some hooligan, and the sound vanished.

## 29

The sun rose higher in the sky. The car parks filled up and people started to gather and mill in the High Street. Arts and crafts were represented in profusion from all over the country. Rugs from Winchester, pottery clocks from Bath, baby clothes from Exeter, stuffed toys and dancing plants from Taiwan. The galleries and gift shops flung wide their doors. The stall with the coffee and doughnuts started a trend and much money changed hands for calories to fuel the day's wandering about.

The fairground started whirring and whizzing people into states of macho indigestion behind the council offices, and by 9.30 things were generally under way.

Bounty Sound Radio were doing an all-day feature from their outside-broadcast caravan stationed in Waitrose's car park. The DJ was waxing lyrical about the day and slipping on another classically golden, boring record as the crowd peered at him curiously.

'OK, it's nine thirty... er... er... seven in the jolly old A.M. and that was "Sugar, Sugar" by the Archies, I'm sure you all remember that one, fantastic track, right well I'm talking to you from Waitrose car park in Godalming here at the Godalming Festival and it's a fantasmagorical day weather-wise, good people, the sky is blue and the sun is a piece of cheese, as my mother used to say, and we are looking forward to speaking to Mr Phil Collins later on when he pops in to open the musical events of the day so if you want to come down to see Phil get down here right away and now here's another great track from the sixties it's the Nineteen Ten Fruit Gum Company...'

The record spun and the DJ finally inhaled.

Bernadette, Frog and Jules marched up to the Pepper Pot, bright and breezy.

'How's it going?' said Bernadette to Graham, who was munching a doughnut.

'Pretty well, all things considered,' he mumbled through the dough. 'Thank you both very much for stepping in at such short notice.'

'No problem at all,' said Frog. 'So, what's the plan?'

Graham fished out his programme and handed it to Frog, who glanced down at it.

'Bloody hell!' he said. 'That's a lot of performers; where are you going to put them all?'

'They'll take turns,' said Graham, defensively.

'But there must be about five hundred people, and you don't have any gaps in the programme.'

Graham took back the programme and looked for non-existent gaps. 'Well, I'm sure we'll muddle through,' he said.

The crowds were gathering around the Pepper Pot in expectation of the celebrity visit, together with forty members of the Godalming Opera Company in full costume plus friends, ready to open the show. The street began to fill up. A double-decker bus edged its way down the High Street escorted by a policeman. It stopped a hundred yards back, and sixty student performers, musicians and audience members from the Guildford School of Acting carrying instruments, props and music stands made their way towards the stage. By 10.15 the area was packed and nobody could move.

Graham, who had retreated to the offices of Nabbit and Waite across the street, decided the time had come to get things going. He tried to leave. The door was blocked by the expectant crowd. He shoved and yelled to no avail, and eventually had to lower himself from a window.

Mrs P hove into view, bringing her massed Junior School Choirs to see the great man open the show and position themselves for their performance. Graham spotted her ushering a hundred children plus parents through the outer crowds and tried to head her off at the post office, but he couldn't move and on she came like a demented shepherdess weaving this way and that, trying to find a way through, walloping the legs of people in her way with her walking stick and making giddy-up noises.

The policeman pushed his way through, parted the mob and helped Graham and George Nabbit towards the stage.

'If I were you I would try to disperse the crowd a little, sir,' said the policeman helpfully.

'You couldn't block off the entrances, could you?'

'It's a bit late for that, sir; they're already blocked by people.'

At 10.30 the Borough Hall Art Exhibition was empty, except for one or two officials, the art unadmired. The Bounty Sound DJ was babbling to nobody. The fairground was still. Bridge Street and Queen Street were deserted, the stalls quiet. Even the coffee-and-doughnut stall was unattended. Everyone was up at the Pepper Pot.

Jules, Frog and Bernadette had remained in the Pepper Pot and were watching the developing crisis with some amusement as Graham popped out of the front of the crowd and up on to the stage, followed by George Nabbit. He was a bit rattled but nevertheless defiant. He approached the microphone.

The PA had been supplied by a local sound-hire company and was very loud, but Graham was of the 'won't get me near one of those things' school of thinking when it came to microphones. He felt that the mere existence of a microphone in his near vicinity was good enough to amplify his rich, resonant tones.

He stood at the six-foot-range ring. 'Ladies and gentlemen . . .' he said.

The buzzing, whispering noise passed unnoticed by the throng.

'Stand closer to the microphone,' said Frog.

Graham edged up to the four-foot mark. 'Ladies and gentlemen, if I could have your attention, please.'

Still nothing.

He looked perplexed, and hit the microphone a couple of times to see if it was working. It thudded and squeaked in the affirmative.

Frog stepped up to help. He planted his lips on the microphone head. 'LADIES AND GENTLEMEN, IF WE COULD HAVE YOUR ATTENTION PLEASE,' he said at four megawatts.

The crowd jumped a foot in the air and came down cheering.

Frog stood back and Graham stepped up again for lesson two. 'Thank you very much,' he said, trying not to touch the microphone in case Frog had left any spit on it. They all settled down. 'I should like to thank you all for coming here this morning, such a pleasant one I'm sure you agree, to support this, the first, hopefully, of a long tradition of Godalming Festivals.' There was a ripple of polite applause and some whistling from some rough types at the back.

'It's not very often I have the chance to meet so many of the fundraisers and contributors to our charity cause in person, so I would like to give you a brief rundown of the ways in which the money raised here today will be spent by the National Golfing Widows Support Fund, NAGSUF.'

People shuffled.

'The fund was established in 1965 to help the dependants of those whose family obligations tragically conflict with their social commitments and golfing careers and has done so much to improve the lives of those who must wait in the wings as their loved ones sacrifice that which is most precious in the name of golfing excellence. Many of you may know that my own dear wife has benefited greatly from the generous provisions of the fund and the support of the organization during her recent illness.'

Many people knew that she was, in fact, having it off with the treasurer when Graham was at the golf club.

'In 1965, a man with a wife and three children could expect, on average, twelve weekends of disruption a year due to illness, bereavement and family commitments such as holidays but now, with the judicious use of funds to provide special baby-sitting facilities, nursing care and bargain-break activity holidays for unaccompanied children, the same man can expect no interruptions at all. Greatly improving the quality of life for his family and his handicap at the same time. I'm sure you'll agree this is an astonishing achievement.'

The crowd refused to be astonished.

'Get on with it, Graham,' said an even-less-committed committee member from the crowd, who knew about his wife.

'Where's Phil Collins?' said another.

'Ah,' said Graham, 'I was coming to that.' He drew breath. 'It is with great regret, ladies and gentlemen, that I have to announce that Mr Collins is unable to be with us this morning due to pressure of work and other commitments, but he does send his best wishes and has expressed a wish to join us next year.'

'He's probably playing golf,' said another voice from the crowd. 'Quick, send him some money!'

'However,' said Graham firmly, 'however, I'm sure you will join with me in welcoming the new rising star of pop music, Mr

Jules Charlie, who has stepped in at short notice to fill the gap.'
He applauded as he backed away from the microphone and Jules
stepped forward.

The crowd were not best pleased, and would probably have
left if any of them could have moved at all, but they couldn't.
They stared at Jules and tried hard to recognize him.

'Ladies and gentlemen,' he began.

'Oy, mate, sing us "The Wild Rover"', said someone who finally
did.

'I'm sorry, I'm not Phil Collins, take my word for it, but it
probably gives me more pleasure than it would him to declare
the Godalming Festival officially open!'

He wielded the giant scissors and cut the string tethering
several hundred helium-filled balloons. They sailed into the blue
sky and headed for Gatwick to bugger up the approach.

The string having been cut, there was a general expectation
that something would then happen. Graham expected the Godalming Opera Company to burst forth. It didn't. He looked around
to find that half of them were still in the crowd, struggling to
get to the stage. There was general scuffling and squeezing until
they were all present, the piano struck up the intro to the *Pirates
of Penzance* and off they went.

It was, by then, 11.25.

As a matter of fact the performances during the day were
extremely good. The audience gradually drifted away, which was
generally a good thing as it allowed breathing among the remainder. But the sun carried right on shining, people scoffed sandwiches, swilled canned drinks of varying potency and cheered
their friends and relatives as they did their bit. The only trouble
was that everything took 50 per cent longer than it should have
because of the late start and the absence of any gaps in the
schedule.

Graham was ducking and diving, making spontaneous programme alterations for all he was worth. Gilbert and Sullivan
weren't through till nearly 12.30, Sondheim wasn't sung till one
o'clock. So the massed Junior School choirs and the Police Brass
Band were cut short in an attempted rescue, but the Old Buggers
played over time and they were back where they started. They
got stuck in a rendition of 'Mama Don't Allow' and the solos
went round and round because they couldn't remember who'd
had one and who hadn't and they didn't want to offend anyone

by leaving them out. The Barber Shop were then extremely surprised to be cut out altogether.

The String Quartet sawed their way to 7.30 and the Recorders had to rush on because it was past most of their bedtimes. Eventually *Carmen* was reduced to once round the Toreador song and Graham finally got the day over at nine o'clock.

The rock session was in doubt. It had always been a controversial event. Bernadette had forced the issue to encourage young people to support it and there were a lot of hairy types hanging around, waiting for their moment. Besides, Jules and Frog had been booked specially.

Jules and Frog looked around at the hairy types and doubted whether they would really fit in, but they felt it ought to go ahead.

'Well, it'll have to be cut short. We can't go past 10.30 or we'll have complaints about the noise,' said Graham.

'Well, we've got to do something or we'll have a hairy riot on our hands,' said Jules.

The original concept had been for a competition. Several local bands were to compete for some tickets to see Def Leppard.

'Bin the competition, raffle the tickets and let's just get the bands to do fifteen minutes each,' said Frog. 'How many are there?'

'Three,' said Bernadette.

'Well, there you go. You could probably get all three bands set up together on the stage, then there won't be so much hassle changing over.'

The bands were happy enough because they only really had three songs each anyway, and they set about cramming all of the gear on to the stage. The PA was already set up, which cut down the crisis factor considerably and they were ready by 9.30.

Ten miles away, the Mayor of Guildford was just settling into bed with a good book and a steaming mug of Horlicks.

Damner 'Ed were not exactly a young band. The drummer had not cut his hair since his fifteenth birthday so, by measuring the overall length and counting the colour rings, you might take a guess that he was probably forty. The bass player was definitely of the same era, but the guitar player and the vocalist were much younger, which brought the average below the sort of age where you can just about get away with saying it's twenty-nine.

The floodlights struck the Pepper Pot, making the tiny building seem huge in the darkness. The stage was aglow. Damner 'Ed belted out the first number into the still night. The crowd came back out of the pubs and filled the streets again. Crack went the bass drum, thud went the bass, scream went the guitar and the singer together.

Ten miles away, the Mayor's Horlicks began to froth and the lampshade swayed.

Six miles away, Mrs Stickleback and the Treasurer fell out of bed.

Three miles away, there was a power cut, two miles, a tornado took off the roofs of some houses. Within two miles you were at the gig and that was that.

The Guildford digital telephone exchange did not click and whirr because software doesn't do that any more, but if it could have, it would have done it very loudly as hundreds of telephone calls funnelled into it and tried to get back out again to the Godalming Police Station.

Damner 'Ed screeched to a halt fifteen minutes later and handed the baton to Duffy, a lanky teenage band who felt they had a mission to melt electronic funk and rock music together at high volume to produce a funkadelic fusion of style (man). They cavorted about with much serious head-banging but it was still crap. Deafer Than That lived up to their name and played one song with a fifteen-minute drum solo. As the last chord died away you could just hear the Mayor of Guildford swearing down the telephone in the distance.

The audience loved it and chanted for more. Jules and Frog got nervously on to the stage. It was 10.15.

'I'm going to tell you a secret,' said Jules to the crowd. 'We were only booked to play here today because they couldn't get Sooty and Sweep and I don't think you really want to hear the live version of our Euromission Songfest entry.'

Loud agreement.

'This has been a short gig at the end of a very weird day and what I would like to do as the finale is invite some of the guys from each band back up on stage for a fifteen-minute jam. Is that OK with you?'

Loud agreement.

Jules and Frog had agreed that the guitarist and the singer from Damner 'Ed were pretty good and together with the drummer from Deafer Than That and Duffy from Duffy they started a twelve-bar rock-and-roll riff in the key of E.

As it began, nobody had the slightest clue where it was going to go. The drummer whacked out a mid-tempo 6/8 and Frog planted a bass line on to the familiar pattern. The guitarist played a comfortable riff and settled down and Jules stepped up and sang verse one while the other vocalists listened and clapped in time or played tambourine.

There has been a struggle over the last few decades to find an international language. The English say it's English and, after a bit of a debate, the Americans agree. The French say it's French and the Japanese smile nicely and sell you stuff in any language. Esperanto was an inspired but doomed attempt to take away national self-interest, but it's all irrelevant because there is already an international language: the twelve-bar blues.

You can take any rock-and-roll musicians from any country, born since World War Two, put them into random groups, kick off a twelve-bar blues and the music will go on for ever. Actually, that is precisely what it has done.

That is precisely what it did in Godalming that night. Jules sang a one-line, 'woke up this morning' kind of verse structure and a hanging, one-word chorus in a rock style. The others leapt on to the idea and pulled the verses this way and that to suit their own interpretation. Verses alternated with solos and endless choruses. The crowd picked it up and sang along in unaccompanied shouting and screaming as the left side tried to be louder than the right side. It was just like a real rock gig.

The music was not exactly polished, but the spontaneity was intoxicating. They probably would have played for ever if Graham Stickleback hadn't turned up with the police, who promptly arrested the band.

# 30

Press reports in the following edition of the *Bugle* concentrated on the School Choir and Recorder recitals, with barely a mention of the public-order problems later on. Bernadette did, however, get a piece into the *News of the World* about a riot in Godalming and sexual misdemeanours among the festival organizers.

Jules and Frog were trying to put it behind them as they turned up at the MusikSat television studios in Wapping the following week to do their next gig live to ten million people. Well, live-ish anyway.

The producer was not sympathetic. Pre-publicity is forbidden in the contract, which also has a clause about the ceremonial beheading of the party of the first part if the party of the second part gets pissed off.

After a nasty moment or two, during which she consulted the other acts as to their fate, she reluctantly accepted the situation as a *'fait accompli'* and stormed off, muttering darkly about compensation.


British television is internationally renowned. It has a reputation for the highest standards in broadcasting, which meant that the show was run a bit like a prison camp.

The Beeb had never screwed up Eurovision and MusikSat were not about to give them a chance to say 'I told you so'.

Live shows are high-risk and the schedule is ruthlessly maintained. Earnest assistants with headphones, clipboards and cattle prods scurried about rounding everyone up and herding them back and forth from their dressing rooms for all the different lighting, camera and sound rehearsals. These people could definitely be entered for 'One Man and His Dog'.

As has been said, pop music and television are an uneasy mix, particularly live music on live television. Videos are easy; they're just like records – you just stick them in the machine and play them – but shows like this are different.

In the good old days, there was never a problem. Originally the studio orchestra did all the accompaniment and that was that. They were all set up in the pit or behind the screens, depending upon how ugly they were, bung on the next bit of sheet music and away you go.

But pop music has moved on a bit since the late 1950s, and bands no longer sound like Ronnie Hazelhurst. They use all sorts of dodgy technology to make their noises.

Amplifiers, effects, sampled sounds, multi-layered keyboards all played by one guy and a few Midi leads, sequenced or digitally recorded backing tracks generated and controlled by computers. It's a far cry from the traditional orchestra, and requires a degree in computer engineering to set it all up. The average band takes all afternoon to set up and soundcheck, but the show demands a three-minute turn-round on a single stage.

The Musicians' Union takes a position on this sort of thing. Basically, they want to stop TV producers taking a short cut and using actors who only pretend to play while miming to a backing tape. The *Singing in the Rain* scenario. So they insist on real musicians and the producer insists on a three-minute changeover. A bit of a sticky one, that.

A compromise was reached. Miming, they finally agreed, is OK, but only by real musicians and only to backing tapes they had made themselves under strict union supervision.

The Musicians' Union are also concerned about the increasing use of technology and the impact it has on the traditional musician's lot, and go to some lengths to contain it. No sequencers, no midi, no drum machines and the like. I dare say players of the Hollow Log would have thought a modern piano a bit of a cheat. They should relax. The instruments may change but music flourishes.

Jules, Frog and the Dodgy Boilers hung out all day in full make-up trying to be angelic to make up for the fuss they had caused. Glenna popped in from time to time, but she felt safer out of the way. They played Scrabble, Black Jack, Triv and I Spy to exhaustion and tried not to think about the gradually tightening knot in their stomachs. The lavatory did as much work as the production assistants. Live television should be bottled and sold as a laxative.

Everyone was coping with the stress in their own way. Jules went very quiet and yawned a lot. Frog talked faster and faster. Someone was screaming abuse at the make-up ladies (a very bad move), the actor types smote their brows with the back of an anguished hand, the muso types smoked a lot and made increasingly feeble macho jokes about the actor types.

There is a certain atmosphere generated by this level of collective fear. It has often been remarked upon in war novels about the honest Tommy about to go over the top – that kind of thing – and it may seem fatuous to compare them, but most people would rather die than make a total prat of themselves in front of ten million other people. Or so it seemed to the heroes of round one of the Euromission Songfest as the presenter rehearsed the introduction.

Wogan has made Eurovision his own. It is rumoured that he actually likes doing it and, considering how many times Ireland have won, this is not altogether surprising.

He refused a great deal of money from MusikSat to do the Songfest, which says something for his loyalty and something else about his bank balance. This left them with something of a problem. To most people the anchorman is the show. They needed a charismatic front man to carry the whole thing off.

So why they picked Dave Temple is hard to imagine. He was not charismatic. He was not even well-known. His only claim to fame was that he had had an extremely dodgy hit record of his own when he was eighteen and didn't know any better, and he had presented perhaps the most hilarious of the Brit Awards ceremonies when Rolf Harris had unaccountably been given the award for longstanding service to the industry and Keith Harris had turned up to collect it.

But Dave had done all right. His natural naïveté won through. No matter what happened, he just shrugged and did his impression of Ronald Reagan. Actually, the impression was so good people thought for a while it was Ronald Reagan, including Ronald Reagan. The first year had been a bit shaky, but he had gone from strength to strength and now he was a household name because of it.

The format of the show was based upon the original, with just enough changes to avoid legal action.

Basically, it had been spiced up a bit.

If the Song for Europe Show was a game of croquet on the

rectory lawn before tea, Songfest was a gladiatorial contest. A fight to the death.

Each act appeared in turn to sing their song. So far so similar. Between the songs, to cover the changeover, there were the reviews, and this was where the old and the new shows diverged.

Out with those friendly reviewers that made encouraging remarks like 'Well, I could tap my foot to that one' or 'Now that's the kind of song you might hear people whistle in the street.'

In with the hatchet men.

'That one made me want to puke! If these people can't write better songs than that, they should have their hands ripped off. Singers? I've heard better singers down at London Zoo being thrown fish. Don't give me impartial; you'd have to be deaf to vote for that one.'

David Temple had a long stick with a boxing glove on the end of it. If he felt the act wasn't going down too well during the performance, he could rush on and stir things up a bit.

The writer of each song was asked a few questions at the end and invited to criticize the other entries, after which the song was given a ten-second reprise and the members of the audience asked to vote, using buttons on the arm of their seats labelled Good, Fair, Poor and Crap.

The viewers were also asked to vote using a cunningly devised telephone voting system in which hundreds of thousands of 6p phone votes were cast into a black box and assimilated using complex computer algorithms by a blind guy who stuck a pin into a list.

The result was produced at the end of the one-hour show. The winners sang their song and marched onward to the international final in Brussels, and the losers were pelted with fruit and vegetables by the studio audience, joined for the occasion by the winning entry. The entry receiving the fewest votes was finally plunged into a vat of gunge.

All in all, MusikSat felt they had brought out the best in the show and the ratings only went to prove it.


As the time drew near, Jules and the rest of the band sat in the assembly area with all the others and waited. The acts were a mixed bunch of likely and unlikely candidates to represent the good old Royaume Uni.

In the good old days a well-known artist would sing all of the songs to provide a fixed point of reference for the comparison. No one can quite remember when, but at a critical point along the divergent paths of Eurovision and the rest of the commercial music industry, the supply of willing artists ran out.

As a result, the Beeb were reduced to taking what they could get; usually a motley collage of OK and not-so-OK artists whose only qualification was that they had either written the song or that they were 'between jobs'. This has resulted in some pretty dire acts and, as the standard fell, the whole thing degenerated into a singer rather than a song contest. The best song in the world can be murdered by a poor singer. Just think of that embarrassing uncle doing 'My Way' at Christmas parties.

In recent times the Beeb has reinstated the old formula but MusikSat realized that this element of comedy was an important part of the show, as it considerably increased the chances of one of the acts falling over or forgetting the words, and so kept it as a feature for the Songfest.

This particular year they had some classics.

Most of the smart money was on a girly duo singing a bouncy little number about sisterly love. It was a catchy tune with a thinly disguised European-unity message and just the kind of thing that was likely to do well. They hadn't written the song, but had been chosen from a drama school to do the full song-and-dance routine that had become standard since Bucks Fizz whipped the skirts off the girls in 1903.

Unfortunately, the two girls hated each other. They also hated the band, the production assistants and the make-up ladies. One micro-second after the perfectly choreographed hug at the end of the routine and they were at each other's throats all the way to the dressing room.

There was a girl with enormous tits and a boy-girl duo who sang a very sincere ballad directly into each other's eyes, which kept making them crack up. A holiday-camp entertainer who made everyone wince by winking at the camera and a cred band who were seriously 'right on', wearing t-shirts and ripped jeans and giving everyone the impression that they might at any time revert to type and gob on the audience.

Then there was Max deVegas. Max had had a minor hit in 1971 with a song no one could quite remember. He made a couple of quid from royalties every so often when it appeared on pop quiz programmes to perplex Mike Read. He sang like

Engelbert Humperdinck, and he'd been doing the clubs and moving to countries where he might squeeze the last drops of fame from it ever since.

He was very philosophical about it. 'I've made a good living,' he would say. 'I didn't exactly hit the big time, but it pays the mortgage. I don't mind doing things like this. The money is good and it's nice to be remembered.'

He had a ten-penny song and a 500-quid suit, which he refused to sit down in. He stood and watched the Gruesome Twosome do the hugging song and wondered which country he should move to next.

Everybody knew that the G.T. were likely to win, but they were getting so far up everyone's nose they could have started a bogey farm. Jules and Frog discussed how much they hated them for an hour to take their mind off the pain.

# 31

With enough emotional static to light the building, everyone positioned themselves for the real thing. Act one on the stage, act two in the wings, act three down the back, Jules and Co. in the number-four position by the door.

Then it was all happening.

David Temple stepped forward. Applause, applause. Grin grin. 'Waffle, waffle, blah, blah, blah, great pleasure and a privilege, waffle, waffle, blah, blah, telephone voting, waffle, blah, waffle, blah, celebrity panel, blah, blah, blah, final in Brussels, blah, waffle, corny joke, take the piss, point the finger, here he is. Act number one!' Applause.

The cameras glide into position, in comes the band, Joe Holiday Camp winks at the camera and struts his funky stuff.

This business with the miming and the backing tapes gives each act the choice between cramming the stage with their own people, throwing caution to the wind and relying on the live studio band, or a combination of the two.

Joe Holiday Camp's song was a bit of an oom-pah romp, so he opted for the complete studio-band treatment with no musicians on stage. The Creds, on the other hand, were not about to let someone who looked like their grandad have anything to do with their song, and so they shuffled six people on to the stage plus instruments as Joe Holiday Camp came off and David Temple engaged one of the celebrities in the diversionary chat disguised as a review of song number one.

'Meana, what did you think of song number one?'

'Well, I mean, David. Do you really have to ask? It had no discernible melody, the words were banal and didn't rhyme. The man himself was unspeakable, he winked at the camera for God's sake.'

The audience were thrilled. They clapped and cheered. It was going to be a bloodbath.

Wham, bam and on with the Creds. They leapt about all over the stage miming to their backing tape while the studio band popped out for a quick one at the local.

David thought he hadn't had a big enough laugh so far that night, so he pranced on during the second verse brandishing the boxing glove and headed for the lead singer. The singer dodged out of the way and David fell over the drum riser to tremendous applause.

He popped out again after the band had left the stage.

'Adolf, how did you feel about that?'

'Well, I thought you were about the best part, David.'

Big laugh, more frantic applause and David waved the boxing glove.

More waffle, act number three. Jules and the guys were standing silently in the wings, smiling lamely at each other and feeling awful.

Act three was the girl with the enormous tits. She had an exceptionally bad song, but she managed to expose most of her erogenous zones in the three minutes and consequently went down extremely well.

Applause, waffle, on they go.

Jules's song called for the most difficult of all backing, half and half. The studio bandleader dons his headphones and listens to the pre-recorded half, including a secret metronomic click, and conducts the band along with it. Both halves are mixed and broadcast together along with the live vocal. Now there's one for 'The Generation Game'.

Click goes the metronome. Pow goes the brass section and Jules and Frog step into the limelight.

They did OK. Not exactly a sparkling performance, but Jules remembered all of the words and which camera to sing to. They all made it through their stage movements without looking too wooden and nobody's head wobbled. Frog managed to avoid falling over the step which wasn't there at rehearsal and that bastard Temple stayed off the stage.

Applause, applause. RELIEF!!!!!

In a gushing euphoria the knots vanished, the smiles came back for real as they waved to the crowd and walked off the stage, completely elated and talking nineteen to the dozen. They were greeted by Joe and all the other recently relieved with cheering and much slapping of backs and they all settled down to watch the rest of the show on the monitors as the production assistants tried to keep them quiet and prevent any early alcoholic celebration.

They made certain gestures at the monitor as some moron slagged them off for not smiling enough, and on went the show.

The songs were sung, acts moved on and off the stage, Temple fawned, the celebs bitched. Everything was going right.

The Gruesome Twosome were flawless from the skirt-twirling beginning to the final embrace, which put a bit of a damper on the proceedings. They came offstage and walked straight through the assembly area to their dressing rooms while Max deVegas did his Engelbert Humperdinck impression one last time at the end.

David Temple was a bit disappointed at the reprise, when none of the writers would slag off any of the others. With the exception of the G.T., they had all agreed privately that the hatchet mob didn't need any help, so they kept it positive.

The audience felt no shame about it and hissed, booed and cheered on command as the ten-second bursts of song gave everyone a last chance to vote.

'Waffle, waffle,' went David Temple. 'Blah, blah, blah, telephone voting, waffle, waffle.'

Glenna was in the audience with Brian Payedwell. She'd kept her nerve, avoided fainting, chucking up, spitting at the celebs or clocking Brian, although he talked almost continuously for the whole hour.

'I've got a few mates, right, who've got them new phones with redial on 'em.' He chuckled at his ingenuity. ''An they've been dialling our number, right, right the way through the show. That's twenty blokes, right, it takes about ten seconds to dial the number, that's six per minute times twenty blokes times sixty minutes that's over seven thousand votes. I reckon we're gonna win this, Glenny.'

'Gee! I wonder if any of the others have thought of that,' said Glenna sarcastically.

Brian was not deterred. 'In the bag Glenny, you mark my words. I reckon we should phone the office now and book our tickets to Brussels before the rush.'

The production assistants hovered like jail warders, but the crowd had got the party mood and began to break out. Pandemonium! People were quaffing illicit booze smuggled in earlier in the day. The producer had come down to give everyone a lecture. It was right out of *Tom Brown's Schooldays*. If she had had a cane someone would have got a damn good thrashing.

The mood would not be suppressed. The exquisite relief of simply getting through the show was intoxicating. There was a genuine sense of cameraderie. Jules, Frog and the rest of the band pinged about in the throng. Frog, who had a hipflask with about a gallon of whisky in it, tried to persuade the girl with the enormous tits to run away with him.

The G.T. were conspicuous by their absence. Having disappeared immediately after their performance, they popped down to repair their make-up and move their drum kit next to the stage in anticipation of their victory reprise.

The scoreboard was at the ready, the roving camera was lurking backstage in the assembly area to catch excitement and disappointment on the faces of the contestants.

On the monitors they watched and listened as David called for the voting on Joe.

'And votes cast for act number one...' said a disembodied voice, 'nineteen thousand, seven hundred and two!'

The audience clapped and cheered and the roving camera focused on Joe. He winked at it.

'Moving right along,' said David, aware that there were no losers to make fun of at this stage.

'The votes cast for act number two...' said the disembodied voice, 'sixteen thousand and eleven!'

Applause, applause.

David smirked, as did the producer as she called for the roving camera shot of the Creds to rub their noses in defeat. The Creds waved their illegal beer cans at the camera and one of them fell off a chair.

Things were moving quite nicely, with Joe still in the lead.

The disembodied voice, which sounded for all the world like someone standing behind the scoreboard with a clothespeg on their nose, twanged on. 'And the votes cast for act number three... twenty-seven thousand, four hundred and sixteen!!!'

More applause. A new leader. Joe looked dispirited, but winked at the camera anyway and the girl with enormous tits wobbled them dangerously as the camera lingered. She smiled, but nobody was looking that far up.

The voting was going fine, tension building in textbook style; the bad guys had been trounced and the lead was still controversial.

Jules and Frog were leaning next to each other against the coffee machine as the roving cameraman pushed towards them. Would they lead? Would they lose? All the pain, all the effort focused on a single moment.

Mr Nose continued, 'The votes cast for act number four...'

Jules held his breath. Frog held the hand of the girl with the enormous tits.

'Twenty-six thousand, five hundred and forty-nine!!!!'

Shit!

The bastard with the roving camera shoved the lens up to Jules's face to capture the moment, and the producer smiled her secret smile again.

The camera panned left for another cleavage shot.

The audience clapped and cheered as David Temple recapped the scores at the halfway point, but Jules and Frog weren't listening.

They did not look at each other but sank into their own gloom.

Songfest isn't much in global terms but, Olympics or school football, losing is still a bummer.

They should never have agreed; what would all their mates say? What would James Deek do? Is there life after a credectomy?

Jules re-emerged from his private gloom in time to hear the votes for act number seven.

So far, no one had beaten twenty-seven thousand, so the tits were still in the lead, but now was the real test. How had the public reacted to the perfect Euro song? There was a hush.

'Seventy-six thousand, two hundred and sixty-six!!!!!!'

The assembled crowd was stunned. The audience went wild, clapping, cheering and stamping their feet. David gushed with surprise and delight. A new leader, and what a lead! Fifty thousand votes. It was a rout.

The girl with the enormous tits burst into tears for the pleasure of the crowd.

The G.T. did not smile in case they cracked their make-up, but moved nearer the door.

The rest of the team suppressed the urge to boo.

'So now,' said David with a 'let's get on with it' tone in his voice, 'can we have the votes for act number eight?'

'Certainly David,' whined the invisible sinus. 'The votes cast for act number eight, the final act this evening...'

The hush settled once again.

'NINETY-EIGHT THOUSAND, NINE HUNDRED AND ONE!!!!!!!!!!!!!'

The assembly area exploded in ecstatic delight. A huge, spontaneous cheer burst out which was clearly audible in the studio. All personal disappointment was carried away on a wave of poetic justice. The Gruesome Twosome had fallen at the last fence as Max deVegas pulled it off against all the odds. They shot each other a murderous look and walked out of the assembly area, never to be seen again. The rest cheered them out.

Max was truly stunned. His face was a picture as he was led back onstage to collect the handshake and sing his song to finish the show. Disbelief trembled a bit in his voice, but he sang it great anyway. He even forgot to throw his vegetable as the audience clapped and waved over the closing credits and the Creds got the gunge.

The viewers must really miss old Engelbert.

The producer smiled her smile once again.

## 32

Mike Delta watched the show on TV and generally considered that Jules had had the best result in the circumstances.

Since returning from his holiday he had had a bit of a lie-in. He had slept off his hangover, slept off his jet lag, slept off his tan and slept off his lethargy.

He was greatly amused by the way his joke had turned out but, seeing Jules's look of anguish, he felt a pang of remorse. The effect of the joke on Jules had never really occurred to him. Until seeing him on MTV's preview show, he had had no concept of him as a person at all. He was just a demo tape.

He examined his conscience. Does the placer of the whoopie cushion think about the effect of the joke on the cushion? He thought not.

He also thought maybe whoopie cushions deserved a bit of consideration after all, and decided to call a few people to see what he could do.

## 33

Jules and Glenna were *incommunicado* for the next forty-eight hours, during which he moped and she comforted. There was a bit of an upset when they reconnected the phone because everybody called to commiserate and complain that they had been unable to vote because the line had always been engaged and that they therefore assumed Jules must be winning.

This seemed logical to Jules, too, because he didn't know about the guy with the pin round the back but, after some tentative enquiries, he decided to let it drop. No one likes a bad loser.

Brian was outraged.

'We were stitched up!' he said. 'My blokes could only get through a couple of times. One of 'em didn't get through at all. If I find out how they did it I'm gonna have someone's bollocks for breakfast!'

'You're only pissed off because you've been outstitched,' said Glenna. 'Whatever they might have done, if you'd thought of it first, you'd have put it down to a smart business move. Let it drop, it's not important.'

'Of course it's important,' said Brian. 'Because, right, it was going to be the cornerstone of Jules's launch.'

'I think,' said Glenna very deliberately, 'it's time we had a discussion about that.'

'About what?' said Brian.

'About what's going on. The plan. Where's the money? I'm very curious about the whole record-deal thing. Nobody has seen or heard from James Deek for months except you. All inquiries about the money are swiftly brushed aside and, if the cornerstone of the launch was supposed to be the Euromission Songfest, I'd like to know what he proposes to do now.'

'And who the hell are you to be asking questions like that?' said Brian defensively.

'Who the hell do you have to be?' said Glenna.

Jules, who had been watching the conversation like a spectator at a tennis match with his head following the ball, was alarmed to find both of them turned to face him.

'Who's doing the managing here, Jules, me or her?'

'I don't see why we can't discuss it now she's brought it up.' Jules was fed up with all the evasion. 'Is there a problem with that?'

'Jules, you should trust me; I know what I'm doing. Business is my game, right; I have got it sorted.'

'Not good enough, Brian, I want to know what's going on.'

Brian grinned and sat back in his chair. 'Well, all right,' he said. 'Since you ask, I'll tell you what's been going on. I was going to keep it a surprise but, what the 'ell, you forced it out of me.'

Brian enjoyed a big announcement. He had put a full-page advert in *The Times* when his daughter passed her GCSEs.

'I've had that bugger Deek over a barrel, right, and I've rolled him over. We are going to make a total fortune.'

'That's where we came in,' said Jules. 'We already had a total fortune.'

'Peanuts, mate,' said Brian. 'I've done my homework, right, and I've figured it out. That deal was OK, I'll give you that, but, forgetting the advance money for a sec' 'cos you were going to 'ave to repay that anyway, you were really only working for CBA. They were making all the really big money. You, right, were on 18 per cent and they, right, were on 82 per cent. EIGHTY-TWO PER CENT!'

He banged the desk in 3/4.

'So,' he shrugged in a matter-of-fact kind of a way, 'I've had a deal.'

'What kind of a deal?' asked Jules nervously.

'I've only reversed the situation,' said Brian triumphantly. 'We get the 82 and they get the 18. What about that?'

Glenna and Jules watched Brian do a lap of honour round his office waving an imaginary World Cup.

'And how the hell did you do that?' asked Jules when Brian had sat down again. 'They were trying to get out of the deal a few months ago.'

'Easy,' said Brian. 'I've set you up as a fully independent record company in your own right, right, which is licensed through CBA. I was thinking, right, it is always better to control the means of production, I read that in a book once, and you're the product, right, so I got Deeky to sell me back your contract. You are now signed to your own record company. Perfect! A self-employed mega-star!'

'You, you gave him back the money?' Jules slumped back into his chair distracted by childhood memories of *Jack and the Beanstalk*. 'Beans?' he said absently.

'Eh?'

'How much did it cost to buy back the contract?'

'Two hundred and fifty grand. Which is a great deal, right, 'cos he paid us three hundred and fifty.'

'So we've got a hundred grand left.'

'Not exactly.'

Jules was numb.

''Cos in another brilliant move, right, I've bought that old studio as well! No more loony studio bills; we can make all our records there and we can rent it out when we're not using it.'

'So there is nothing left.'

'I 'ad to borrow a bit to get the studio, but, yeah, in round figures. But we're set to make a fortune. Is that a deal or what?'

Brian stood, arms out waiting for congratulation.

Silence.

'Well, don't all thank me at once!'

## 34

Jules, Frog and Glenna met in the pub and drank in respectful silence. They wanted to think. Jules often went to the pub to think but usually only ended up thunk.

'I was rich,' muttered Jules mournfully.

More silence.

'At least you've got a studio,' said Frog, groping for plus points.

'The studio is in debt and so am I.'

More silence.

'Three hundred and fifty grand. I had three hundred and fifty grand and it's all bloody-well gone.'

'Where are we with the album?' said Glenna. 'If we can get that mastered we've still got a chance.'

'CBA are never going to release this album,' said Jules into his beer. 'James Deek has got his money and his cred back, he pissed all over us and all we have is a worthless piece of paper giving us 82 per cent of nothing.'

'If it's a good album, somebody'll like it.'

'The vaults of the music industry are knee-deep in stuff that somebody likes. The question is, will they get behind it and spend money? I think not.'

'The question is, are you just going to roll over and play dead?' said Glenna, wagging her finger at Jules.

'I hate it when you do that,' said Jules from inside the beer glass. 'I think we should sue Brian and get our money back.'

'Sue a solicitor? Get real. You've always wanted to make records, so make one. What's to lose? I can try to get the studio some work and make some money. Keep the bank manager off our backs for a while.' Glenna put on her thoughtful look. 'Jules, what's the situation with your publishing?'

'It was included in the original deal with CBA so I guess I've got it back.'

'Well, there you go, then. I know this publisher guy, he used to be really good, maybe we can get an advance against your publishing. That would keep us going till we've finished the album.'

'Do they do that kind of thing?' said Frog, who'd always lumped publishing companies and record companies together.

'They might.'

There was a general concurrence and the minutes of this, the first meeting of the Let's Make a Really Good Record, Get Famous and Piss Off James Deek Club, showed that, after some round-table discussion, the motion to make a really good record, get famous and piss off James Deek was unanimously and enthusiastically carried.

# 35

Long ago, when there was no electricity, beasts roamed the musical deserts. There was the Composeratops, a mighty scaled reptile with a tiny, prehistoric mind full of musical notes, but it knew not how to play and neither did it know language. Then there was the Authoropterus, which had half a brain with words in it, but no ears. These beasts were mortal enemies for many centuries, scribing great music and poetry respectively and completely ignoring each other, until one day a young Authoropterus, who should have known better, could contain himself no longer and walked right up to a Composeratops and poked it in the ribs.

'Excuse me?' said the Authoropterus.

'WHAT' bellowed the Composeratops, 'DO YOU WANT?'

'Only, I've just had this mind-blowing idea, on account of some prehistoric mushrooms I've just had for lunch, that if we put your mighty music and my powerful poetry together we could have something radically groovy.'

'Like what?'

'I thought we could call it a Song!'

'It would pollute my music.'

'No, it wouldn't, it would be great, Compo.'

'How shall we know this when I cannot play and you cannot hear?'

'What we need is a couple of them Musicianosaurus characters.'

The Musicianosaurus was the third of the mighty beasts of the wilderness. It had no brain at all but had fiery emotions, large elephantine ears, strong hands and beautiful voices with which it could interpret the silent cipherings of the other beasts, to speak and play them and give life unto them.

And thus it was that the Musicianosauruses did sing and play the songs, and the peoples of the wilderness rejoiced and said unto themselves, 'This is really brilliant, we should have a song contest.'

'So, Compo,' said the Authoropterus. 'What do you reckon?'

'Well, OK,' said the mighty Composeratops. 'But we'll have to get separate deals from the publisher.'

All went well for the next few thousand years until a cave-dweller accidentally invented the piano. As a matter of fact, he was trying to invent a soup-strainer for his dearly beloved, who could never get the bones out of her ferret stew, but when she hit him on the head with it, it sounded a most excellent polyphonic chord and there it was.

And he said to one of the Musicianosauruses, 'Get this, mate, a whole new sound.'

'But the Composeratops and Authoropterus haven't written any music for it.'

'You could redo one of their old tunes.'

'And could you scribe it for me to read?'

'I reckon we could come to an arrangement,' said the cave dweller. And he was so fascinated by the idea of adapting old music for different instruments he completely forgot to patent the piano.

So composers composed, authors authored, arrangers arranged and musicians played, each depending on the others to make music and each getting a share of the cake until a bespectacled descendant of the forgotten piano inventor went to a record company in 1950-something and said, 'Hi, I'm a singer/songwriter.' And the old order collapsed.

This new person didn't need the beasts of the old world because he did everything for himself. And his manager was well pleased, saying unto him, 'Who needs those other dudes? Your royalties will be vast and my cut likewise.'

The new fashion took hold, the producer replaced the singer/songwriter as king of the 1980s technology jungle, and the composers and authors dwindled and the arrangers hid for fear of ridicule.

Publishing companies refused to adjust. 'The world may change,' they said, 'but the royalties get paid just the same.' And they gave them all to the all-new 'package man' who didn't know what they were for, exactly, but took them all the same.

One of the peculiar side-effects of the confusion crops up to baffle and enrage bands that are about to sign a publishing deal.

Picture the scene. A bunch of unruly mates have been playing together since they were at school. They practise in the garage and drive the neighbours bananas with old Marc Bolan songs until one of them says he's got a song of his own. He tells them how it goes and plays the keyboard part, while the others get the hang of it and kick in with the drums and bass and everything and, by the end of the afternoon, there it is, an original song. Dreadful, but original, more or less. They do this a few times, get good, get noticed and are then picked up by one of the record companies, who want to take them on.

Cut to the record-company offices.

'So, guys,' says the suited one, waving a fist full of royalty percentages, 'who actually writes the songs?'

There follows a shouting match and a band falling-out. The guy who brought the songs in the first place says he does, the singer says he changed the melody because he couldn't hit the really high note, the guitar player says they'd be nothing without his brilliant riffs and then everybody else points out that they wrote their own parts, so they should all get their share.

Most publishing companies sign everyone, including the roadies, just in case.

Only dinosaurs can remember the difference between content and style, but if anyone worked it out, there would be a lot less stress in band politics.

## 36

'So, guys, who actually writes the songs?' Nark Sleeper of Black Hole Publishing smiled at them over his desk.

'I do,' said Jules.

'We do,' said Frog simultaneously.

Nark looked back and forth between them.

'Well, you know, I do, like, the melody and the words,' said Jules defensively.

'So what's the rest of the track?'

He let the debate ramble on for a while. 'It's tricky to define, but I always say the song is the part you can sing in the bath,' he said finally.

Jules looked satisfied. Frog did not.

They waited for Nark to speak again. They waited a bit longer and a bit longer after that. He said nothing, he just sort of hung there, frozen in the about-to-say-something position.

After thirty rather embarrassing seconds, Frog said, 'Excuse me?' and Nark suddenly snapped out of it and jerked back to attention. 'WOA, SHIT!' he said. 'Did I go again? That keeps happening to me these days. I must get some sleep. Listen, guys, some of these songs are great. You say you're making an album?'

'Yes, at Rock Green.'

'Oh, right, the Shit Factory. Bloody hell, are you the guy that was signed to CBA?'

They both nodded and launched into a series of overlapping excuses.

'I thought I recognized your names. Let me see, who was it told me about this...?'

Another frozen moment.

'Ahem!'

'WOA, SHIT! Gone again. Yeah, right, I think I read about it in *Music Week*. Who's releasing it?'

'No one at the moment. That's why we came to you.'

'Well, you've come to the right man. I got...'
They waited. 'AHEM?!'
'DANK MCDREW!' snapped Nark, shaking his head as he crashed back from planet Zog. 'I got Dank McDrew his deal, you know. Look, I like the stuff and I think I can help you with a small advance to keep you going and take a provisional interest in the publishing. Say five grand?'

Jules tried not to look overjoyed. 'Five grand would be great, Nark; do we need to sign anything?'

'Not for the minute, mate, I can't give it to you yet. I've just got to get the rubber stamp from er...'

Frog hit him.

'JAKE!'

'Jake. Right. Who's Jake?'

'Jake? He's the MD. Don't worry about him, he'll love it. I really like that third one, what was it? I reckon I might be able to get the record signed. We might get you a couple of covers out of it.'

Jules pinged out of Nark's office feeling much encouraged.

'Five grand will definitely keep us going till we finish the album. It couldn't be better,' said Jules.

'Weird person.'

'If he coughs the cabbage, he can be as weird as he likes.'

The two of them made their way back to Waterloo and got on the Portsmouth train. Jules was rambling, on but Frog was troubled.

'Jules,' he said after a bit of a silence, 'can we clear something up for my benefit?'

'Sure. What?'

'Where do I stand with you and all this? I mean, I know it was your deal and everything, but we've never discussed it properly and it was all a bit of a laugh, but I'd just like to know. That's all.'

'You're in, you're completely in, Frog. We've always worked together and I want you to be a part of all this.'

'Yes, but what does that mean? The only money we've earned has been from gigs and we've always split that down the middle, so what's the deal now?'

'You get 50 per cent of the artist fees and royalties.'

'Not Nark's five grand, then.'

'The five grand will go into the pot, but the point is you don't actually write any songs.'

It was true. Frog had never written songs and Jules had always written them. He had started in the usual way with pathetic ballads about why Rosemary Stacy persistently refused to have anything to do with him, even though he'd gone to the trouble of learning to play the guitar just for her. Frog, who was usually getting laid while Jules was getting morbid, didn't have the time or indeed the inclination. That's the key. People start writing songs to get laid. If you're already getting laid you don't. It's as simple as that.

When they started to play together they were distracted by the need to make a few quid and they rarely played any of Jules's pathetic ballads in the pubs because they would have been bad for business. As time went on, Jules got a passion for it and started recording. Frog had no time for the classic attic stuff, but he loved to play in the studio and he felt an obligation to keep Jules out of trouble.

The train jerked forward and clanked as it gathered speed along the platform.

'I guess you can't expect to sing bass parts in the bath,' said Frog.

'We could co-write some stuff if you want; it's just that I never thought you were interested. You're a player. There's nothing wrong with that.'

'Nah!' said Frog. 'I'm no good with words and I haven't really got the time, what with one thing and another.'

Jules stared out of the grimy window and they didn't speak much more during the journey. After a lifetime's friendship they had become good at overlooking their differences, but they'd suddenly glimpsed the gap between them and it was wider than they had imagined. Some of the cosiness fell into it.

## 37

The new air of optimism down at the studio was only slightly dented by the publicity surrounding the promotion of James Deek to permanent managing director of CBA. Being a managing director he did, of course, have a lot more meetings to attend, which is why he never took another call from Jules, Brian, Glenna, Frog or indeed anyone from Godalming ever again, including his mother.

It was his mother who blew the gaff on the Jules and Glenna situation. She sent him a copy of the article in the *Godalming Bugle* for his scrapbook of press cuttings with his name in and there was the photograph of Glenna getting out of Jules's car at his flat. He confronted Glenna and they were both relieved when she resigned.

'Who are they?' asked his innocent new secretary as she put down the phone for the hundredth time, having explained to Brian Payedwell about James being in a meeting.

'They are bad news, Chicago,' said James from over his very important newspaper. 'They tried to stitch us up. Tried and failed, love. Don't worry, they'll get tired and give up soon. Hey, listen, would you volunteer to make some coffee?'

The music press had noted James's revival of fortune and gossiped about the downfall of Jules Charlie. There was a short editorial about the state of the Euromission Songfest and its irrelevance to the pop and rock industry, but the full stop at the end contained the real message for Jules.

Jules and Frog were philosophical, they had been in this spot before. In fact, they had always been in this spot. It was like meeting an old friend after you've been out of the country for a couple of years, and they got down to work on the album. Mike Delta went out and about trying to revive interest in the project and Glenna threw herself into sorting out the studio problems.

Brian took it the worst.

'I do not believe it!' he said as he put down the receiver. 'That bloke is always in a bloody meeting.'

Glenna looked at him pitifully. 'So, what does your secretary tell people you don't want to talk to?'

'I only want to know, right, what the 'ell's going on. We had a deal, a good deal come to that, struck over a hundred-quid curry for Chrissake and now he's in a bloody meeting for three weeks!'

'He was playing his own game, Brian.'

'I'll sue the bastard!'

'Brian, if you want to get the bastard back, help us. If we can get this project off the ground and make some money it will piss James Deek off far more than high-grade legal bullshit. Anyway, what if you did sue him? Jules would be dead in the water. No one would touch him. I reckon he's done his bit for the revenge business.'

'You're only right, Glenny,' said Brian.

Glenna circled the date in her diary and wrote, 'Brian admits to fallibility, call the Vatican.'

Nark Sleeper popped into the studio from time to time, but the five thousand quid never materialized.

'Jake just won't go for it,' he complained. 'I just don't get it. He normally just, you know . . .'

'NARK!'

'WOA, shit! . . . Er, he, you know, lets me get on with it.'

After that he was too embarrassed to return their calls. Either that or he'd fallen permanently asleep and no one at Black Hole had noticed.

## 38

If success is being in the right place at the right time, Jules's answerphone made yet another brilliant career move, for it had, once again, chosen to stay at home, just in case there was an important call, instead of going down the pub for a drink with everyone else.

The little red light blinked smugly. Jules liked messages on the answerphone. They usually meant good things. Envelopes on the doormat are devalued currency, but tax inspectors, double-glazing salesmen and bank managers almost never leave messages on your answerphone because they know it's a waste of time.

'Jules, hi, you don't know me. My name is Mike Delta and we need to talk about your record deal.' He gave his number and emphasized the need to call him right back.

'Mike Delta was the managing director at CBA. He's the one who got you signed in the first place,' said Glenna.

'Is that good?'

'Not necessarily. He disappeared from the scene after perpetrating his big joke, featuring you as the plastic dog turd, and no one has seen him since. He popped up in the States, I gather, but only at parties. Perhaps he wants to laugh at us down the phone.'

Jules called the number and listened to Mike Delta for several minutes without saying anything.

'He wants to meet us,' he said to Glenna thoughtfully.

Glenna sat down with a bump.

## 39

Cars clogged up the small parking area outside Rock Green the following day while their owners gathered in the games room, which had a large round table in it and several almost matching chairs. Spring had launched gloriously into summer and the sun cast shadows in dappled light through a large window and bathed the room.

They had arranged the meeting at the studio to give an impression of work in progress. The whole team were there to meet the architect of their misfortune. Even Brian. Jules had mixed feelings. He felt badly about what had happened but, after all, whatever his motives, all Mike had really done was get him signed to CBA. Surely James Deek was the bad guy here.

Mike Delta was doing a good job of pouring oil over troubled waters, wearing a fetching little outfit of sackcloth and ashes.

'I admit it was a bit beano,' he said to the assembled crowd and Jules in particular. 'I had no idea things would get this far out of hand when I stitched up CBA and, in any case, I never realized what a pain in the bum it would be from your point of view. So please accept my apologies.'

The crowd was soothed.

'I've been thinking about it a lot in the last few weeks and I think there is still a prospect here. The bottom line is that I would like to help you finish the job. Make the album, release it and get your money back if I can.'

The crowd was on his side.

'I don't have a label and I don't have any money, but I know a lot of people and I do know the business.'

The crowd were enthusiastic.

'So you would be the manager?' asked Jules.

'Yes, I would. And I would also be the executive producer of the record. The creative input comes from you of course, the songs, the sounds, arrangements and performances. This will be an in-house production, but I have the vision of the commercial direction, so I would like the final say on the mixes and the choice of tracks at the end of the day, so that I can sell it. You may love it on artistic grounds, but remember it won't count as revenge if it doesn't make money.'

There was a long silence.

'So, what do you say?'

'I say, what about Brian?' said Jules.

'Good point, Julesey.'

'I mean, he may be the wally that dropped us in this particular bedpan, but don't forget he's still holding all the contractual loose ends.'

Brian looked less comfortable.

'It's up to you, guys,' said Mike. 'I need the authority to do what I have to do, but if you feel he has a part to play, it'll probably make things easier. In any case, you should clarify things with CBA, see if there's anything you can rescue.'

They asked Mike to leave the room while they discussed his offer, but there was no real doubt.

'Do it, Julesey,' said Brian. 'What's to lose? I'll be OK, I've gone off the music business a bit, to tell you the truth.'

'Don't be stupid, Bri, we'll need someone to hump the gear,' said Frog.

'You're a bastard, Froggy.'

'Let's do it!' said Jules as Mike put his head back through the door.

## 40

For all their renewed commitment, the studio recordings still didn't gel. The harder they tried, the more it veered out of control. They started new tracks, scrapped old ones, revived old ones, scrapped new ones and still there was no discernible theme. Nothing to hold it together.

Jules and Frog argued a good deal and Jules became restless and distracted. Niggles over who had written what and what would happen to royalty payments cropped up more and more frequently and the tension, although not exactly tangible, created a muted atmosphere in the studio which made it difficult to work.

Glenna didn't actually live with Jules, although casual observers would have disputed this. Since the previous September she had been his lover, his critic and his consort. She would drive down most weekends, and she kept an extensive selection of clothes at the flat but this, she maintained, did not constitute living together.

She found Jules attractive but enormously frustrating. He was always kind and considerate, but she never knew exactly which planet he might be on. When he was recording he was on planet confusion, when he was writing he was on planet vacant, when he was gigging it was planet angry. When he wasn't doing any of the above it was planet 'Z'.

'Do you want to eat something?' Glenna said as Jules stared out of the window at the streetlights blinking on one at a time in the brilliant view.

'Sorry. What was that?'

'Food?'

'Yeah, definitely.'

'Yeah, definitely what?'

'Please?'

'Let's go for a pizza. We've had curry twice this week. I'm beginning to sweat passanda.'

'Do you want to go for a curry, then?'

'A pizza! I would like a pizza.'

Jules turned back from the window to face her. 'We'll go for a pizza if you like.'

They walked down the hill heading for the Pizza Place. The evening air was cold. Jules bounced along holding Glenna's hand, falling off the kerb from time to time and occasionally walking into lamp posts.

Avoiding the cemetery, they walked up Church Street and past the Pepper Pot, which still bore the scars of recent events.

They stood for a few minutes in the doorway of the restaurant wondering if they should just sit down, but eventually a cheerful girl came out of the kitchen and showed them to a table.

They sat down. She was never seen again.

The cold air had woken Jules up a bit and they chatted aimlessly about domestrivia. What had happened to all of hairy leftovers he had been saving in the fridge; wasn't it about time he got some curtains for the bedroom; the pleasures of dog ownership; an update on the 'EastEnders' plot line, etc. They weren't really paying attention, but about half an hour later they felt a twinge of hunger and began to wonder what was going on.

There was evidently some kind of disagreement in the open-plan kitchen. The chef was talking very loudly in Cockney English and gesticulating loudly in Italian. It seemed to be an affair of the heart, but although the hands were expressing the trauma, Cockney is not a good language for emotion, so they couldn't really tell. Jules waved at several people as they passed back and forth and eventually slipped out from under his cloak of invisibility long enough for someone to see him.

'Have you ordered?' asked another girl with an unconvincing smile.

'Er, no,' said Jules, who glanced down at the menu only to glance up and find she had wandered off. Actually she had galloped off to rescue her friend, who seemed about to be assaulted by the chef with some pizza dough.

Too late. The dough flew out of the kitchen like an Italian frisbee, splatted on to the window and slid right on to a table where two guys were on their second bottle of vino collapso. The guys were none too pleased and one of them stood up to complain, which was a shame because he copped frisbee number two right in the mush.

As it happened, there were also a fair number of kids in the place from the local public school, and they took this as a general signal for a food fight. Much cheering and lobbing of complimentary garlic bread ensued and the guy with the unsolicited free sample went after the chef to try to give it back. Wielding as much of the gunk as he could scrape off the table, he chased him twice round the restaurant and into the High Street, followed by most of the kids, who saw this as a good opportunity to get away without paying. Jules watched them go and thought he recognized the chef.

A waitress came over to their table. She was wearing some garlic dough sticks and ice cream. 'Have you ordered, sir?' she asked.

'Er, no. What was all that about?' asked Jules.

'The chef had some bad news,' said the waitress. 'You see, although he's a chef by profession he's more of a drummer by inclination. His band have just sacked him.'

'Were they any good?'

'Deafer Than That? They were OK,' said the waitress. 'They had a record deal once.'

Light dawned on a new idea.

The chef reappeared at the door with a large grin and a dough ball stuck to his back.

'Hi,' said Jules. 'I'm Jules Charlie, remember me from the Godalming Festival? This is Glenna. I'm thinking of putting a band together.'

Glenna looked stunned. 'Since when?' she demanded.

'Hi,' said the chef. 'My name is Baseball Batts but you can call me LOUD!'

# 41

'A band? Are you crazy?' Frog looked incredulously at Jules. 'Why not?'

'Because it's a nightmare, that's why not. All that rehearsing, all that arguing, all that "I can't hear myself in the mix, man", all those disgusting gigs lugging six tons of gear in and out of a van you have to get a bank loan to pay for, with the automatic "breaking down on motorways in the middle of the night" feature, all that "where's the money from that last gig, man?" Hassle, hassle, hassle, HASSLE, HASSLE, HASSLE!'

'A real band. Not that poofy miming lot. We can go out and do our own songs. I'm completely pissed off with all this programming shit. Let's get some players. It'll be great. You remember Deafer Than That? I met their drummer in the Pizza Place last night and he says he'll do it.'

Frog was not convinced, but he was convinced that Jules was having one of his funny five minutes and it would be best not to disagree.

Jules and Frog had been in a few bands before. There had been the Velvet Fog.

The Velvet Fog had been a school band that changed personnel faster than an estate agency, and, although they hadn't actually been in it at the same time, they both suffered initiation into band politics under its leader Doug Diggins. Doug, a gifted keyboard player at the age of fourteen, had a profound sense of destiny and was preparing for greatness.

Anyone who joined his band soon found out that, if Doug was going to be famous, he was going to be a famous con-man. He set up dance gigs, printed tickets and got the band to sell them to all their schoolmates. After the dance, he would disappear with the money and then reappear a few days later with a new piece of 'essential' equipment for the band, which he would keep at his house.

He would also fail to pay the venue, pointing out that fourteen-year-olds were too young to sign contracts anyway and then move on.

His charming personality and a constant supply of suckers allowed him to survive fifteen years as a musician, during which he perpetrated variations of the same general scam to all and sundry, including three wives, before he was found dead in a ditch. The killer was never found and the case was closed after six months because the list of suspects began to overload the Police National Computer database.

Jules and Frog always felt nostalgic for these good old days and even now, years later, new friendships could still be founded on the strength of a bond based on a mutual loathing of Doug.

'Don't tell me that bastard owed you money as well!'

They always talked of having t-shirts made with I.O.U. on the front and ONE THOUSAND POUNDS on the back with Doug's signature at the bottom.

Jules was still owed a one-third share of a bass guitar from 1968.

More recently, there had been Dream Streets.

Dream Streets was a bit more cred and did at least stand half a chance of commercial success. It was founded by a couple of guys who had themselves been in several other bands.

John Donald and James Barnes owned the famous Godalming recording studio, Bridge2Far. Bridge2Far was a brilliant studio and the two guys made brilliant recordings. They ought to have been very successful but they were buggered by arithmetic. They charged 8.00 pounds per hour and, no matter what they did, the running cost was never less than 16.00 pounds per hour. They therefore went bankrupt at 100 miles per hour.

Jules had met them somewhere in the middle between the 'enthusiastic' and the 'despondent' phases. He had arrived one day at the studio in the middle of a conversation centred upon what they were going to do with Doug Diggins when they found him.

'Don't tell me that bastard owes you money as well!'

It transpired that he had settled a long-overdue studio bill by trading it against a keyboard which it later turned out he didn't actually own, a fact that became apparent only when a tearful girl arrived at the studio asking for it back. The luckless girl had been persuaded to sign as guarantor for a loan on the strength of his promise to marry her. 'Double D', who was already married in any case, had failed to keep up the payments and the finance company were about to repossess it. She never saw him again.

It is possible she saw him once more, but the police could never prove it.

They became friends.

Jules made some demos there, they went on to write some songs and, when James and John decided to put a new band together, they asked Jules to sing.

It was out-and-out rock. John Donald played guitar, James played keyboards, Dingle (what's a metronome?) Dell played drums and Frog played bass. They wrote some great songs and made some great demos. A few encouraging noises from record companies later and the band were on the road. Well, on the Godalming road anyway. They played a few pubs, a few universities and set up a few of their own concerts in local halls.

If they had ever sounded as good live as their demos, they might have succeeded. In the studio the sound was clean and clear. The songs, the production and the performances fused together, leapt out of the speakers, grabbed you by the nuts and made you listen.

On stage, they were the acoustic equivalent of the M25. Busy. Jules kept losing his voice, James kept losing his cool and nobody could hear anything for all the noise.

Record-company interest faded away, arguments broke out over creative direction, demos that had sparkled were worked and worked until all you could hear was desperation. The Local Residents' Action Committee, Godalming Against Loud Music, got an injunction which effectively stopped the studio from trading, the bank asked for their money back and everything went into decline.

When the studio finally died, so did the band.

Jules and Frog went back to duo gigs in the clubs.

'You know where you are with duo gigs,' Frog had said as he wiped the beer off the amp and picked broken glass out of his guitar case.

'Yeah, nowhere,' said Jules.

# 42

Life is not fair for drummers. In a band situation, they are the heartbeat, they are the foundation, they have to be good.

A vocalist can carry off any kind of talentectomy by developing an attitude and calling it style, the guitar player can still get away with Bert Weedon's Play in a Day, and there is virtually nothing a keyboard player can't do with technology, but the drummer is stuffed. If the drummer is crap, the band goes down the toilet.

Crap comes in two basic drumming flavours, tempo-flavoured and volume-flavoured. The former usually causes the last bar of the song to be played 50 per cent faster than the first and the latter causes volume-control warfare on stage as each member of the band cranks up the level to hear themselves above the din until the audience's ears are bleeding and the vocalist's tonsils are spontaneously launched over the crowd, a trick perfected in the punk era.

Baseball Batts was a terrific drummer. He was not too busy and he had a great feel, but he did get through half a dozen sticks and a skin or two every time he played.

Jules and Frog agreed that two out of three was good enough.

Frog phoned Juno Jones. Juno Jones was a black American, who had married an English girl and settled down well enough to feel at home, but managed to keep a distinctly American style. He was also a wicked guitar player. He had the ropiest-looking Fender Stratocaster, but it sounded great when he played it. Frog had met him when he was 'doing a dep' and playing with this Blues Brothers cover band. The Blues Brothers are now an institution, and knowledge of the film script, the songs and the dress code is compulsory. Since then The Commitments have fanned the flames and there are several great bands on the British circuit doing nothing else. Frog, who actually only knew one Blues Brothers song at the time, lied and said he could do it because he needed the cash.

The keyboard player from the BBCB was Alec French. He had a DX7 keyboard that was excavated at an archaeological dig near Glastonbury, and ridiculous hair which he normally kept tied in a ponytail, but which occasionally exploded vertically like an anti-personnel mine to make him one foot six inches taller. Alec was a matter-of-fact kind of musician. 'Yeah, mate, I'll do it if it's any good.'

They set to work.

The new line-up sat in the studio for three days and listened to the tracks Jules and Frog had laid down over the past few months. It was a bit sketchy, but enough to get the general idea.

'The style hasn't really settled down, so maybe we could think that through and work on that,' said Jules.

'So, what are you looking for, man?' said Juno. 'I mean do you want class, you know what I'm saying, some kinda smooth kinda thing or are you into energy?'

Alec filled his pipe. 'No, I think I get it. It's more a natural thing. Wild as in wilderness rather than crazy wild.'

Jules hadn't a clue what they were talking about, but he agreed anyway so that they would play and he could find out.

They set up their instruments in the live room and began. Music was heard through the studio doors for the first time in a quite a while. It went on for quite a while.

Rehearsals are a tricky problem.

The performance of music is generally accepted as good. A cultural benefit or good way to get laid, depending upon your age and sensitivity, but undeniably an entertainment for audiences and performers alike.

There is, of course, wide disagreement about the merits of different types of music, but they all have this in common. Any kind of music has to be learnt before it can be performed, be it by some spotty kid learning to play the trombone, a concert pianist learning a new piece for the repertoire, the soprano from the local amateur operatic company, or a pop band preparing for a tour. It may come as a shock to regular viewers of 'Top of the Pops', but everyone rehearses.

Rehearsals are generally accepted as a pain in the arse.

Apart from being very hard work for the performer, they are acutely irritating for any non-participant who happens to overhear them, and therein lies the problem.

It's not so much the noise, although they can be pretty noisy, as the mind-numbing repetition. Over and over again the performers struggle with annoyingly small sections of music and if lucky listeners liked the piece at the beginning they will certainly hate both the piece and the performer by the end.

'No, no,' protests the uninitiated rehearsal witness, 'I'm into the music, I'll just listen.' And they settle back expecting a concert with a few bum notes.

It's another by-product of the Hollywood myth. Anyone who has seen *Singing in the Rain, Holiday Inn, 42nd Street, Fame*, etc., thinks they know what to expect. In a ninety-minute film there is only so much time for comical tripping over, forgetting the words and general getting it wrong before you cut directly to the getting-it-right bit. It normally took Jules ninety minutes to tune up.

'AAAAARRGHHHH!' says the newly initiated rehearsal witness as he runs from the building following four or five hours of setting up the PA, fixing the PA because the amp is humming very loudly, aimless musical twiddlings by various bored musicians while others attempt to tune up, repair strings, connect twenty five midi leads, swear at each other about any or all of the above irritations, drink drinks of various potencies and smoke cigarettes of variable legal status and then play one song over and over and over again.

'AAAAARRGHHHH!' says the neighbour, who wasn't into the music in the first place.

'AAAAARRGHHHH!' says the policeman as he comes to tell you to shut up for the fiftieth time on behalf of the recently deaf.

'AAAAARRGHHHH!' says the council together with the magistrate who slaps on the injunction.

Performers solve this problem as best they can.

It's easy for the rich and famous. For those at the top of the tree, there is always a luxuriously appointed, efficiently soundproofed palace that can be rented for the purpose of confining the offensive noises to those who need to be offended. The rest of them just have to lump it.

There are those who really don't give a toss about what the neighbours think because they do DIY at eight o'clock on a Sunday morning. These people start riots and wars and the only thing to do is keep away from them as much as possible. Musicians generally, however, struggle with their consciences.

They hide away as much as possible and blag rehearsal space in village halls, other people's houses, garages, etc., just to spread the problem around, hopefully to prevent any individual neighbour from reaching boiling point and committing actual bodily harm.

It is a futile hope.

Fortune had smiled upon Jules in this respect, for one of the by-products of having bought the studio was that they did at least have a harmless place to perpetrate their rehearsals.

Recording and rehearsing are not the same thing, but the rehearsals sparked the recording which sparked the rehearsals which sparked the recording and slowly but surely the songs, the set and the album glued themselves together.

They all loved the album when it was finished. A rare feat. Jules loved what had happened to the songs. Frog and the band had turned the songs into sounds and then played them like angels. They all loved the way it sounded.

They felt they were ready.

## 43

'Why have I got to do it?'

Jules was driving the dogmobile down to the studio with Frog. Frog was having to get used to driving dogs now that he no longer worked in the motor trade.

'Because it's got to be done,' said Frog.

'I hate those gigs we did for Sherman.'

Frog winced as the car bounced off the kerb while Jules groped over his shoulder for the seatbelt.

'Face it, Jules, we need the money.'

'We've got a proper band now, we've got some great songs, we should be doing gigs with them.'

'Who for?'

'I don't know, someone.'

'It's straight arithmetic, Jock, my old cock. One of Sherman's gigs pays about a hundred and twenty quid. On the other hand, original bands playing original stuff get paid precisely zero.'

'Arithmetic is bollocks.'

'Suckmuckdoo!'

'You always say that.'

'But I'm right though, aren't I?'

The prospect of doing more of Sherman's gigs horrified Jules. He preferred to think of himself as a writer and playing other peoples' songs that you had long since got bored with, to a bunch of people who had long since got bored with you, seemed a bit beside the point. On the other hand, a hundred and twenty quid is a hundred and twenty quid.

'I'll do you a deal,' said Jules.

'Woah!' Frog threw his hands up in mock surprise.

'Yes, I'll do the Sherman gigs if we can also do some real gigs with the band and play the new stuff.'

## 44

Mike Delta loved the album, but for slightly different reasons. Enthusiasm and spontaneity don't necessarily equal commercial success, but in this case he was sure they had got the balance right. He hadn't had much to do with the recording in the end, appearing once in a while to nod and then go out to lunch with Brian or Glenna, but it felt good to be making real records again and he was in a buoyant mood.

Glenna loved the fact that Songfest gloom had evaporated and everyone was so 'up' all the time. Jules and Frog went out three or four evenings a week doing Sherman's poxy gigs while she was busy trying to fix some dates for a couple of showcases.

The plan was to divide and conquer. Wow the sceptics in the record companies in small groups and then try to license the record territory by territory. If they could start in the UK, then the rest of Europe would surely follow suit and, she hoped, if they could get half a hit or two, they would finally get the USA. The first step was definitely going to be the hardest.

There are very few decent clubs left in London and of those that remain still fewer are regarded as cred by the music business.

Glenna was negotiating with the Sad Sax. It was not so much a negotiation as an unconditional surrender. However, as the management of the Sad Sax, mindful of their favoured position with the music business and of the desperation of the would-be 'great' to attract their attention, laid down their standard contract conditions.

'Send us a tape, love, and we'll see what we can do,' said the manager of the Sad Sax. 'If we do go for it we expect 100 quid up front as a deposit against ticket sales to cover the cost of the PA and the lights, we give you 200 tickets that you sell for whatever you can get, then we give them a quid discount on the door, count the ones with your name on and if you get more than a hundred in we give you your deposit back.'

Glenna wrote all this down and promised the man a cassette.

'Do you mean we have to pay them for working at their club and sell the tickets for them?' said an outraged Jules when they discussed it later that day.

''Fraid so, Jules. That is the way it works.'

'Perhaps we're also expected to work behind the bar, wash the glasses and sweep up after closing time.'

'We couldn't afford it.'

The cassette was a formality. The manager of the Sad Sax said yes to anyone who was prepared to take his ridiculous contract. He didn't really care who they were, what kind of music they played or whether they were any good. All he had to do was put on seven acts a night and he made a profit. He made his real money over the bar, and he never returned anyone's deposit because he employed very large guys to count tickets and no one ever disagreed when they only counted ninety-eight.

The bands never actually sell tickets to their mates, of course, because it's hard enough to get them down to the umpteenth gig that month in the first place, never mind asking them to pay twice, so they just give them away and take the loss.

Desperation and gullibility mean that there is a never-ending supply of bands who will go for this, so unscrupulous venues always get away with it, which is a shame because unsigned bands can't keep it up for long and so, good, bad or indifferent, they fade away.

The system doesn't favour quality. The poorer the show, the smaller the audiences, the smaller the audiences, the fewer the venues. Round and round, down and down. These clubs are so busy making money out of the bands they have forgotten the audience altogether.

One day, there will be one band and one venue but the manager of the Sad Sax thinks it will be him, so he's OK.

## 45

Having accepted the ridiculous contract, Jules, Frog and the band put their irritation aside and became enthusiastic about their debut gig. Frog even changed his guitar strings.

By the day itself, the tension was unbearable. Worse than the Songfest.

Glenna and Frog lodged themselves in the caravan and smoked each other's cigarettes until the M25 fog detectors went off, while Jules yawned his head completely inside out and went vacant.

'Who's coming?' asked Frog for the second time that cigarette.

'Everybody,' said Glenna with confidence. 'Mike has done the rounds and everybody wants to see what all the fuss is about.'

'I hope that bastard Deek hasn't been invited.'

'Except him.'

'Brian has been on the phone for the last week and guarantees over a hundred punters so we should get our deposit back.'

'Who?'

'Just mates.'

'I hope they're not all solicitors. A hundred solicitors in one room is asking for trouble. I'd be tempted to torch the place myself.'

Jules yawned again.

'Not keeping you up, are we?' said Frog.

'What?'

'Never mind,' said Frog and nicked another of Glenna's cigarettes.

'I can't help it,' said Jules, coming back to earth. 'I always get like this when I'm wound up. Anyway, I reckon if you're going to lose control of a bodily function in a crisis, the yawn reflex is definitely one of the soft options.'

'I think Baseball has lost control of one of the others,' said

Frog, glancing at the smoke coming out of the lavatory window. 'He must have been in there for half an hour.'

'I'll ring the cesspit company in the morning for a collection,' said Glenna, absently.

'I'd ring them now,' said Frog, 'or we'll all be floating to the gig.'

Brian arrived at 2.30 with the van.

'Aren't you ready yet?' he said, looking around at the gear half in and half out of cases and spread around the inside of the studio. 'We're supposed to be there by four o'clock.'

Baseball was persuaded to come out of the lavatory and they all loaded the van. Jules counted everything, Glenna led the sherpa's team and Frog took 'shotgun and jigsaw' in the back of the van to make it all fit. He always enjoyed this task and was conducting an experiment with the concepts of 'spatial optimization' and 'dimensional dilation' with the general aim of getting all the gear into a one-metre cube which did not rattle.

The van bounced away over the uneven drive and the gear rattled just as it always did. It rattled up the A3, rattled into Putney, it stopped rattling for the usual twenty minutes of steering-wheel pounding, fuming and swearing up the High Street, then rattled over the bridge and up the King's Road and finally stopped outside the Sad Sax at 4.15.

The decorators of the Sad Sax had a fixation with the colour black. The front is painted 'Cred Black' with the name picked out in dark grey. The interior is even blacker because there is no natural light to spoil the effect. When the place is open they switch on those special lights that make it darker, but at that time in the afternoon it was bathed in fluorescent light which exposed the true magnitude of its tackiness and made you realize why they went to so much trouble to stop people from ever seeing it.

At one end of the black room was a large black stage flanked by black speakers, and in the middle was a large circular bar. Between the bar and the stage was the mixing desk, cunningly positioned so that the engineer was never in any danger of running out of alcohol.

The engineer was standing at the desk looking annoyed.

'Where the fuck have you been?' he inquired as Jules staggered in carrying three guitars.

'Er, I'm sorry we're late,' mumbled Jules. 'The traffic was terrible.'

'The traffic is always terrible. You shoulda foughta that before you pissed about with my afternoon. I've got free other bands to do before eight o'clock.'

It wasn't a personal attack. The engineer was permanently annoyed with everything and everybody. He had been the house engineer at the Sad Sax for five years and had worked with hundreds of bands. Thousands of musicians with a million different ideas about sound. He resolved any argument by insult and it had become a habit.

He was annoyed that he had been working for so long for so little and still hadn't been asked to work for a major band, annoyed that the band he used to be in had never been signed, annoyed that several really crap bands it had been his displeasure to work with had been. He was bitter and, of course, almost completely deaf.

'Oh, my Christ, not another one of them!' he said as Frog pulled his bass guitar from the case. 'You're not another wanker who thinks he's Mark King, are you?'

'What?' said Frog.

'Never mind. I'll deal with it.'

And so on until all the gear was out, the stage was set and they were ready to soundcheck.

'Give me the "kick",' shouted Smiley down the intercom.

Baseball obliged. Ten seconds later the bass-drum sound could have dwarfed Concorde.

'Right, now give me the snare.'

Volleys of cannon fire filled the air.

'Right, now go round the toms.'

Baseball did.

'No, no! Fuckin' hit them,' complained Smiley. 'Look, I'll show you.' He left the crow's nest, jumped up on the stage and pushed Baseball out from behind the kit.

There followed an earthquake. The room and all the fittings and fixtures vibrated. Everything that wasn't screwed down fell down. When he had been the drummer in a band no one ever said they could hear it. Not at first, anyway; six months later they couldn't hear anything.

'That's how you get a sound, son.'

The soundcheck continued. Smiley got the bass and guitars to sound like a steel mill and chainsaws respectively. The combined effect was more industrial than musical.

'OK, now give me a bit of lead vocal.'

Jules sang on his own. A thin wispy sound struggled out of the speakers. Smiley turned the EQ knobs this way and that for a moment.

'Again?'

It got worse.

'Perfect.' Smiley pronounced himself satisfied. 'Give me a number.'

Jules was far from happy, but they counted in the first number and launched into it as enthusiastically as they could.

It sounded terrible and they stopped halfway through.

'I can't hear the vocals at all,' said Jules.

'Well stand closer to the fucking mike,' said Smiley. 'That's all you get; the next band have been waiting half an hour as it is because they were here on time.' And he waved at the next band who gushed in through the door and started putting gear up on the stage before anyone could protest.

Jules and Frog sat in the pub next to the club staring into space. Glenna had gone off with Brian to find a more sensible place to park the van. Baseball, Alec and Juno decided to check out the boats in Chelsea Harbour.

'Could you hear the vocals?'

'All I could hear was the drums and a kind of hum. I think it was my ears.'

'I may be wrong, but I think it's going to be a disaster.'

'What time are we going on?'

'Nine-thirty.'

'If we leg it for the station and take the train to Gatwick we might just be able to buy a ticket, get on the plane and be out of the country before anyone noticed we were gone.'

'Jules, we have to do this and we have to be good.'

'How can we be good when it sounds like shit?'

'We leap around and pretend that it's supposed to be like that.'

'But it isn't. I want it to sound like it does in the studio. The way we rehearsed it. Why can't it sound like that?'

'Get real, Jules, it never sounds like that. Face it, the punters don't care. You've played enough gigs to know. Someone comes up to you and says, "Oy, mate, can you play 'Stairway to 'eaven?'", you play him a couple of bars on an accordion, he'll be happy as Larry. He doesn't care if it doesn't sound right, he just wants to be reminded of it.'

'This doesn't remind me of anything.'

'All we have to do is behave like we're in control and people will take the rest for granted. If we look confused, people just get embarrassed. It's all bullshit; this is a very image-oriented industry.'

'Do you think anyone in the entire history of rock and roll ever got a good sound on stage?'

'No.'

'It's good to feel a part of such a great tradition.'

'Suckmuckdoo!'

# 46

Brian and Glenna were standing at the back of the club watching the end of the previous band's set when Mike wandered in.

'Did somebody die?' said Mike, looking around at the sparse audience.

'Only those guys,' said Glenna, nodding at the band.

The noise stopped and the band's fifteen mates at the front went wild and demanded an encore. The vast and empty space behind them said nothing.

Smiley banged down the faders and began to set up for Jules, thus preventing the band onstage from getting ideas about doing an encore and screwing up his schedule.

'Where is everyone?' asked Mike. 'I thought you said you could get a couple of hundred to fill the place up.'

'They're in the pub, Mikey, don't worry, they'll be here in a minute.' Brian waved at the stage. 'We'll 'ave more than that load a prats anyway.'

'Where are the A&R guys?' countered Glenna.

'I spoke to them all this afternoon; they'll be here.'

Mike looked around. 'God, this place has gone downhill. I haven't been here for years.'

'I don't find that a particularly reassuring thought, bearing in mind your previous job,' said Glenna. 'I'm going to check on the guys. Get me a beer if you're thinking of going to the bar.' She strode purposefully towards the dressing-room door, trying not to look like a groupie.

She put her head round the door and nearly fell down.

'My God, what have you done?' She surveyed the scene in disbelief.

'We've decided on a more outrageous approach,' said Jules.

'I see.'

'Make an impression, you said.'
'You will.'
Glenna left and headed back to the bar.

# 47

Glenna needn't have worried.

Not that she needn't have worried about Jules. Jules was without doubt stepping firmly out to lunch and probably wouldn't be back for a while. Not that she needn't have worried about him looking a total prat in fifteen minutes' time. She should definitely have worried about those things, but she needn't have worried about him screwing up in front of all those important music-business people, because there were none there.

In a hotel in Paris a party was going on. It was chic, it was expensive, it was loud, it was drunken and James Deek was a proud man.

James Deek had laid on free air travel and overnight accommodation for every European and American record-industry person he had ever met, together with several hundred he had not, for an irresistible celebration of the renaissance of CBA Records in style.

Irresistible for several reasons. First of all, it was largely free, completely free if you didn't drink anything, not very likely, but anyway... Second, it was in an exotic location to which you could take some impressionable secretary and 'widen her horizons' on expenses, and third it was a good lig.

To 'lig' is a show-business sport, which involves going to parties and hanging out with famous people as if you know them. It's also a career path. Accomplished liggers move up the pecking order by standing behind the stars and getting into their photographs. At any show-business party the ratio of liggers to real guests is in the region of 100–1. The whole thing has been raised to an artform in Los Angeles, where they run degree courses in it at UCLA, but all you really need for social climbing is a pair of big boots and a head for heights.

Famous people were going to be at James's party, followed, as ever, by the paparazzi, and you therefore stood a good chance of a double whammy. Several of the label's bands were playing the gig, but the real stroke, and the reason most people had turned up, was that the headliner was the incredible Neil Down.

Neil Down was a phenomenon. Big in the 1960s when he was young and rebellious, now, in his late forties, he was famous for his music, his relationships and his assaults on journalists. He made a record every two years or so which sold by the million and in between times he made a few movies and guested on everybody else's records.

The ageing process, plus one or two cosmetic operations, had been kind to him. He had fared well.

It isn't easy to grow old gracefully in show business. In the 1960s, rock stars had a certain image to live up to. They had to be alcoholic substance-abusers with a hyperactive social life. Neil was a conscientious rocker and was never to be seen without a bottle of Jack Daniels in one hand and his other one down the front of some groupie's tie-dye. It was a survival test. It looked a blast, but life could be pretty shitty. They smoked it, ate it and generally wallowed in it. The Crapped-on Factor, as it were.

Any that made it to 1975 with only minimal brain damage were allowed to sleep it off for ten years or so, at which point, when their social consciences were awoken by Bob Geldof, they were allowed back into society, provided they became politically and environmentally aware. The sensible rock star was born.

Neil made it. He awoke, bemused, to face the greater challenge. Rock and roll on orange juice and muesli. It's tough at the top.

He was a longstanding mate of Cagg Brown, which was why he signed to CBA for his return album. It sold three million copies, and his tour went on for the following two years, during which he was seen by an estimated 10 per cent of the planet's population. He looked set to gig for ever, but it all came to a sudden halt in 1987 when he was shot and wounded on stage at Wembley by a particularly dedicated fan during the encore.

He hadn't made a public appearance since, but he was here now and playing for James Deek.

James was not just the luckiest son-of-a-bitch A&R man that ever made a living without signing a single artist, but he was now the most influential. Not only had he put together the most outrageous music-business party of the year and got Neil Down to play, but he had also kept it secret from Mike Delta. An ingenious trick accomplished by telling everyone that the party was in his honour. He smiled to himself.

He had never made such an effort over anything before, but spite had made him strong and he was beginning to enjoy the feeling.

'Game, set and match to me I think,' he said to himself as he surveyed the assembled throng. And he walked down the steps to the sunken bar and sank a very large Scotch.

The room was vast and was set with streams of converging red and white lights in the floor and walls to give the effect of the night traffic flowing up and down the Champs Elysees. The eye was drawn down the perspective to the stage, upon which a combination of lights, photographs and structures created a majestic Arc de Triomphe.

To complete the effect, the bar prices were extortionate.

Dance music thudded from the sound system and the stage at the base of the Arc was in darkness as the crew removed the previous band's equipment and prepared for the gig of the decade. The audience swayed, danced, drank and yelled at each other over the din. Even though they were largely professional cynics, there was a definite buzz. A sense of anticipation. People wanted to see whether he could still do it. A teenage hero is still a teenage hero no matter how cynical you are.

The press were out in force, waiting to see whether he would get shot again. Several were carrying guns of their own just in case no one else was going to do it.

Pin-sized red lights on the front of bits of equipment glowed and blinked in the darkness as the crew walked around the stage. The audience suddenly went quiet as figures appeared carrying instruments and then began to chant and clap disapprovingly when it transpired they were only more roadies.


Back at the Sad Sax, Smiley the engineer, fag dangling from the lower lip and scratching his arse, stood up at the mixing desk and invited the previous band to get their gear off the fucking stage.

It was 11.15 in Paris and a quarter-past the Stone Age in London.

In Paris the dance music stopped. The audience held its collective breath, which was no bad thing considering the amount of garlic in the fish soup. A well-known French DJ walked on from the wings to introduce the act and the audience booed in a good-natured, get-on-with-it sort of a way.

A lighting technician, balancing up the rig manning a follow spot, who hadn't had the fish soup, caught the enthusiastic garlic blast full in the face and narrowly avoided falling off. The audience put the barracking track on pause for a moment and listened.

At the Sad Sax a coachload of drunken solicitors led by Brian Payedwell fell in through the double doors at the back and headed for the bar.

As the French DJ charmed his way through a two-minute build-up, Smiley was fog-horning at Jules and Co. to get their act together. Jacques de Lacques shone, Smiley ranted, Paris held its breath, London belched and bought another round.

At precisely 11.42 (everybody's time in Europe except England), 10.42 (real time), the opening chord for each performance was struck.

In Paris, the band powered into the opening of one of Neil Down's biggest ever hits. The riff hit the air in perfect time, at perfect pitch and in perfect balance. Huge guitars played the exquisite melody, the drums cracked and the sky melted. The lights exploded on to the stage with the power of a solar flare and there was Neil Down in full body armour.

He sang. The audience went crazy.

Smiley whammed up the faders as the first song of Jules's set struggled for lift-off. There was a deafening feedback squeal. Jules winced and backed off the mike. The guitars squeaked and buzzed, the drums beat an uncertain rhythm at 7.5 on the Richter scale.

He sang. The audience couldn't hear him.

There are those who think that Jules's idea of dressing the entire band in duffle coats and hush puppies was a masterstroke. There are also those who stand at Clapham Junction in rain-soaked anoraks and write down train numbers.

The effect was fairly dramatic. They looked like a bunch of Paddington Bear fans on an outing. The completely appalling sound made it seem faintly punky, but overall it was a good deal more hilarious than sexy. Despite everything, the band did not falter. They jumped, sang and twanged their way through the set for all the world as though it was supposed to sound like that and came off after forty-five minutes, sweating profusely under the weight.

The audience, consisting as it did largely of Brian's friends, shouted and cheered loyally, but the room oozed indifference. There were precious few people in it, no one there that the band hadn't invited and, of course, no A&R people at all.

Smiley swore and the next band scurried around them as they prepared for their set. Jules, Frog and the rest of the guys lugged their gear off the stage and retreated to the dressing room.

They reappeared half an hour later in the bar, minus the duffle coats.

'That was magic!' said Brian to Frog. 'Fancy a drink? You should meet some of these guys I brought down.' And he steered him into a gaggle of people. Frog looked as though he might kill Brian, but he plastered on a quick-fit smile and dropped into polite conversation. He was good at that.

Jules was not good at it. He fussed with the equipment and spoke briefly to Glenna, but kept out of the back-slapping scene. He was horribly disappointed and couldn't keep it out of his mind or off his face.

They loaded the van in silence and left at two in the morning without their deposit.

# 48

The next day they all turned up at the studio late, but the row started early.

'It was a bloody disaster,' said Frog. 'How much did we lose?'

'Two hundred and fifty quid, including the coach and the bar tab,' said Jules.

'It wasn't that bad,' said Brian. 'My mates said it was OK. All right, it was a bit empty, but we're only just starting, we can build on that, right, get it up to a couple of hundred regular punters and then start charging the venues.'

'There's a revolutionary thought.'

'Why duffle coats?' Glenna appealed to Jules. 'What in the world made you think this would be a good idea?'

'It was a joke, Glenna. Not a very good one, I know. To tell you the truth I'm not sure I wasn't just trying to piss everybody off,' said Jules dejectedly. 'I've suddenly lost track of the point of all this. We put ourselves into debt, take abuse from wankers in record-company offices, wankers in the press, wankers at venues, and for what? To impress another bunch of wankers who couldn't even be bothered to turn up!'

He paced up and down the caravan. 'Where were they? I thought Mike had this covered.'

'We were Deeked!' said Mike, stepping out of the rain and into the warm caravan.

'What does that mean?' said Jules.

'It means that James Deek sabotaged the gig by setting up a better one.' He waved the paper at them.

The front cover had a large photograph of Neil Down walking out of the hotel after the gig and, half a pace behind, James, grinning like a demented Cheshire cat.

'He flew the entire music industry to Paris for a freebie. It must have cost hundreds of thousands of pounds. You should be honoured, Jules.'

'He did all that just to get even with me?'

'Me, I think.'

Frog came in from the rain with a tray of coffee and they both steamed as Mike read out the details of the event from the gossip column, and they all steamed gently as they tried to come to terms with what had happened.

'Didn't you know about this?'

Mike was nettled. 'No, I didn't know about it. I might have my ear to the ground, but I'm not bloody clairvoyant.'

'How can you not know about a party that big?' asked Jules.

'How could you wear duffle coats at a gig?'

Depression set in.

'Well, he stuffed us,' said Baseball, who was hitting his knee with a couple of heavy-gauge drumsticks.

'What the hell are we going to do?' said Jules. 'It's hard enough trying to do this when nobody cares who you are; it's impossible if they're actually out to get you.'

'I'm going to talk to her,' said Mike, looking closely at the photograph.

'Who?' said Jules.

'Just a friend of mine.'

A flicker of reassurance floated about the conversation for a while, but nobody was convinced. Optimism was marked absent on the register and pessimism put up a camp bed in the spare room of Jules's life. There seemed no point in staying, so he picked up his jacket and walked out into the rain. Frog followed.

'We need to talk, Jules,' said Frog, falling into step as he walked towards the car.

'I couldn't cope with another arithmetic lesson, Frog.'

'We're skint,' said Frog earnestly. 'You need money, Jules; I need money.'

'That's it, isn't it?' Jules stopped walking and looked at Frog. 'I have had the worst five months of my life and you are going to suggest we do another tuppenny-ha'penny gig at one of Sherman's poxy clubs where the audience consists of drunks and children who hate us.'

'You don't have to tell me, I was there. Anyway, it's not tuppenny-ha'penny.'

'Well, thruppenny-ha'penny then. I don't care. I am not doing another one of those poxy gigs!'

Jules turned to walk away and Frog grabbed his jacket to stop him.

'Well, what are you going to do, for God's sake? Just listen for a minute, Jules, it's not another poxy gig for Sherman, OK? It was one of Brian's friends at the gig last night. He represents that guy Rantin who has all the holiday camps.'

Jules eyed Frog suspiciously.

'He wants to give us a contract.'

'So now we're Red Coats?'

'No, the band. He wants us to play the winter season in his golfing place in Spain. Fifteen grand! That's three grand each.'

Jules looked skywards. 'Three grand to be a bloody Red Coat. I think I preferred working at the hospital.'

'This is real money. Not a music-industry mirage. It's three grand to be a musician. For Christ's sake, Jules. Isn't that what you wanted?'

'No... fucking... way!'

'You owe me, Jules. I'm into this for a few quid too, you know, all this poncing about doesn't pay my mortgage. Just think about it.'

'I don't need to think about it. It's a crap idea and I'm not doing it!'

'Well, what are you going to do?'

'Not that, OK? Just not that.'

Frog lost patience. 'Well, it's better than this bowel movement you've got us into. Face it, Jules, it's over. The fantasy is over, welcome back to real life, wake up and smell the manure.' He waved in the general direction of some mud.

'Frog, I've been working for this my whole life. It's not over. I would know if it was over.'

'Would you?'

There was a long silence.

'Look, Jules, we've discussed this in the band and we reckon it's a good gig. We should do it.'

Jules was in an ugly frame of mind and saw no reason to disguise his contempt. 'Well, just go and play the gig. Take the band and play the fucking gig because I'm not going to Spain to be a prat, I can do that quite easily right here.' He strode off sulkily through the mud.

Frog watched him as he slammed the door of the car and reversed out the car park and a great many other things besides.

## 49

Frog, living as he did in the flat above Jules, saved a great deal of money on telephone bills, but it was rather embarrassing when they occasionally fell out as they had to time their arrivals and departures carefully to avoid meeting in the stairwell.

After the row outside the studio, he went straight back to his flat because he knew Jules would drive about for a few hours to calm down.

He searched around in his 'important things' drawer and produced an elderly passport. He threw it down on the coffee table.

He fetched the portable end of his portable phone and fished out his diary.

He called Brian Payedwell.

'You and Julesey ''aving a bit of a tiff?'

'He doesn't want to do that gig in Spain, Brian, but don't blow it out just yet, I want to see if I can fix something up.'

He pressed the 'out' button and put the phone back down. He lit a cigarette. Turning the pages at the back of his diary, he produced a folded piece of paper with a short, handwritten message in two parts. The first part said Terri and gave a phone number. The second was in his own handwriting and it read '(the girl with the enormous tits)'.

He spoke for over three cigarettes, after which he glanced at his watch and headed for the bathroom to take a shower.

It seemed to him that Jules had finally and completely flipped out. Knowing him as well as he did, he was fairly well tuned to his eccentricities, but he was frankly baffled. The guy was facing bankruptcy and didn't want to know about a fifteen-grand gig. He hoped Jules would wake up soon, before it was too late.

## 50

Deek woke.
It was a slow process, one of those awakenings that slip back and forth over a very fuzzy boundary of consciousness. One where you don't know whether you are dreaming that you feel like a corpse that's been given a day off or whether you actually are a corpse that's been given the day off.

Eventually he decided he was that corpse.

He put his hand to his head to hold his eyes in while he contorted the rest of his face as a headache test. The headache passed the test and Deek passed out again. He slipped back into the land of the living again a few minutes later and tried to remember not to do it again.

He moved his other hand slowly, trying not to disturb his head again while he checked his watch.

It was at this point that he made another significant discovery. He was not alone. He touched skin that was quite definitely not his own.

He recoiled in confusion, trying to piece together the previous evening and remember who the skin might belong to, but nothing came to him.

He remembered everything up to the point at which he had been a very important record-industry person fighting off brown-nosers hard enough to allow himself to breathe, but not so hard that he ever had to buy a drink. That part was OK, it fitted his current self-image of Superman meets J.R. Ewing, but Superman does not go on to get pissed and wake up the next day with a head that felt as if it had been drawn by Picasso and a surprise friend.

The surprise friend rolled over, farted and fell out of the bed, taking the duvet as it went.

Deek raised himself painfully on one elbow and peered over the edge of the bed at the shape under the duvet.

The shape groaned and moved about, trying to find an air hole. Slowly, a head appeared and looked unsteadily back at James Deek. Two pairs of eyes challenging the very definition of the word bloodshot.

It spoke.

'Bloody hell. Don't you look like a wanker with no clothes on!'

Deek fell off his elbow.

## 51

Helen Denture was a striking woman. She was a tall, slim and elegant woman in her mid-thirties with dark hair cut into a kind of manic bob. She was a hard-drinking, hard-partying 'one of the guys' kind of a girl with an anarchic sense of humour and a laugh like a machine-gun. The daughter of a Sheffield steelworker, she was fair of face, charmingly blunt and disarmingly obscene. She played men at their own game, usually cheated and usually won.

She was one of the most successful women in the music business, Head of A&R at Luggage Records, one of the last small independent labels, with her own (male) secretary and one scout. She had a rich and colourful reputation for doing anything for anybody, with anybody or to anybody, and now she had apparently done it to James Deek.

Her acquaintance with the music business had begun at a Neil Down gig. It was the first real rock-and-roll gig she had ever been to, and she fell in love with the whole thing. The noise, the smell, the sweat, the hype, the show and the party. She forced her way backstage, found the great man and told him that she should be his personal assistant. In the drunken post-gig euphoria, and with a completely different notion of what personal assistance she might provide, he agreed to this, but she managed to sidestep the following lunge and leave again before he could get really stuck into their first meeting. By then he had given her his personal number.

She called him the following day and every day thereafter for the following month until he agreed, sober and in the presence of witnesses, to give her a job.

There are surprisingly few people in any organization that actually do anything and, at that time, there were precisely none in the Neil Down Machine. She was brilliant. The office never recovered. Stuff happened. Tours were booked, recording projects were arranged and then completed. Buses, aeroplanes, PAs, studios, venues, catering, booze and prostitutes fell into place like magic and the band were bailed out from local prisons when required. She was clever enough never to sleep with Neil and never to get involved in the drugs, and soon she was more or less running things.

By the time Neil went underground she was launched.

She stood up and walked uncertainly towards the bathroom, still clutching the duvet and groping for a packet of Gauloises as she passed the table.

Deek lay on the bed with his eyes still closed, wracked with the insecurity of amnesia, trying to work out why he had jumped Helen Denture of all people. Christ, she knew everybody.

He hadn't jumped her, of course, she had jumped him, which is an entirely different thing, but he couldn't remember that part.

He eased himself into the sitting position on the edge of the bed and fumbled for a pair of boxer shorts to cover the most embarrassing parts of his body, which amounted to most of it. He cranked himself into the vertical and tottered across the room to open the curtains. The midday sunlight caused a relapse in the headache and temporary blindness, but he stood in the window anyway and looked at the view with his eyes closed.

The view he did not see was worth unscrewing your eyes for. The Parisian sun had washed most of the colours to white but the staggering architecture tumbled away northwards across the river and rose to meet the Sacré Coeur as it smiled down at the rest of the city from the top of the hill.

The Sacré Coeur smiled back at the staggering architecture, it smiled at the ridiculous traffic, it smiled at the tourists, it smiled at the 'entrepreneurs' ripping off the tourists, and at the artists that were busy doing yet another painting of a Montmartre café scene and it smiled at the microscopic figure of a record-company executive in a distant hotel window with a face like a dried chamois trying to cope with the daylight.

After a few minutes trying to open his eyes he gave in and turned back into the room.

'I'm going to get some coffee,' he said to the bathroom door. 'Do you feel like anything?'

A towelled head with a toothbrush in it appeared.

'I feel like shit,' it said.

'You look like shit,' said Deek, who was not so delicate that he didn't spot a good opportunity to turn the psychological tables.

'I hope you don't read anything into this,' said Helen, as she dunked another wad of croissant into an Olympic-sized cup of coffee twenty minutes later.

'Into what?'

'Because this is just, you know, casual with me, James. I mean you are a nice guy, well, basically nice.' She glanced at the bed and some rather obvious footmarks high up the wall. 'Nice, but weird. You know I'm not surprised your wife left you, but anyway I'm not ready for any kind of commitment to a steady relationship.'

Deek sputtered. 'I assure you I have no intention...'

'Well that's good, James, let's just keep it light. We get along, we do business, I fuck you, you fuck me. It's just a game, right?'

Deek spluttered some more but no further words were spoken, no further glances exchanged.

They parted at the hotel door an hour later and made their separate ways to the airport. Deek knew he had made a big mistake and determined that Helen would pay for it. He made a mental note to review the distribution deal Luggage Records had with CBA.

## 52

Life on the road is known to be for animals and adolescent males only.

The tour bus is a multi-functional facility. It provides transport, of course, for the band and the equipment and is designed to be airtight so that the disgusting body odours and flatulence are not inflicted upon innocent bystanders.

The windows, if present, should be blacked out, but at least one should be capable of opening to allow for the disposal of beer bottles, used condoms, members of the band who fart too much and the display of the rare Greater Spotted, White Hairy Drummer's Buttocks when all else fails to get a laugh.

But it is also the bedroom, changing room and occasionally the lavatory. Frog's elderly Transit would have to do.

Frog had been on tour once and, though this didn't count as an actual tour, he was willing to bet that Theresa was going to complicate matters on the drive to Spain.

She had been thrilled when Frog called. 'Well, I've got nothing on,' she'd said, and laughed very loudly.

Five days of travel in Frog's van. Five days, four blokes and two enormous tits. The vibration alone would probably be enough to put Baseball into a sexual coma.

At six o'clock in the morning two weeks, later Alec, Juno and Baseball emerged from Rock Green, where they had crashed overnight.

Clutching mugs of coffee, they blinked in the dawn's early light.

'So this is six o'clock, man, I knew I wouldn't like it.'

Glenna arrived to see them off.

'How's Jules?' said Frog.

'Seething,' said Glenna. 'Maybe he'll calm down when you've actually gone.'

Terri arrived in a boiler suit. Pretty but unrevealing. Frog breathed a sigh of relief. 'OK, campers, let's get going.'

They pulled out of the studio drive five minutes later, the van lying low on the axles. Terri squeaked with excitement, 'I can't believe we're actually going.'

'Neither can I,' said Frog, who'd just done a service on the van.

Glenna watched them turn out of the drive and disappear round the bend in the lane. She locked the studio gate behind them.

## 53

August and September were unhappy months for Jules. The few showcases the band had struggled on to do had been an expensive, largely unattended waste of time. The album had been completely blanked and when the gig-tab got over two thousand pounds they'd just given up.

Jules was all for carrying on, but when Frog and the rest of the band had gone to Spain there seemed little point. Mike Delta had dropped out of circulation and, despite Glenna's efforts, the studio remained largely unused. Even Brian had found an excuse to visit Spain and had not been seen for eight weeks.

The bills heaped up, the money ran out. Jules did not handle it well. The rows about money were like icebergs in his relationship with Glenna, which eventually hit one and sank.

'You are bitter, boring and broke,' she had said. 'You'd better decide what you want and how you're going to survive. Meanwhile, don't expect me to hang around watching you torture yourself. Call me when you have a sentence to say that doesn't include the words "that bastard Deek".'

And that was that.

That was when he decided to go to Nashville.

It wasn't that he particularly liked country music. As an acoustic-guitar player, he was always irritated by the general assumption that, unless they have just stepped to the front of a stage filled with smoke and a very hairy rock band, acoustic-guitar players are either folk or country. Jules was not much into folk music either.

Country music suffers greatly from being popular. Like Benidorm or Niagara Falls, it has been visited so often that the thing of beauty which made it worth the trip has been all but destroyed. But Nashville remains a monument to its past and a Mecca for songwriters.

He had heard stories. Stories of musical fusion. Artists and writers, famous, infamous and anonymous colliding in a creative meltdown. Of fame and wealth, of overnight success. These stories were clearly dung, but at least it seemed that his kind of personal madness was acceptable, if not compulsory.

His only real connection with Nashville was an old schoolfriend called Stephanie something. They hadn't exactly been close, but the few months she had been at Jules's secondary school had left an impression on him. If only he could remember her second name. Stephanie something was a brilliant piano player. She was a star pupil and singled out for much attention. She played classical pieces to the school every morning in assembly, had a great deal of private tuition from old 'Letch' Fletcher the music teacher who could see, not only a Royal College of Music scholar on his list of teaching achievements, but also, if he stood just behind her while she played, right down the front of her blouse.

But she was best remembered by the rest of the school for her impromptu lunchtime rock-and-roll sessions and the occasion, at the end of the year, when she had sneaked a copy of the 'Liberty Bell March' past the headmaster as the morning-assembly classical piece. The Headmaster didn't twig. He liked military music. It stirred the soul, stiffed the resolve and gave him a hard-on for the good old days when you could thrash a lad for not wearing his cap on the way to school. Morning assemblies were pretty tedious so, given its cult status, when Stephanie burst into the theme tune to 'Monty Python's Flying Circus' there was a riot. She was sent to his study and Mr Crumble had to have severe words with the rest of the school about respect and the perils of watching television.

Stephanie eventually did go to the Royal College, but never made much headway in classical music and finally ended up in Nashville as a session player. After some fairly sketchy research, Jules had managed to find someone who remembered her second name.

'Chisholm? Stephanie Chisholm. I think that's the girl you mean. I couldn't tell you where she's living,' said the secretary at the college. 'Anyway, she might've got married by now.'

'Thanks, I'll figure it out.'

And so he'd blown the last few quid in his overdraft on a cheap air ticket to Nashville. He had no idea what he was going to do there, he just knew he had to go and make something happen.

## 54

Dreadnaught Sea Freight and Marine Hire were a solid firm of very normal people. After some thorough checking, Glenna satisfied herself that none of the employees was a frustrated musician or songwriter. There were no family connections with rock stars or record-company executives. They didn't even play the radio in the office.

'I'll take the job,' she said.

'When can you start?' said her new boss.

Dreadnaught was based in Staines, but it did business worldwide, mostly with the offshore oil exploration business and nothing to do with the record business. It also gave her an opportunity to move back into her parents' house and save the rent for a while. Glenna got on well with her parents, who had a house in Virginia Water. It was certainly large enough for them to survive the occasional family reunion and they lived there only six months of the year anyway.

She emptied her suitcase on to the bed and hung her stuff in the wardrobe while her mother hovered.

'Do you want to talk about it, dear?'

'No thanks, Mum, if it's all the same to you, I think I'll just nurse the anger, beat myself up a bit and get it out that way.'

'Whatever you think best.'

Her job was fairly menial, but that was OK. All she wanted was normality. She was basically the secretary for the managing director, but it was a small company and there were no real lines of demarcation. She quickly found herself taking client orders, doing the customs forms, making tea, doing a bit of accounts, whatever the next phonecall happened to be about.

Jeff, her boss, was a nice guy to work for. He was flexible and charming, he didn't shout and he didn't chase her round the desk. A good egg. Quite attractive. Shame about the beard.

She stood at the filing cabinet struggling with an armful of paper.

'You must find this a bit dull after working in the record business.'

'Dull is fine; I like dull.'

'You don't miss it, then?'

'No, not a bit.'

'I just wondered because you've organized our client records under seven-inch and twelve-inch.'

'Well, I thought, longstanding and recent clients, Jeff. You know, for the discount rates.'

'Thank God. I thought you'd been checking out their, (hee-haw) inside-leg measurements. Hhhhhuh. And er...'

Few people 'hee-haw' these days; it used to be considered hilarious in the 1920s, but Jeff had it off pat. He always did it halfway through the punchline of a joke and it was just as well, because Jeff's jokes were so amazingly unfunny that you would never otherwise have spotted them. For this reason he also finished up with his own version of a laugh to cover the embarrassing silence, followed by a kind of speculative new sentence to change the subject, which itself petered out just as embarrassingly.

Glenna groaned, 'You get worse.'

'I'm just trying to cheer you up, lovey.'

'Don't think I'm not grateful, Jeff, but if you really want to cheer me up all you have to do is tell me to shred this week's paperwork.'

'I couldn't do that, lovey, not that I wouldn't like to but (hee-haw) I like milk and sugar on my shredded weeks. Hhhhhuh. And er...'

She gave him a look.

She brooded a lot at the weekends, visiting the nearby riding stables, occasionally going for rides and frequently going for long walks with her parents' mad spaniel, Snoopy, who was the only one that thought life had taken a significant turn for the better.

Snoopy had a good attitude. All dogs think they're really people and they must get a bit pissed off with continually getting the raw end of the deal, but it never stops them from getting down and partying at the drop of a snack. Snoopy partied. He threw himself at her every morning with his special hurricane welcome, belted round the house doing his wall-of-death routine on top of the furniture, he ate her underwear, and got the shits.

What more could you want? The walks were good for him, too. He chased the ducks, jumped in and out of the lake and frightened little old ladies by appearing like the creature from the deep in the middle of picnics.

After four weeks, he felt he had persuaded Glenna to relax.

'So, what do you think I should do, Snoopy?' she said as he trotted beside her.

'Well, myself, I think you should follow your instincts and marry the bloke. This success/failure music thing is just a phase. He'll work it out sooner or later and you guys will have a ball. He sounds like a nice bloke. If you love the guy, call him.'

There was a bit of an embarrassing pause. Glenna looked at Snoopy, Snoopy looked at Glenna.

'If only you could talk,' said Glenna.

'If only you would bloody listen,' said Snoopy and wandered off to find some month-old foxes do's to roll in. 'Man, I should get my own couch and start a psychoanalysis gig. People are so screwed up.'

# 55

Having seen her behind James Deek in the newspaper photograph, Mike had spent a fair amount of time with Helen Denture. She had worked for him once, and he held her in high regard. He badly needed an ally and thought she might help. He also fancied her to death.

Mike Delta raised his wine glass. 'I definitely love you,' he promised with an extremely dodgy grin.

'No you bloody don't,' said Helen Denture. 'What are we going to eat?'

The two of them ordered a couple of hundredweight of junk food and junk wine and shortened their lives on it.

He explained his plan in detail.

The idea had come to him while watching a particularly depressing 'Top of the Pops' show. A year out of the mainstream of the music business and he didn't recognize anyone. He squinted at the various artists trying to find some he knew or a record he liked, and eventually he just turned the sound down.

'It's brilliant,' she said. 'Without doubt the most creative commercial music idea I have heard for a long time,' she mumbled through her Double Massive Cholesterol Burger. 'Plus, it stuffs up old Deeky. You know he dropped our distribution. Frankly, I'm chuffed you've asked me.'

'Helen, there has never been anyone else, you know that.'

'You're more full of shit than an aeroplane toilet,' she said, laughing her machine-gun laugh and firing random bits of burger across the table. 'So what do you need from us?'

'Marketing and distribution. I assume you have distribution.'

'No problem, Chook. When are we going to do it?'

'No time like the present. I want to press twenty thousand next week and get it in the shops the week after. It's only a week till November, Radio One are already doing a sweep on the Christmas number one; I want it to be us. Can you get the wind-up going by then?'

'I love all this seat-of-the-pants stuff. Don't worry about that, they're going to lap it up.'

'OK, you do Radio One, the regionals, TV, etc., and leave the press to me. One thing, Welly, don't mention it to Jules. He'd have a heart attack.'

'Whatever you say, Mikey, whatever you say. Where is the poor love anyway?'

'He's gone to Nashville.'

'Nashville? What for?'

'At least a month if we're lucky.'


A week later, down in the cutting room, the engineer listened to the master as he set up the lathe for the cut.

'There's nothing on this one, squire,' he said. 'Are you sure this is the right tape?'

'Oh, yes,' said Mike. 'Quite sure.'

## 56

Jules peered out of the steamed-up windows of the Heathrow shuttle coach at the trees alongside the M25. The sun was making a brave attempt to chase away the autumn mist. The yellow and brown leaves trembled and dripped as they clung obstinately to the branches.

He was just getting into a lyrical idea that the leaf was some kind of personal metaphor when he remembered that it would fall off and die in a couple more weeks so he started thinking about himself as the tree instead.

A spring of nervous tension started to wind up as they approached the airport. He hated flying. He was a nervous passenger and remained fundamentally unconvinced by the theory of aerodynamics, but more than that, he really hated airports.

Airports are like sewers; they're supposed to flow. Smelly at the best of times, if they get blocked up you're suddenly up to your neck in shit.

Jules's palms were appropriately clammy as he hauled his bags and his guitar out from the bowels of the coach and turned to face the enemy.

Terminal four. Thousands of airport and airline workers, each with a mission to disorientate and confuse him. Five-mile check-in queues, misleading advice, obscured signs, missing signs, muffled, unintelligible announcements and all the time a whispered, subliminal message in the air. 'You're going to miss the plane, you're going to miss the plane, you're going to miss the plane . . . YOU'RE GOING TO MISS THE PLANE!!'

He closed his eyes and chanted back the traveller's mantra, 'Money, tickets, passport, money, tickets, passport . . .', crossed himself, took a deep breath of aviation fuel and diesel fumes and plunged through the automatic doors into the battle.

He walked the length of the concourse, looking for his flight number on a check-in desk. He walked back. The departure area was seething with people. He collided with most of them as he peered over the sea of heads to read the labels at the front.

And there it was. A queue to end all queues. The M25 without cars. All four hundred people flying to Washington were in it. People would live out their lives in it. Raise their children, grow old, retire and die as it stretched out in time like a civilization and wallowed in the misery of human stress.

'You're going to miss the plane, you're going to miss the plane...' went the terminal.

'Money, tickets, passport...' said Jules to himself, planting himself at the end of the queue and patting the different pockets for the thousandth time.

People at the front of the queue, presumably the descendants of those that had joined the back long before, screamed in frustration at the check-in girl. They waved their arms about, but they still needed the aeroplane to make them fly so they eventually calmed down, gathered themselves and wandered off in search of the next queue. The rest of them shuffled forward. Jules fished out the ticket, to read again the check-in instructions. 'No later than two hours before the departure time,' it said. He looked at his watch. Oh God! Only one hour fifty minutes.

'You're going to miss the plane, you're going to miss the plane...' the frenzy continued.

'Money, tickets, passport, money, tickets, passport... Ouch!' he said as the umpteenth person pushed their trolley into his legs.

The queue edged forward like a snail on Valium while each person in front of him fumbled for tickets, lost their passports, checked in three hundredweight of excess baggage, negotiated to buy shares in the airline. Why, oh why, does it always take so long?

After forty minutes Jules was almost at the front and the stress was unbearable. The subliminal message was deafening in his ears and the nervous pocket-patting had become so violent he was making dust.

The check-in girl patiently explained to the man ahead that, no, he couldn't take his bicycle as hand baggage, and then he was gone. Jules had made it.

Relief.

'Ticket and passport please,' said the girl and smiled her cheery smile at him. Jules smiled wearily back. He was already exhausted and he'd travelled only twenty-five miles.

He pulled the ticket from his jeans and plonked it down on the desk but, reaching into the pocket he had been patting for the last hour, he produced only his diary. Panic! He patted all his pockets again, rummaging through each, turning out loose change, old train tickets and crusty tissues but no passport. He ripped open his bag in a frenzy, sending three novels and twenty cassettes into the girl's lap. She turned not a hair.

'Is this it?' she said, gathering the debris and picking out the battered booklet.

'Ah,' said Jules. 'Yes.'

He checked in his big bag and his guitar, which was labelled fragile, placed gently on to the conveyer and rattled down the chute behind her.

One down and one hour to go.

Stuffing bits of paper back into his pockets, he headed for passport control.

Four paces and another queue.

'You're going to miss the plane, you're going to miss the plane . . .' The tension clicked another notch.

This queue spread down from passport control like molten lava. It oozed between the security gates and through the X-ray machines, welling up in the departure lounge. Jules oozed right along with it. He thrust his hand baggage into the X-ray machine and walked through the terrorist trap.

'Beep!' went the machine.

'Shit!' went Jules.

'Please take out any metal objects from your pockets.'

He placed a few coins on a plastic tray and popped in and out of the electric door frame once again.

No bleep!

The friendly security woman rummaged under his jacket, discreetly around his nether regions and up and down each leg.

On he went.

'Excuse me sir?' said another friendly soul.

'I'm sorry?'

'What have you got in the bag?'

The man on the X-ray machine was squinting at his monitor. He wound the conveyer back a couple of feet to get another look.

'A few cassettes, a couple of books, paper, that kind of stuff. Why?'

'No metal then?'

'Er, no.'

The security man turned his head on one side and looked again.

'Records?'

'No.'

'Belt?'

'No.'

'Nothing of a curly nature, would you say?'

Jules was baffled, the security man was baffled. They sent for another security man and he was also baffled and Jules was obliged to empty the contents on the counter to find the weird thing that was perplexing them so. A packet of guitar strings does look very peculiar on an X-ray machine.

Jules was stuffing everything back into the bag as they announced the boarding of his flight.

He ran up the moving walkway to the gate and took his place at the end of yet another queue shuffling towards the aeroplane itself. 'Thank God,' he said, 'I'm on my way.' And he allowed himself a secret smile.

'BING!'

'Ladies and gentlemen, we regret to announce that flight 217 has been delayed for one hour. If you would all take your seats again we will board the aircraft in approximately forty-five minutes. We would like to apologize for any inconvenience, raising your blood pressure, shortening of your life expectancy, but it really isn't our fault so if you are considering violence then kindly blame those bastards in air-traffic control. Thank you.'

The crowd sagged. Jules also sagged, but at least he could now see the aeroplane out of the window and he felt that if he kept it in sight then it couldn't leave without him.

## 57

Outside the window, down at the aircraft's side, Ron 'The Case' Casey was also having a tough day.

'Where's my bloody catering?' he screamed down the radio. 'Don't tell me the truck's left there, you silly sod, that does not help the situation, you said that half an hour ago, I do not want to know where it's not, I want to know where it is! . . . I know you've dispatched the truck, I'm not arguing with you about that . . . I'm not arguing with you about that . . . No, I'm not arguing with you about that. Look, I know you've dispatched the truck but where's the bastard gone?'

'Oy, Case! We found the rest of the baggage,' said a voice from under the wing on the far side of the aircraft. 'It was up the next cul de sac.'

'Find the bloody catering truck and call me back!' spluttered Case into the radio. 'What?' he said, turning to face the other voice.

'We found the rest of the bags, they were trying to put 'em on the 317.'

'Well, get 'em back and put them on this one!'

Aeroplanes need a lot of things to happen to them between the time they arrive and the time they leave again, and it was Case's job to see that they did.

First of all everything has to get off. The passengers, the baggage, the rubbish, the sewage, the crew, etc. Then the aircraft has to be checked, refuelled, cleaned and reloaded with all of the above. They don't actually reload the sewage, of course, that arrives in the catering truck.

'I won't be able to get 'em on before ten-past,' said the voice. 'You won't make your departure time. Why don't we put 'em on the next one?'

'Make 'em wait,' said Case. 'Baggage cock-ups are definitely our fault, but delays we can put down to air-traffic control.'

# 58

Jules finally sank into seat 47A. That is to say his lower body sank and his knees rode up the back of the seat in front, but at least he was mostly in a seat. He spotted the nearest emergency exit, looked out of the window, counted the engines and checked for loose rivets. There were none, but there was definitely a suspicious puddle under the fuel tank and he was considering reporting it to the stewardess when someone sat down in 47C.

"Allo,' said the person. 'Is someone sitting in this seat?' He waved at the empty seat between them.

'I have no idea,' said Jules cautiously.

'They quite often leave a gap when allocating for people travelling alone,' said the stranger. 'All the better for us if they have, eh?' He proceeded to spread his personal effects over the spare seat. Jules raised his eyes heavenwards and then shut them tight.

'Bloody air-traffic-control delays, eh?' said Mr Informative. 'I don't think! I bet they lost the bags. They always tell you it's ATC. I'm Reg, by the way, Reg Spottiswood, I'm an air-traffic controller.'

'Good God!' said Jules, opening his eyes again. 'I had no idea it was a personal service. I thought you guys worked in that glass tower thingy.'

'No, no, you wally, I'm on my day off.'

'Ah,' said Jules. 'Hi, I'm Jules Charlie, songwriter.'

Reg was a short, jolly man with no hair, no sensitivity and no inhibitions. He babbled on about everything he thought Jules ought to know about air-traffic control and the aviation industry.

Jules closed his eyes again. The engines whined and the aircraft rolled forwards. He looked outside to see the terminal building sliding away. It looked so peaceful from the outside, but he knew the battle would still be raging.

The stewards and stewardesses did their pointing at the emergency exits and pretend inflation of the life jackets routine as they trundled on towards the runway for take-off. Jules tried to memorize the safety instructions.

'Songwriter, eh, what've you written then?' said Reg. 'Anything I know?'

'I doubt it,' said Jules candidly.

'Not too good, then,' said Reg. 'Don't worry, I expect you'll get the hang of it. Bloody 'ell, look at that!'

Reg pointed out of the window next to Jules at another aircraft.

'That was a bit close. They shouldn't've given us line-up till that one cleared the intersection, I can tell you.'

'Do you work here at the airport?' asked Jules as calmly as he could.

'Me? No, I'm a centre man myself. I work at the old London Air Traffic Control Centre. You know, the one with that computer that keeps breaking down,' he chuckled.

Jules groaned and clutched his stomach to stop it churning.

The aircraft surged forward and they were both pressed back into their seats as tons of metal accelerated down the concrete to do its impossible trick on thin air.

Roar went the engines, twang went Jules's nerves, whine went Reg and faintly, and in the distance behind them, Jules thought he heard the terminal saying, 'I bet you wish you had missed the plane now.'

'This is where it's going to happen one day.'

Jules opened one eye and looked out of the window as the plane climbed westwards across the Staines reservoirs and up the M4.

'Compton,' said Reg, nodding earthwards. 'Spaghetti Junction in the sky. A friend of mine had a really nasty one round here a few months ago. Two at 33. The sector was going under, the radar was nothing but a green glow, lost the picture completely. Just as well the conflict alert was on.'

'You mean a near miss?'

'Bloody near. It's too busy these days. You don't know if you're on your arse or your elbow. I don't mind telling you, I've had a few scares myself. I've been telling them for years, but do they listen? Pigs might file a flight plan!'

The truth about air-traffic control is that nobody wants to know the truth about air-traffic control. If airports are like a sewer then air-traffic control is like Dyno Rod. People gotta go,

planes gotta flow. You don't want to know how they do it, as long as they do it. Some guy turns up to unblock the drain, you don't want him to show you a handful of the stuff when he's finished.
Jules did not want to know about air-traffic control.
Reg told him anyway.

The green wasn't exactly aglow on the radars of the London Air Traffic Control Centre at that particular moment on that particular day. There were, in fact, several counties between the very few aircraft that sailed up that bit of the troposphere known as the Bristol Sector.

The Sector Controller lifted the corner of his newspaper, glanced down at that bit of the radar it was concealing and said hello to Jules's flight. He leaned over to the adjacent radar controller and tapped the flight strip.

'Fill yer boots,' said the second controller, which is air-traffic-control speak for 'I haven't got any aeroplanes at all so do whatever you want and leave me alone.'

'Speedbird 217 climb to flight level 310,' said the first into his headset microphone, and he wrote the level on his own strip in blood red. He reached over to the second controller's strip and coloured that one as well, then plopped the paper back down on the radar tube and carried on reading the sports page.

'Isn't that the flight Reg is on?' said the Crew Chief.

'Old Reggie Spotter? Yeah,' said the sports fan. 'Skiving bastard got a cheapie from the Guild. Wants me to speak to the captain, see if I can get him upgraded in exchange for a direct routing.'

'Cheeky sod!'

'He's probably up on the flightdeck now telling them he's the General Manager and promising them "free flow" till next autumn.'

'He's only being "user-friendly".'

'Yup. If they're friendly, he uses 'em.'

Flow management is the art of matching ATC demand with ATC capacity. It is the subject of much controversy in the aviation business, as its principal effect is delay. Airlines get fed up because ATC delays cost them a lot of money. Passengers get fed up because they get to spend more of their lives wedged into airport terminals or aeroplanes.

Years ago there was a music-hall act called plate-spinning. Air-traffic control is a lot like plate-spinning. The point is you can't go on adding plates indefinitely. Sooner or later, you won't get back to one of the wobblers in time and, whoops! it's one of those disappointing trip situations.

Aviation boomed in the 1980s, ATC was swamped and delays became endemic. Everyone got fed up, but the argument goes that it is better to experience the terminal than to have a terminal experience. Flow management, however, is more of a black art than a science, somewhere between meteorology and astrology.

Earlier in the day the sky had been crammed with aluminium as the sector creaked and groaned under the weight of the early-morning traffic. The oceanic inbounds were late because of a slower than average jet stream and they all got muddled up with the commuters rushing in and out of London to Brussels, Amsterdam and Paris. Fog had complicated matters and the plates wobbled dangerously as aeroplanes stacked up all over the place.

'Flow' had snapped into action. Three every fifteen minutes through Bristol. Delays built up and, four hours later, aircraft were waiting for up to an hour to use the sector one at a time.

The Crew Chief's phone rang.

'Yo, Flow. This is the Bristol Chief.'

'Hi,' said a harassed voice. 'Um, we've got a bit of a backlog through your sector, could you take a couple of extras?'

The Crew Chief peeped under the newspaper and looked at Jules's lonely blip.

'I guess we can take a couple of extras.'

'Great.' Click . . .

Thirty minutes later the sector was completely deluged. The controller's nose was glued to the radar and he was talking like an auctioneer on speed.

'Sod' is an air-traffic controller and he works at West Drayton.

By then, Jules was far out over the North Atlantic, well into his second Scotch and beginning not to mind about the prospect of a seven-hour aviation lecture.

Many people have speculated about why it takes seven hours to fly to the USA and only six to fly back. Is it the rotation of the Earth? The higher octane rating of American aviation fuel? Is it downhill on the way back? What?

Now it can be revealed. It is nothing but a shoddy trick

perpetrated by the airlines to make up time on their schedules. It also makes the disgusting night crossing seem faster and takes the economy passengers' minds off the fact that the guy in front has reclined his seat on to their noses or that the people on either side have annexed their arm rests. These problems do not, of course, affect first-class passengers, who are allowed to take the full seven hours for the eastbound crossing so that they can sleep.

Jules took one westbound earphone off.

'... and another thing,' went Reg. 'These "fly-by-wire" jobbies, they're not safe, you know, I had one the other day...'

Jules replaced the earphone, watched his lips move briefly and nodded a couple of times.

# 59

The plugger sat on the edge of the desk.

'You've got to play it, John, it's a total blast, people will just die!' He waved Jules Charlie's record under his nose.

'Have you given it to anyone else?'

'No, mate, if this is going to work it's got to be exclusive and it's got to be on the "John Friendly Show".'

'OK, I'll give it a play, see what the reaction is, but if I get heat from the producer, I'll deny all knowledge and blame you.'

'Hey, that's what I'm here for, mate. By the way, are you still on for the skiing next week?'

It is a curious irony that the success of BBC Radio One FM has debunked its most sacred principle.

They are, on the one hand, entirely independent, non-commercial and commercial-free. On the other hand, every record they play is a commercial. A commercial for the record itself, the album it comes from, the film, the book, the artist generally and the tour they happen to be in the middle of.

Radio One dominates national pop-music listening and, therefore, it also dominates pop-music marketing. While Radio One airplay doesn't actually guarantee a hit, you can't have one without it, a fact which gives them considerable influence over the charts, which are the basis of programme planning in the first place.

It is a circular relationship. Airplay means sales, means chart position, means airplay. Moreover, a hit in the UK will almost certainly be a hit in the rest of Europe. This makes Radio One producers very popular with the record companies.

Pluggers are the middlemen. Employed by the record companies and tolerated by the BBC, their only qualification is that they have to be 'best mates' with as many producers and DJs as possible.

Most new records have to be vetted at the weekly playlist meetings, but the more established DJs have some flexibility and can sometimes slip one through if they think there is some credibility in the exclusive or that the playlisting is a foregone conclusion.

John Friendly was about to get an exclusive first laugh.

## 60

Jules dropped his bags and guitar on the floor of his hotel room and fell on to the bed. It was 10pm local time and four o'clock in the morning personal time.

To get a deal on the airfare, he had flown to Washington, Dulles, taken the train into the city and taken an internal flight from National.

Getting into the USA is a very tedious business. The immigration authorities were not at all convinced he was really on a holiday. Immigration authorities are populated by a special breed of people carefully selected from those who are considered too suspicious by nature to be tax inspectors.

'You gotta be kidding me,' said the woman behind the desk at the front of another hour-long queue. 'It says right here on your passport you're a musician, you're going to Nashville and you want me to believe this is a vacation?' She looked him over. 'I will bet the house you're some no-hope singer tryin' to make it in show business. I get about twenty a day through here, you guys are all the same.' She fixed him with a look designed to boil wetbacks.

'I will give you two weeks. If you ain't outta there by then 'armo send an official down there to shoot yo ass. Have a nice day.' She stamped the form, pinned it to his passport and waved him through.

Dulles Airport is aptly named; you do not want to hang out there if you want to avoid brain-death. Nothing ever happens. *Die Hard 2* didn't fool anyone. He took a cab down town to National, checked his bags in once again and waited for his connection in the bar. It was late. He drank beer and watched a baseball game on television. Having avoided English sport his entire life, Jules had none of the usual preconceptions about American sport. After three beers, he was captivated and became possibly the first Englishman to come to terms with the rules of baseball before cricket, something he had to keep to himself in later life as, in certain parts of the UK, this is still a hanging offence.

The one-hour-and-thirty-minute flight to Nashville eventually landed at 8.30pm.

'How y'all doin today?' inquired the bus driver as Jules fumbled for the fare and jammed his guitar under the seat.

'Fine, thanks,' said Jules
'Y'all from outta town?'
'Yes, I'm from England.'
'Really? That's great. I have a friend in London, let's see, his name is John Davidson.'
'I don't think we've met.'
'I guess not. You just visiting?'
'I'm a songwriter.'
'Yeah? Me too.'

The bus jerked out of the airport and joined the evening traffic.

Jules was surprised by the coincidence, but he was tired, so he let it go. He drank in the city scenery as he watched it go by. Like most people, he was familiar with Movie America. Real America was clearly too big to fit into Panavision. Bigger roads, bigger cars, bigger traffic jams, bigger billboards, bigger buildings, bigger graffiti. It was loud, colourful and unashamedly tacky.

The hotel was cheap and just as tacky, but Jules was too tired to notice and too tired to care. He was too tired to eat, too tired to unpack and too tired to undress. He just checked in and crashed out.

He woke up, ready to go, at 3.30 in the morning and had to wait three and a half hours for breakfast.

# 61

Jules took his clothes off and sat in bed watching television for an hour. He found out who won the baseball game, who was ahead in the Presidential election campaign, but most of all he found out what coffee he should drink, what car he should buy, what breakfast snacks he should give the kids and which lawyer he should call if someone ran him over while using all of the above simultaneously. At seven, he showered, changed and went downstairs in search of food.

There was no restaurant. Tragedy. Actually, there were a couple of tables in a semi-detatched deli kind of thing, but it looked a bit low-key and Jules was feeling hungry. He decided to look further afield. This is America, he told himself, someone somewhere will sell me breakfast.

He didn't have to venture far. Across the street was a neon sign. 'Dave's 24-hour Diner', it sparked. 'Our prices cain't be beat, c'mon in and eat.'

>    Bacon and Grits.....................................$1.49
>    2 Eggs, Bacon and Grits.......................$1.99
>    2 Eggs, Bacon, Sausage and Grits.......$2.49
>    2 Eggs, Bacon, Sausage, Hash Browns
>                    and Grits..................$2.99
>    2 Eggs, Bacon, Hash Browns, Sausage,
>             Grits, Waffles, Syrup,
>                    Juice and Coffee.....$4.99
>          (Heart disease our specialty)

Jules looked over his British right shoulder, stepped off the kerb and was nearly mown down by a car coming from his American left. It screeched, he jumped and scampered to the far pavement, spinning his head at 100rpm to be on the safe side. The driver smacked her hand on her forehead in mock exasperation and drove on.

Inside Dave's Diner were a load of happy, munching people lined up on stools at a formica-topped counter. The waitress zapped up to meet him as he sat down.

'How y'all doin today?' she drawled, pen poised over the pad.
'Fine, thanks,' said Jules.
'Can I get you anything?'
'Coffee?'
'Sure, honey. You want cream and sugar with that?'
'Just milk, please.'
She looked uncertain.
'Cream?'
'Yes, er, no sugar. Thanks.'
She returned a moment later with a mug. Jules consulted the menu.
'What are grits?'
'Grits are light, white and fluffy. A great way to start your day. You want some?'
'I don't know. What are they made of?'
She frowned in an effort to remember. 'Do you know, I have no idea,' she concluded after a moment. 'Grits is just, well, grits I guess.'

Jules went for the full 'thrombo combo', grits included. She struggled to get all the codewords out of him, but she eventually went away with a pad full of meaningful squiggles which she tore off and stuck on the hood over the hotplate for the chef.

He watched in fascination as the chef juggled dishes, pans, utensils, toasters, waffle-makers and food in exquisite choreography. Moments later, the plate arrived, actually it was two plates, because it didn't all fit on one. Two plates overflowing with America. Jules jumped right in and rushed around, eating anything he passed.

The grits was a mistake. It reminded him of wallpaper paste, only without the flavour but, thirty minutes and two coffee refills later, he was all done and ready for the day.

'Y'all from outta town?' asked the waitress as he paid his $4.99 and bunged down the extra dollar to ensure safe passage out of the door.

'Yes, England.'
'Just visiting?'
'Yes, I'm a songwriter,' said Jules proudly.

'Really? Me too,' said the waitress.

'Good grief,' said Jules. 'Maybe we could...' but she had already zapped off for her next customer.

Jules went back to his room to begin his search for Stephanie Chisholm. He was nervous about it, but he more or less depended on finding her to make the connection with the Nashville music scene. He'd tried to find her from England, but the phone bill got to three pages. It had to be cheaper from here. He took a deep breath and picked up the phone.

During the rest of the day he spoke to a large number of bemused strangers, left messages for many more and ran up a large telephone bill, all to no avail. 'Hi, my name is Jules Charlie, I'm trying to trace a Stephanie Chisholm from Godalming, England. If you're her could you give me a call etc., etc.' The sun rose and fell in the blue sky and by evening he was still nowhere. He decided to find a club and get something to eat. Printers Alley was a few blocks away and he wandered down to see what he could find in the way of a steak surrounded by chips, a large beer and some music.

His luck was in. You can't fall down in Printers Alley without rolling into such a place. He rolled into the Circle Club.

It was early, but there were fifteen or so partakers of the happy hour lined up at the bar and dotted about at the tables.

'Hi. How y'all doin today?' said a waitress.

'Fine, thanks,' said Jules. 'Do you do steaks?'

'We sure do, honey. We also breathe air, piss water and play country music.'

'I guess you could call that a varied menu,' he said, 'lead the way.'

She showed him to a table.

The steak was in fact a whole cow. Jules surveyed it. He took a bearing off the t-bone, made base camp on the lower slopes and clambered up the previously unconquered north face. He stood on the summit gazing down at the french fries. He ate for twenty minutes and then stood back to see what kind of impression he had made. Almost none. He ate for another twenty. Yes, you could just see where some of the plate was showing. It was delicious but, after an hour, he had to give in.

'Y'all want another beer?'

'Yes please,' said Jules. 'And a bigger chair.'

'I can get you a doggie-bag if you wanna take that home.'

'Thanks, no, I don't have a dog. Do you have a dog?'

'Hell, no, but I could trim it up a little and give it to my ol' man,' she laughed. 'Y'all new in town?'

'I arrived last night.'

'Songwriter, right?'

'Isn't everyone?'

'Takes one to know one. You should meet Jed, he's just got himself a record deal.'

Jed was the warm-up act for the band. He was tuning up on a small but impressive stage filled with sound equipment and lights. He stood up to the microphone.

'Folks, it sure is good to see y'all here tonight. I'm gonna be singing a couple of tunes for you, I hope you like 'em and I hope you might stick around a while, see the band and have yourself a blast.' He played the chord of A.

'Woa, darlin',' he began.

The audience clapped wildly.

''Preciate it, 'preciate it.' He crooned and smoothed his way into the song which seemed to be about a girl whom he loved so much that his tears had watered the crops and made them grow in the shape of a heart.

'Y'all know "Bobby MacNut"?' yelled a member of the audience as he bunged five dollars into a glass jar placed at his feet for the purpose.

'Sure do,' smiled Jed and played the chord of A. 'Woa, Darlin'...' More wild applause as he sang a song about a girl that he loved so much that the crops had failed.

Jules thought perhaps he should get together with the first bloke.

'Anything by Jim Bob Coolidge?'

'Why, surely.' Chord of A. 'Darlin'... Another heart-rending tale of love so true.

'And now here's a tune I wrote myself. Woa darlin'...'

More wild applause, fivers and Woa darlin's followed in profusion as Jed sang. He could not go wrong. Every song was just like the last. Every song was everybody's favourite. At the end he told them all how much he 'preciated their warmth, their applause and the jar full of money and left the stage.

Jules was very impressed. Here was a man who had found a way to make one song last an entire set. If he ever went to England his grasp on the 'Wild Rover' Endurance Record was definitely under threat.

He was finishing his beer when a voice squealed so loudly in his ear he nearly jumped out of his skin. Which would have been a shame because he was just growing into it.

'JULES CHARLIE!!!!' said the squeal 'EEEE-EEEEEAAAAAAEEEEEAAAAA WHAT ARE YOU DOING HERE?'

'Stephanie?' said Jules, rubbing his ear, trying to massage life back into his cochlea.

'Beverley, you prat, Beverley Chisel.'

Much jumping up and down and hugging later, they sat back down.

Beverly was small but powerfully built. Not heavy, but she definitely looked as though she worked out with weights, as Jules discovered when she slapped him on the back a few times, winding him and shooting him out of his chair and on to the floor.

'You're looking great,' she said. 'So what's the story here? To what do I owe the pleasure of this coincidence?' said Beverley when her voice had descended back into the audible range.

'Looking for you, actually.'

'Well, you found me, but why, for heaven's sake?'

'Have you got a few days?'

'Well, not right now, I have to do the gig.' She pointed at the stage. 'But stick around and we can talk later. This is so great. Tell me, did you ever make it with Rosemary Stacy?'

Beverley and the rest of the band lugged the gear on to the stage and plugged themselves into the PA. Jules felt a load off his mind. He watched the gig with fascination. Basically, it was more of the same old suckmuckdoo, but the players were great, Beverley was faberoony and he was beginning to feel more at home. Hell, another couple of beers and he might even be able to tell the songs apart.

The band got offstage around one and Jules and Beverley sat and talked till two-thirty. There was a lot of missing history for both of them.

'I just couldn't see myself as a concert pianist,' she said. 'I'd always have wanted to play the "Liberty Bell".' That's what makes me tick musically, you know, the funny stuff. It's been great here. My father was American, so there were no problems with the green card. I just moved in and started playing. Word got around and I started getting sessions. There's a lot of work. Everybody round here is recording something. Even the drains play country.'

Jules gave her the short version of the previous ten years and the full version of the last twelve months. She was impressed.

'My God, aren't you the pop star?' she chided. 'Listen, I'm only kidding. I think it's great that you've come over. I'll do what I can, Jules, introduce you to some people if I can, tell you some places to go, but this is a town full of songwriters, you're not exactly going to stand out.'

'I'm getting the hang of that, but what the hell, I'm here now. I might as well give it my all-American best shot.'

'A toast to blind optimism.' She held up her glass. 'May ignorance always be bliss.' She dumped the rest of her beer down her throat. Jules dumped likewise.

'I don't want to be rude, but I'm totally knackered,' said Jules eventually. 'I'd better get some sleep. My body clock is still only about halfway across the Atlantic. What are you doing tomorrow?'

'I got a ten and a two at United Artists. You wanna come along?'

'Love to. What the hell are you talking about?'

'Sessions, you plonker. Sessions in Nashville run to a schedule. I've got one at ten o'clock and one at two o'clock.' She wrote down the address on a napkin and squealed a bit more about seeing him after all this time.

Jules walked slowly back up Union Street and wondered what she would have done if they'd actually been friends.

## 62

The following day he didn't wake up till six o'clock. Breakfast at the diner was a tad more conservative and 100 per cent grits-free.

The historically suspect trolley buses do not run until midday at that time of year, and so Jules found himself walking the three-quarters of a mile up to Music Row. The streets were wide, the buildings mountainous and the pavements deserted.

It is a seemingly strange contradiction that Americans, who will jog for miles, won't walk more than a block. The reason has nothing to do with exercise and everything to do with traffic. Three-quarters of a mile will involve several hundred road crossings at least half of which will be eight lanes or more. The pavements are, therefore, mostly empty, except for muggers and English tourists who say 'Pooh! It's only three-quarters of a mile,' and get splatted by traffic coming from the wrong direction. Jules ran the gauntlet, diced with death, dusted himself off and found himself in Music Row.

Music Row is the shop window of the country music megastore. Shrines and gift shops, museums and snack bars. Music twanging out of every doorway. Country records, country singers. A young cowboy wearing boots and a stetson was singing his sentimental heart out to passing strangers in a parking lot, the instrumental breaks in the backing tape providing him with the opportunity to advertise his latest album, take some money and sign some autographs.

'Who is that?' Jules asked a recent purchaser.

'I have no idea,' said the woman, putting the cassette into her bag along with a few hundred other souvenirs. 'But he sings so pretty.' And she scurried off to the Barbara Mandrell All Year Round Christmas Shop.

Jules checked his tourist map and carried on up the street, past the stand where Elvis still apparently buys his hotdogs and into Music Square. Music Square is the country music megastore. The $3 billion engine that drives the machine: all the major record companies, publishers, all kinds of services, recording studios, artist management companies and law offices. Jules walked as slowly as he could but nobody offered him a deal.

He finally arrived at the United Artists Tower, a building that looks like a ten-storey heap of giant thru'penny bits. There was no one in the lobby, so he followed his directions up to the third floor and into the studio. He stopped at the door of the mixing room and looked at the engineer. Barging into someone else's session is naff in anybody's studio.

The engineer looked up. 'Hi?' he said.

'I'm here to see Beverley. Is she here?'

He waved through the double glazing. 'Right there. Y'all wanna wait?' He signalled a chair.

'If you don't mind.'

Beverley, who was mucking around with some chords on the piano, looked up and waved at him madly. He sat quietly on a chair at the back.

The room was filled with the band. Beverley by the piano, a round man in his late fifties, balancing an acoustic guitar on top of a substantial paunch, an electric guitar player with a sideways haircut, the world's wrinkliest pedal-steel player and Jack-the-Lad on bass were all jammed in together. A bored drummer and a serious vocalist were each in separate booths off to the side.

A lively discussion was in progress.

'I don't know,' said the sideways haircut, 'I think we could half the tag and push the song a little harder on the tempo and kinda hit the dirt running.'

'But I really like the tag,' said Mr Serious.

'I like the tag,' agreed Jack.

'Song's too long, man,' said the paunch.

'Well maybe so, but it's a slow song. We can't go crashing round it like the Kentucky Derby.' Mr Serious was slipping into Mr Grimble.

'Can't do the song too long, man. It's the law.'

There was a pause in the debate. Gum was chewed thoughtfully.

'Know what I think?' said the drummer in a bored tone. 'I think there is a lotta love in this room.'

'Let's just play the song, lover boy,' said the engineer.

They played.

A count-in on the sticks and the band played country. Bursting into life, like the seven dwarfs digging for diamonds, and the man sang. Three minutes and thirty-seven seconds later they all stopped. Silence.

'How was that?' said the singer.

'Three minutes, thirty-seven. It's a take. Let's go on to the next one,' said the engineer down the intercom.

'Because, you know, I thought the guitar player was a bit slow in the last chorus,' continued the singer.

'I think it was you guys who sped up,' said the guitar player.

'I did not speed up,' said the drummer.

'Know what I think?' said the bass player.

'There's a lotta love in this room,' chorused the crowd.

Everyone laughed and they shuffled the paperwork for the next track. And so the morning wore on. Four hours, five masters. Brian Payedwell would have been ecstatic.

'This town has a style, in case you hadn't noticed,' said Beverley over a can of lunchtime Diet Coke. 'You don't come here unless you want it, but if you do want it, it's a piece of cake. The players just know how to deliver it. We get a chord sheet in the Nashville number system. Actually I believe it was invented by Bach, Johnny Sebastian Bach. You remember him. He was really big in the country scene. They probably have a museum for him somewhere. Anyway, so you get the chords and quick listen to some demo and then, pow, you do what you do.'

'Isn't it a bit dull?' said Jules, who was getting the teensiest bit bored already.

'Drives me crazy, but the work is regular, the pay is OK and, well, there is so much love in that room.' She rolled her eyes and flashed her smile. 'The songs are the same, the musicians are the same. I have a feeling that nobody's touched the mixing desk since 1955. I mean, why change it just when it's perfect? The only things that change are the key and the tempo.' She finished her Coke. 'Come on, then. There's no one in the studio at the moment; play me some of your stuff.'

Jules was glad of the opportunity to play. He picked up a guitar, sat next to the piano and sang a song. After a verse and a chorus, she played a perfect country arrangement right over it.

'There you go,' she said. 'Country music. You want it, all you have to do is turn it on. We'll have this album finished by this evening. Nice song, by the way.'

'Thanks.'

The rest of the magnificent seven drifted back into the studio for the B-side, so Jules had to stop.

'Did y'all like that last one?' said the serious singer as Jules stood up to leave the room.

'It was very . . . interesting,' he said carefully.

'Was it too fast, did you think?'

'It was just fine.'

He smiled.

'Only I got the idea when I was looking at that great big, blue sky and I thought my love is as big as the sky is blue.' He looked all misty-eyed. 'That's why I called it "My Love is as Big as the Sky is Blue".'

'I think there's a lot of love in that song,' said Jules.

Beverly bounced to his rescue. 'Don't feel you have to hang round all day,' she said. 'I'll be down at the Circle again tonight. Why don't we get together then?'

Jules agreed and made his excuses. The engineer and the band braced themselves for another ballad.

Jules walked back along Music Row wondering what Frog and Glenna would have made of Nashville. The thought troubled him. He bought two of the tackiest postcards he could find and sat down outside a café with a beer and wrote a cheery note on the back of each. He gazed up at the blue sky and thought of rainy England. As the sun warmed his face the mists of anger and righteous indignation he'd been nursing of late gradually burned away, leaving leaving him feeling stupid. Stupid about a lot of things, but particularly about Frog and Glenna. He signed both cards 'Stupid of Nashville'.

He hesitated by the mailbox. Holding the cards above the chute, uncertain about whether to send them. After a few minutes somebody else wanted to post something so he had to drop them in or look even more stupid.

## 63

'Oy! Do you know that "Birdy Song"?'

The drunk leaned on Terri's microphone stand.

'Course we do,' said Terri and turned to Frog to see if it was true. 'This bloke says he wants the "Birdy Song".'

'Yes, all right,' said Frog, gritting his teeth at the punter over her shoulder.

'How do the words go, then?'

'They go "quack, quack, quack, quack".'

'Oh.'

The drunk walked away, waggling his elbows happily to his mates and going, 'Quack, quack, quack, quack.'

'Three thousand quid, three thousand quid, three thousand quid,' said Frog quietly to himself.

# 64

Zenon I. Tychniowzygielski (Jr) was known as Chuck. Zenon Tychniowzygielski was a stupid name and anyone who could pronounce it only took the piss out of it, so Chuck it was.

Chuck ran the Nashville Songwriters' Showdown, a club for undiscovered songwriters down at the Steel Bar. Every Tuesday night, half a dozen hopefuls would stand up and sing their three best songs in the belief that one day a record-company executive, an artist or a producer would be out there in the audience, sign them up and make them famous.

Such is the optimism of American people that, although this is just one of a dozen or so similar clubs in the town, Chuck fielded around fifty calls a week from would-be stars all over the country who would travel thousands of miles just to appear on his show for free.

Thousands of people had played on the tiny stage. In ten years, he had seen a lot of disappointment, but Jim Bob Coolidge had been discovered in that very bar in 1966 and that was enough.

The club was for writers rather than performers, although most of them wanted to be both. It had writers' nights, open-mike nights, writers-in-the-round nights, writers-who-only-play-three-chords nights (very popular), guest nights, good nights, bad nights and 'Knights in White Satin'. It was small, seating sixty or seventy people around a stage which had room for no more than three performers. There was a piano, a couple of microphones and an amp for a guitar. Backing tapes, drum machines and sequencers were forbidden, but you were allowed to use anything else you could carry on and off between sets.

It was designed for simplicity, the idea being that if the song didn't work without a million-dollar studio in the house you might want to rethink your material.

His telephone rang. It was Jules.

'You wanna come over from England?' he said. 'You must be crazy! Oh, I get it, OK, well get yourself down here this lunchtime, we're over on Hillsboro Road. I do auditions from 12.30 till 3.00 and I'll see what I can do for you.'

Chuck did a fair impression of a good ol' country boy. Tall and slim with a deep tan, he wore the stetson well. He had arrived in Nashville from New York fifteen years before with the idea of becoming the first Polish/American country and western star. Fate had not been kind to him, but he had a genuine sympathy for kids trying the same dream and he did what he could to help. Besides, he might make it even yet. You never knew.

Jules was early. Beverly had spent most of her spare time with him and shown him round the town over the last few days. Taken him to see the Nashville extremes of gutter and glitz. She suggested he audition at the club, but she was doing some gig in Iowa so she was out of town till the weekend.

He stood at the back of the club and watched as two others played their songs. Chuck did not make decisions at the audition. He made notes and taped the songs on a cheap portable so that he could listen to them later.

'OK, let's talk,' he said to each in turn. 'The Showdown is at eight o'clock on a Tuesday down here at the Steel Bar. I recommend you come down this week to see what the form is and I will call you when I want you to appear. Do I have a number where I can reach you?'

His words were practised and reassuring as he explained to them what was required for the performance.

'Mr Charlie, if you would like to take the stage... Mr Charlie?' Chuck shielded his eyes and peered over his shoulder towards the back of the room.

Jules was dreaming. England suddenly seemed a very long way away. He was suddenly aware of the strangeness of the things that had happened to him over the past nine months. Each step had seemed so logical at the time, but looking back it was almost incomprehensible. A year ago, he had been a minor-league eccentric with a job, the usual overdraft and a passion for recording songs that no one liked. Now he wasn't at all sure who he was or what he was doing. The only certainty was debt.

He looked around the bar, at the dark wooden benches and booths, at all the unfamiliar objects on the walls and the ceiling.

He tried to picture his local pub and panicked when he couldn't remember all the beer pumps along the bar.

'Mr Charlie?'

Jules crashed back to planet Earth, picked up his guitar, walked on to the stage and sang. He didn't have anything country, so he sang the simplest song he could think of. The PA system was not used for the auditions and, unfettered by amplifiers and microphones, the song took wing and flew.

As the last chord faded into the back wall there was a silence. Jules was uncomfortable. Chuck said nothing for a full minute and a half. He switched off the tape machine and wrote some notes on a pad.

'Did you come all the way over here just to do that for me?'

'Er, yes.'

'Shit!'

'I'm sorry?'

'Kid, the song is great. I'm gonna put you on the fast track. I can get you a slot in about eight weeks. What are you doing after Christmas?'

'Christmas? I have to leave in ten days.'

'Ten days? Are you kidding? I'm booked up through April.'

## 65

After the auditions, Jules sat at the bar and spoke to Chuck about Nashville. Nashville people, Nashville music, Nashville writers.

'Tell me, kid, what did you think of those two before you at the audition?'

'Well, I thought they were, you know, inexperienced. I thought they had something,' said Jules diplomatically.

'Be honest, kid, they were crap. You know it and I know it. What they have are stars in their eyes. Nashville is full of those people.' He rolled back in his chair. 'They come down here sold on the American dream. Anyone can be anything they damn-well want if they put their mind to it.' He emptied his beer. 'Don't get me wrong, I believe it too. Anyone can succeed, but you gotta find your own strength if you want to win. Mostly they come down here trying to be someone else.'

'Jim Bob Coolidge?' said Jules, remembering the name from a faded poster on the door.

'Jim Bob, Hank, Elvis. You name 'em. You would not believe how bad some of them can be.'

'So why do you do it?'

'Well, we ain't exactly the Bluebird Café but everyone deserves a break. You can't tell shit if you try to deal with the world through a closed door. You gotta open up and invite people in. Sure, most people are as bad as you thought they would be, but you have to ride with the disappointments and keep an open mind because every once in a while you get surprised.'

He waved at the bartender for more beer.

'You, for example. You look like some kind of sad-ass disaster, but you really sang that song. A pretty song too. I did not expect it.'

'You and the rest of the world.'

'So what exactly is your story, kid? Why did you come here?'
Jules gave him a blow-by-blow account. He hunched over his beer and poured out the tale of woe.
Chuck was impressed. 'That is a weird story, kid, and I ain't lying. So what do you want here?'
'I've been asking myself that a lot lately.'
'You've come a long way not to know. If you don't know what you want, how you gonna know if you get it?'
Jules had always found cowboy philosophy hard to deal with. Simple truth seemed to him to be a contradiction. He was much more at home with uncertainty.
He squinted into the middle distance. 'I think I need to prove myself, you know, to be accepted. I've been mucking around, writing and playing most of my life. I need to know that I haven't been wasting my time.'
'You ain't ever been to California, have you? They talk like that down there all the time. You gotta stop looking inward and get on with your life. That song you played me showed you have passion, kid; anyone who has passion has life. Why look any further?'
Jules shrugged.
'Well, while you go tryin' to find yourself, I guess I could introduce you to a few people who might be able to help you with your career. That is, if you're interested. If we get a cancellation, maybe I can get you on the Showcase before you have to go back to England.'
'I think I need all the help I can get.'
'We all do, kid, we all do.'

## 66

Jules switched off the television, which was still wittering away from the night before. He felt calm and refreshed. He showered, dressed and sat in the window watching the early-morning traffic on the expressway as the sun came up. It was a beautiful morning. Good weather is good for the soul. The uncertainty of the previous afternoon had ebbed away.

He picked up the guitar and thought about writing a song. As a rule the last thing you need when writing a song is the distraction of an inspiring view, but he hadn't written anything much lately and he felt optimistic.

Distractions come in all forms. A phonecall, the plumber, TV soap operas, an interesting stain on the wall and so on, but getting lost in a great view is probably one of the best ever excuses for not actually writing anything. It has the advantage of giving the writer the appearance of profound thought while allowing free rein to consider how long it is till lunchtime.

It's said that you need only three things to be a writer: a wad of paper, a pencil and a tube of glue. You use the glue to stick your arse to a chair in front of the other two.

Jules had the little pad of hotel notepaper and free hotel pen in front of him as he played a few chords very quietly as he sketched the idea of a song in his head. The key, the tempo, the feel. He liked the idea as it was forming. He liked the way it sounded as it vibrated out of the guitar and back into his head again. He sang a few notes with the chords and he liked those too.

He carried on lah'ing, and dum de-dumming for half an hour until he'd worked various ideas into a coherent format that he could sing right the way through.

The traffic outside the window got slower and slower as the sun rose in the sky, but Jules had ceased to notice.

The song was now lodged in his head and driving him crazy.

Round and round, over and over. It sounded good so far, now all he had to do was finish it. He paced the room as lyrical ideas floated around in his head with the melody. Good ideas, bad ideas, iffy ideas. When a song started well he felt an intense pressure not to let it down. He found a line, then another and another. Great, there was the chorus. Now at least he knew what the song was about.

He sang them and listened to them. Sometimes in his head, sometimes out loud. Over and over, three lines round and round. What did they sound like, what did they mean? Up and down, up and down the room he paced, lost in concentration.

The spell was finally broken when he paced into the bathroom and tripped over the toilet.

He sat up and looked at his watch; it was 9.15. Breakfast time. Great! He went down to the diner.

'How y'all doin today?'

'I'm feeling fine, thank you.'

'Coffee?'

'Yup, coffee with everything on it.'

'Even the croissants?'

He waddled back up to his room half an hour later and sat back down on the bed. Picking up the guitar, he glanced down at the three lines on the notepad.

He planted his left hand for the first chord, raised his right, drew breath and realized he had completely forgotten how the song went.

More pacing and head pounding while he remembered the melody. At least he thought he'd remembered it. He couldn't be absolutely sure. Once, he had forgotten a completed song and never remembered it again to his satisfaction and, although he was forced to admit it couldn't have been exactly memorable, he was always haunted by the thought that he had lost a masterpiece.

He made no further progress over the next half-hour so he went out and took a tour bus round the city, but he didn't really take much in. The Grand Ol' Opry, the Jim Reeves Museum and the Hall of Fame all passed in front of him bathed in the sunlight, but his eyes had that blank look that told those who knew him that Jules was writing another song.

He walked back into his room around noon, sat down in front of the notepad, picked up the pen and finished the song in one five-minute frenzy. It just gushed out of him. Warm and friendly like a successful evacuation of the bowels first thing in the morning, it felt good.

He read it back to himself to catch the sense of it as a whole song and was slightly surprised to find that it had one. The words sat neatly on three small pages of notepaper with no crossings out.

He played it through a dozen times to get the feel of the words in his mouth. Crafting the melody, adding variations here and there to emphasize the lyrics or to sustain the musical progression.

He made the best musical notes he knew how on the lyrics so as not to forget the melody again and then, tucking the notepaper under the strings of the guitar, he put it back into the case and set out for the club to meet up with Chuck.

Even at the time, Jules knew it was a really good song. Jules had written good songs and bad songs. It's always hard to be objective and it normally takes time to put new songs into perspective, but this one just shone from the moment it hit the page.

He played it to Chuck.

'Kid, did you just write that?'

'Yeah, 6.30 this morning.'

'I don't know how I'm gonna do it, but you gotta play that on Tuesday. They are gonna die!'

# 67

The producer of the 'John Friendly Show' was not pleased.
'You stupid sod, John. Did you really play that?'
'I'm not sure, which one was it again?'
'The Jules wassaname record, the one with nothing on it.'
'I guess so, mate. Look, I didn't know what was on it, Scuzzy just told me it was a great record, exclusive, you know, just a bit of a laugh. I thought it would be OK.'
'That bastard plugger. I'm not taking anything from him again. I'll teach him to take the piss. Where was I when this travesty was perpetrated?'
'I don't know, mate, I think you were on the bog or somewhere.'
'This is a stitch-up, John, you broadcast three full minutes of fuck-all on prime-time radio. This record would never get play-listed for Christ's sake; what were you thinking of? It's taking the piss out of us and the punters. If you ever do anything like that again, I'll have your balls. I don't care how popular you are. Now throw the bloody thing away.'

The Radio One switchboard had been jammed when the silent record had been played the previous day. Most people assumed there was a transmitter fault and rang to complain about it. According to a quick survey, something like two million listeners had switched off or retuned their radios for the same reason. Early indications were that most of them had not tuned back.

Them upstairs were very angry.

Being a slow news day, a bored press had had a field-day.

'BEST RECORD ON RADIO ONE' ran one headline.

'POP RADIO FINALLY GETS IT RIGHT' ran another.

'RADIO ONE, F.A.' ran a third.

'The appalling state of popular music was exposed yesterday when Radio One played three minutes of utter silence and the British public, gasping with relief, switched off their radios by the million to extend the pleasure. John Friendly, who played the record, was not available for comment, but we are given to understand that the record was played without being officially playlisted and has now been banned.'

In the next few days, the tabloids used the excuse to rerun stories about artists who didn't sing on their records, couldn't play live or never actually existed at all. There was also a full-page petition signed by many a celebrity, whose records did not get played quite enough for their liking, demanding change.

Scandal and photographs of the famous. It was a story made in heaven. By the end of the week it had risen to the status of a crusade.

The record itself became the symbol of both the joke and the protest. People rushed out to buy it. The presses rolled, the tills rang out. Retailers couldn't get enough. There was even a dance mix which sold very well in Manchester.

The entire story of Jules, CBA Records, the blank tape and the Songfest came out in the Sundays and the press laid siege to the record-company offices to find out who Jules was and to try to get an interview.

In the third week of November, 'Utter Silence' by Jules Charlie entered the charts at number one.

## 68

At one minute to two in the morning Frog and the guys hit the final chord to 'Hi Ho Silver Lining' down at the Old Pub Club, Torremolinos for the fifty-sixth time. Terri bowed low and wobbled her assets. The crowd went wild. As indeed it had every night for the last eight weeks.

They made their way through the crowd towards the sanctuary of the dressing room. Baseball was intercepted by a tall, blonde Black Lace fan and dragged off to the disco, the rest escaped down the stair well.

'What is the world coming to?' Said Alec to nobody in particular as they walked down the steps.

Alec was a naturally cynical person. In the last few weeks he had raised cynicism through levels of mere irritation, above and beyond annoyance, scaled the heights of indignation, reached the summit of outrage and finally brought it to the level of a religion.

'These people do not deserve breath, let alone good music. These people defy nature. They would be more intelligent if you cut their heads off!' He lapsed into multiple sarcasm. 'Yes I'd love to play "American Pie" again, madam. No, no, The Birdy fuckin' Song is my absolute favourite. I live to perform Una Paloma bleedin Blanca ... youuuu wanker!'

'Man, don't these guys ever get tired of the 1960s?' said Juno.

'They don't get tired. They are wankers!' said Alec with the air of someone who has taken the intellectual high ground. 'These people are so stupid they don't even know how to fall down drunk. Even a bloody tree knows how to fall over.'

Juno pulled the pin out of a Spanish beer grenade. 'This nostalgia thing is really a kind of "so-that's-what-I-was-getting-stoned-to" kind of, first time around kind of thing. People ain't trying to rekindle the memory so much as fill in the blank spots.' The can exploded froth. He sucked a fair amount of it into his mouth as the rest spilled on to the floor. 'I'm too young to know, man' he said through his frothy moustache, 'but if I have to play "Silver Lining" one more time I'm gonna kill someone.'

'Death? DEATH!?' Alec's eyebrows were now so far up his forehead they were half-way down his back. 'That won't work. A bloody priest with some garlic's the only thing that'll save us from that lot if you want my opinion.'

Juno and Frog flopped exhausted into the plastic chairs without further comment. They were used to Alec letting off steam after gigs.

Terri clattered down the steps into the dressing room clutching the *Melody Maker*. 'Bloody 'ell, did you see this?' she said, holding up the front cover. 'They've gotta be 'avin a laugh.'

## 69

At ten minutes to eight on Tuesday night, the doors were still closed at the Steel Bar as Chuck and his sound man dragged out the piano and gunned up the PA, but the queue was round the block. At eight, Jules and Beverly were carried inside with the tidal wave as people rushed about, found themselves tables and ordered drinks. He was tense with excitement and nervous energy.

He found Chuck, shoved his guitar under the piano and went to the bar. The format was for each performer to take the stage in turn and play three songs. At the end, an unofficial vote was taken on a poll sample of one (Chuck) and one of the acts would be invited to play an encore.

The order in which people played wasn't supposed to matter but, nevertheless, the later the act the better it seemed to be. Jules was given the last spot.

Beverley chatted to various musicians and writers, squealing occasionally, slapping Jules on the back and introducing him to people. He stood quietly at the back, stony-faced and trying not to yawn as five acts before him stood and played. Some good, some not so good.

'Relax, Jules. Your arse is so tight you'd need a tyre lever to take a dump,' said Beverley and slapped him on the back again.

A girl in a spangled jacket mumbled about lost love, two boys yelled approximately in unison about what they got up to on Saturday nights, another guy had apparently rewritten a couple of Billy Joel songs and yet another played songs that lasted so long Chuck had to jump up in one of the quieter passages and get him off.

The audience was good-humoured and applauded appreciatively.

And then it was Jules's turn. Chuck stood up and gave him a build-up using words like 'international', 'recording' and 'artist'.

The crowd seemed well pleased and applauded enthusiastically as Jules walked on to the stage.

There are occasions when the mechanics of playing and singing take the day off and a performance is carried by the emotion. As if someone else is doing it. Today was such a day for Jules. The guitar stayed in tune, his voice stayed in pitch and he remembered all the words. His heart sang.

He sang to them and they loved it. They whooped and cheered, pounded the tables and shouted for more. Jules was overwhelmed. He had never had such a reception.

At the end of his three songs the encore was a foregone conclusion.

'OK folks,' said Chuck. 'I'm sure you all feel as I do that we have shared something special here tonight and I know you will welcome back Mr Jules Charlie . . .'

They did.

Jules stood on the stage as the applause died down and said nothing for a few moments. He looked at them all. There was a very great deal in his heart at that moment but 'Thank you very much' was all he could think of to say. And then he played the song he had written a few days before.

Afterwards he couldn't quite remember playing that last song. He remembered that he had played it. He remembered the audience standing and cheering, the warmth of their response as it engulfed him and carried him off the stage, but nothing about the song itself.

Chuck was ecstatic. 'Shit, kid, you did it. I knew you could do it. It's that new song; I swear it's a hit and everybody knows it. Did you see how the folks took to it?'

Beverley squealed and launched herself at him in a style reminiscent of Hulk Hogan. 'Brilliant, Jules, completely brilliant,' she said as he gasped for air.

Everyone insisted on shaking his hand. Most were, of course, songwriters themselves. He handed out all the tapes he had brought with him from England and promised to send more to the disappointed. He collected business cards and napkins with numbers hastily scrawled on them. He collected several from women who seemed to have very doubtful connections with the music business, but wanted him to have their numbers anyway. He promised to call everybody the second he got back to England.

The conversations were full of plans for Jules and Jules's songs.

They went on into the night. Over dinner, over drinks, on and on. How could he could get back over to work on the material? Who he could write with? Who should he sign to? Who would the songs best suit? The night was filled with optimism such as Jules could not remember for a long, long time and it felt great.

He lay awake in bed for an hour reliving the evening in all its glorious detail. He had been trying to impress the music business for years. Trying this, trying that, trying anything simply to sneak a way in, all to no avail. Now he had won the hearts of strangers. Well, fifty strangers anyway. Nashville may be a weird place, but he thought the people made up for it.

He fell asleep and dreamed the dreams of success.

He was woken from a deep sleep at 3.00am by the telephone.

'Er, hello?'

'Hi, is that the famous Jules Charlie?' said a voice in a chirpy Scottish accent.

'This is Jules Charlie. Who are you?'

'Hi, Jules, it's Bernadette. I'm calling from London for the *Sunday Score*. Tell me, how does it feel to be the biggest plonker in Britain?'

# 70

Over the following three weeks, 'Utter Silence' by Jules Charlie sold 1.5 million units. It was selling so fast there wasn't time to count them all. It seemed a dead cert for the Christmas number one even though none of the radio stations would play it.

As a matter of fact Mike Delta did attempt to prove that they really were playing it every time you couldn't hear anything else on a station, but the Performing Rights Society wouldn't buy it.

Jules went into hiding.

There were a few photos of him as he arrived at Heathrow, shielding his face and looking like death warmed up, but he had shaken the pack as he left the airport and no one had seen him since. No one knew where he had gone to ground, not even the record company.

His flat was staked out, as was the studio. All his usual haunts. The Batsman was doing a roaring trade by occasionally hinting that Jules had popped in for a pint, but still he remained undiscovered.

Frog, Terri and the guys rushed back from Spain as soon as they realized what was going on, doing occasional interviews about how they didn't know what was going on either and hanging out at all of the most stylish nightspots in London, hoping to get their picture taken so they could protest about invasion of privacy and sue someone.

Money heaped up from sales and royalties at an alarming rate. The financial circumstances of Luggage Records swerved dramatically into the black and members of the band had to employ secretaries to fight off unsolicited calls from financial consultants.

But still no Jules.

Mike started to get annoyed. 'How can I develop this guy's career if he won't show his face? I've got every newspaper, every magazine, television, everyone begging me for interviews and PAs.'

'If I was you, right, I'd stop pratting about, expecting him to pop up and thank you for all this and think more along the lines of an apology.' Brian (I've got a nice tan in the middle of winter) Payedwell wagged his finger at Mike. 'If it was me, I'd 'ave come right out and smacked you up. You've got to let the boy come out and save a bit of face. This is the second time you've stitched him up.'

'All right, point taken, but how can I apologize if I don't know where he is?'

'Good question, Mikey, what about a party?'

'A party?'

'In his honour or something, you daft bugger. Come on, it's Christmas for God's sake, can't you even think of an excuse for a party? How many records 'as 'e sold?'

'About one and a half million.'

'So wassat make it, Silver? Gold? Or what?'

'Triple platinum.'

'Well, there you go. Get all the old mob together and have a real blow-out for that.'

# 71

'Hi, Dreadnaught, can I help you?'
'Glenny! Guess 'oo.'
'My God! It's Brian whoops-where's-my-client-gone? Payedwell.'
'The same. Alive, well and just back from Torremolinos.'
'Sounds like a contradiction in terms.'
'Don't be like that, this club, right, was really good. I've got down to a thirty-seven handicap.'
'Look out Nick Faldo!'
'Don't be like that. Anyway, Glenny, what are you doing over there?'
'I'm leading a normal life for a change. No music, no bullshit. I have this really good arrangement where they tell me what to do, I do it and they pay me. It's that simple.'
'Sounds dull.'
'I like it dull.'
'Listen, I need your help, Glenny. I'm trying to find Jules.'
'You and the rest of the world.'
'No, we're trying to sort out a do for 'is Crippled Platypus or summink. You 'aven't 'eard from him, have you?'
'No, Brian,' she said through clenched teeth, 'I have not heard from him. As I told those wonderful people from the press. I don't know where he is, we've split up. Actually there was an extra bit for the press, but I'll spare you that because there is somebody with me in the office.'
'Haven't you two sorted yourselves out yet? Come on, Glenny, we're only trying to make it up to him.'
Glenna changed her mind, gave him the postscript anyway and slammed down the receiver.
'Heavens, Glenna,' said Jeff. 'I shall have to get some earplugs.'
'I'm sorry, Jeff, I didn't mean to dump my problems on you, but I'm getting seriously harassed.'

'That was Rolf, was it?'
'Sorry?'
'You know, Rolf (hee-haw) Harassed. Hhhhhuh. And er . . .'
After ten minutes and a cup of coffee Glenna thought better of it and called Brian back.

# 72

The Angler's Wrist is a hotel. Not just any hotel; it has a river frontage. And not just any old stretch of stagnation to flush your raw sewage and chemical waste either; this is prime Thames frontage in Windsor. Royal turds pass this way.

Henry Stopp was suspicious. The girl who had booked the banqueting suite had seemed nice enough, but some of the decorative requirements smacked a bit of the music business. Inflatable guitars, whatever next. Inflatable women, I shouldn't wonder. The manager of such an establishment has a tradition to uphold.

Henry Stopp had once had to cancel a party for the McCartneys during all that business with the marijuana in Japan. In jail; wouldn't you know it. And he always looked so clean on the television.

They were extremely lucky to have been able to book it at all, come to that, what with Christmas and everything. Most peculiar the Entropies cancelling that very morning. Such nice people the Entropies. Never mind. Cheer up Henry, he told himself, worse things can happen to a sailor.

# 73

It was 23 December. White Christmas lights were burning brightly in the trees around the hotel as they carried all the bits and pieces in for the party. It was late in the afternoon and darkness was conspiring with the mist to draw in the night.

Glenna and Helen carefully lifted the cake out of the back of the Volvo.

'Don't think you're getting away without carrying 'owt, you lazy bastards!' Helen yelled over her shoulder to Mike and Brian, who were heading for the door. 'There are two more of these in 'ere!'

'Do you reckon he'll show up?' said Glenna.

'Jules? 'Course he will, Chook, no one can resist a bit of grovelling. Has he not called you yet?'

'Not a dickie-bird.'

'I'd dump the bugger.'

'I did dump the bugger.'

'Oh, yes, so you did. But I still think he could have called. Bloody men, eh? They're all the same.'

Everybody knew that the platinum-record presentation was just an excuse for a public apology by the record company. A story about it had appeared in one or two tabloids and Mike felt sure Jules would have got the message.

Glenna had been a godsend. She it was who had conjured up the venue and made all the arrangements. She also drew up the guest list and sent out the invitations.

She sent them all to music-business people. James Deek was extremely surprised when he got one. CBA had been held off the number-one spot with their re-re-re-release of 'In the Winter Time' and the whole episode had soured his relationship with the Nagramiwa Corporation, who were wondering how he had allowed such a golden commercial opportunity to slip through his hands.

He had not replied.

Bernadette MacAlister was also surprised, but she put it down to publicity-seeking. She was always prepared to consider free booze and the chance of a story.

By eight o'clock, all was in place and the types of people who turn up for parties at the time on the invitation started to turn up.

Henry Stopp fussed in the reception area, directing people here and there and trying to keep them out of the public areas. 'No sir, the private bar is through there, that's right, just follow the noise. Sorry madam, can I take that? Just through there, that's right. Heavens! Mo Gordon, love. I didn't expect to see you here.'

By nine o'clock, the place was pretty full. The band was playing and the champagne was sloshing about, but still no Jules.

Henry hovered around Helen and Mike, waiting for the signal to move everybody into the dining room. He wanted to serve the meal before the staff ate it all.

'Shall we say five minutes, Miss Denture?'

'Make it half-past.'

'Well, we did say that it would be 8.30 and I really feel it would be rude to the guests to make them wait . . .'

Helen gave him her withering look. Henry Stopped.

Bernadette was ecstatic. A snub was on the cards here. She scribbled furiously in her notepad. She could see the headline 'CROWNED JULES STILL MISSING'. She circulated over to the bar again.

Glenna, Frog and the rest of the band formed themselves into an exclusive huddle around a small table by the bar, trying to be calm and avoiding Bernadette as best they could.

At 9.40, Helen had to give in and they all gathered at the tables.

The tables were laid with the traditional Christmas bits and pieces. Crackers, balloons, evergreen vegetation and a little present for everyone, which turned out to be a set of earplugs neatly packaged and bearing the legend 'More Silence'. Everyone played with these for a while, sticking them in their ears, up their noses, up other people's noses and finally in each other's drinks.

The meal was pretty average. Not exactly horrible. Thumbs in the soup, elbows in the ear and gravy in the lap were all kept to an absolute minimum, but there was nothing particularly wonderful about it.

The Christmas decorations glittered and swung from a tree the size of Norway. The guests popped poppers, pulled crackers and wore stupid hats, but the atmosphere was muted. Embarrassment tinged with the irritation of being let down when the famous person doesn't turn up at an otherwise good lig.

There was a minor stir at eleven o'clock when James Deek arrived after all, and upstaged the dessert.

'Hi,' he said. 'Sorry I'm late.'

He stood pointedly at the top table and waited while Henry Stopp fluttered about, trying to make room for him.

'Helen, love, how are you? Are you sleeping with any of these charming people or have I got to hide my car keys?'

'Don't worry, I 'aven't 'ad that much to drink, Chook. Sit down, take the weight off your overdraft.'

Henry was still rearranging the cutlery.

'Don't worry,' he said. 'I'll sit in Jules's place, I gather he hasn't shown up. Bad form, if you ask me. Such a lot of trouble. I don't tolerate that kind of thing from my artists.'

'I didn't think you had any living artists these days,' said Mike, shuffling round. 'Such an expense. How are things with Nagramiwa?'

They smiled at each other with calculated politeness.

The in-house sound system was playing the usual selection of Christmas records and nobody was paying much attention, but it was then that the crowd became dimly aware of music outside the room.

It grew louder, apparently coming from the river. They all fell silent. Lights and movement could be seen outside.

Mike stood and walked over to the french windows to find out what was going on. The music was getting louder and now clearly identifiable as 'Screaming for Your Love' by Neil Down. Curiosity got the better of the rest of them and they all crowded round the window and watched as a huge boat slid into view.

The boat put the Christmas tree to shame with white floodlights and whirling pin-spots dancing on the water and the trees around it. Any part of the superstructure not supporting a light supported a loud speaker. The PA spat kilowatts as it pulled up alongside the hotel lawn some twenty yards away from them. The crowd held its collective breath.

Helen and Mike glanced at each other apprehensively and

tried to look as though it was part of the plan. James, sensing the apprehension, had a go at the 'I'm in control' look, but it came out 'Jabba the Hut' as usual.

The crowd were just relieved that a rather boring party had picked up a bit. They fancied it might at least be Father Christmas with some early presents.

Bernadette scribbled fit to bust.

Moments later, the lights on the boat suddenly crashed downwards on to the deck, flooding it with a million candellas and illuminating a band, in front of which was none other than the great Neil Down in person. He screamed and the band played.

The crowd surged through the french windows on to the cold lawn. Bernadette had a spontaneous orgasm and bloody nearly dropped her pint of lager.

Henry Stopp, waving his arms and squealing in protest, got flattened in the stampede.

As everyone gathered on the bank in front of the boat and, as the song got into the second verse, Mike suddenly recognized the guitarist around whose shoulders Neil had draped a chummy arm and was singing in harmony.

'It's Jules!' he yelled at Helen and pointed at the band. 'It's Jules. What an entrance. I love this guy!'

'So that's where he's been. The crafty bugger.'

Jules ponced up and down a bit with Neil, large as life and doing his odd dance. He looked slightly embarrassed but none the less was clearly enjoying the moment. The song rose in its final crescendo, and the wall of sound collapsed into silent rubble. The lights blacked out.

An instant later a single spot picked out Neil as he stood with his arm still around Jules's shoulders.

'I believe you wanted to talk to my friend,' he said.

The crowd cheered and clapped.

Jules stepped forward. 'Ladies and gentlemen,' he said. 'James, Mike, Helen.' He extended an arm in their direction, 'Delta, Deek and Denture.' He giggled. 'Hey, that's a great name for a band. Excuse me for wobbling, by the way, but I found it necessary to partake of the odd Scotch on the way up the river tonight.' He giggled again. 'Anyway, all of you. Those of you from CBA, those from Luggage and those of you from the press. I would like to thank you all for the platinum record and everything and for making this year a very special year for me.'

He bowed low and looked uncertain about how to stand up again. He pulled himself back into the vertical.

'I would thank all of the people who bought the record,' he continued. 'I would like to thank them, but my personal belief is that they're all stark staring bonkers and that therapy is probably the best thing for them.'

At this point astute observers might have noticed the absence of Glenna, Frog and the band from the assembled throng. They might also have noticed that the huge boat was not exactly a river cruiser, but no one did.

'I would also like to apologize for any anxiety my recent absence may have caused any of you, and I would like you to consider this a special tribute from me to you.' He bowed again.

The crowd gave a rousing cheer and clapped enthusiastically. This was turning out to be a great party after all. They edged forward eagerly as the band reappeared on deck and Neil stepped forward once again. The lights powered back on, this time illuminating the lawn.

There was a sound. A deep roaring, rushing sound. For a moment they imagined it was the opening chords of 'Deep and Dirty', a particularly good live track. Some of them started to applaud. But it wasn't that.

It was instead the sound of an industrial-strength, fire-department-approved, diesel-powered marine pump, as they discovered a moment later when 750 gallons a minute of best Thames water exploded from a water cannon mounted on the prow of the boat and into their eager faces.

Water, mud, effluent and small fish were sucked up from the pipes behind the boat and visited upon them as Jules grabbed the cannon and blasted them all off their feet and into a muddy heap. Just like Luke Skywalker in *Star Wars*.

'Yes! Yes! Yes!' Jules cried in his ecstasy.

'AAAARRRRRGGGGGHHHH!' went the muddy mob.

People fell this way and that, tried to stand, fell over, rolled and wriggled, writhed and screamed in sodden surprise. Brian jumped into the river itself, Bernadette lost her shoes, her notepad and her sneaky, secret tape recorder. James Deek ended up underneath Helen Denture again.

Back and forth over the crowd Jules played his watery finale. If anyone looked like getting up, he splatted them back down. He paid particular attention to anyone wearing anything flimsy and managed to defrock the majority of the Luggage secretarial team and delight Mo Gordon.

The roaring and the screaming finally died to silence.

Henry Stopp lifted himself on to one elbow and gazed at the mayhem in stunned disbelief. He decided that unconsciousness was a better bet and passed out again.

Glenna, Frog, Alec and Juno, watching the scene from a safe distance inside the hotel, danced an ecstatic dance and cheered loudly.

Taped Christmas carols were still playing in the background.

'A toast,' said Frog, raising a full glass that might or might not have been his. 'To the Entropies!'

'Yo!' said Juno.

'God bless Mummy and Daddy,' said Glenna.

'Yo, again.'

'To Dreadnaught.'

'And thrice yo.'

'This a great party, man; I love surprises.' He smiled a conspiratorial smile. 'When did Jules call you?'

'When he was still in Nashville.'

'He gets homesick walking to the corner shop.' He surveyed the mudbath outside. 'I didn't know he knew Neil Down.'

'He didn't. Apparently Neil took pity on him when he heard about the gig at the Sad Sax and had him rescued from Heathrow and hidden up at one of his mansions in Maidenhead.'

'You should go into the party business. This was a classic.'

'It was in a good cause.' Glenna smiled a wicked smile and swallowed the rest of her gin and tonic with a flourish. 'So, how is Terri?'

'Don't ask.'

'Suckmuckdoo, mate, that's what I say.'

# 74

The whole event took slightly less than thirty seconds and, before the heap could recover itself, the boat pulled away from the bank. Jules jumped off the deck and on to the lawn as it left.

Mike saw him coming and decided, cowardice being the better part of discretion, to leg it.

Jules gave chase. 'Come back, you shit, I want to talk to you,' he yelled as they both vanished inside the building.

Neil Down was last seen clinging to the mast, videoing the scene for posterity as the boat disappeared back down the river.

Mike, covered in slime, ran through the dining room and into reception. People moved apart like the Red Sea as he burst among them. He looked around to see where the exit was and was about to dive out of it when Jules cut off his escape.

'You record-company whore!' said Jules across the heads of the bemused. 'Stand still and talk to me for once in your life.'

The record-company whore ran back into the dining room, closely followed by Jules.

Jules caught up with him at the cake stand and grabbed his shirt. Mike crashed into the cake, and sprawled in the gunk at Jules's feet.

Jules was breathing hard. 'You made me look a total wanker, arse-wipe; you turned me into Goofy meets Frank fucking Spencer.'

Mike looked at Jules, who was foaming gently at the mouth.

'It had to be done, Jules, it had to be done. Christ! We had a hit with complete silence, doesn't that really make a statement? Doesn't that make you think? I mean, how can you take the music business seriously if someone can have a hit record with nothing on it at all? You've just got to get it in perspective.'

He started picking bits of cake out of his hair.

'You have to decide whose world you want to live in, Jules. Music is big, I mean it's, like, a total phenomenon. The world is full of music and music is full of people. People like the man next door who works at the bank and sings in the Godalming Opera Company, music teachers who play piano badly in assembly, school choirs, folk clubs, jazz clubs, people who whistle in the street, guys beating logs in the jungle.'

He reached up on to the table and took a swig out of a random glass.

'Sure, it also includes the great and the famous, man, but basically there are millions and millions of people playing music just because it's good to do. Why did you do it, for God's sake? Because it was fun, right? Music ... is ... fun!'

He jabbed his finger into Jules's chest on the beat and then wiped his hand on his jacket.

'And over in one microscopic corner' – he pointed at the french windows – 'is the Music Business, where a couple of hundred people make lots of money.'

Jules peered blearily into the garden.

'And that microscopic corner is full of people like James Deek who build high walls around it and like to believe that that's all there is. Don't live in his world, Jules, live in your own. You don't need their permission to be a musician, man, if you play music you ARE a bloody musician. End of story.'

Mike tried to brush the mud off his trousers. 'I hate you for this, man. I really hate you.'

Jules smiled. 'It had to be done, man, it had to be done.'

'OK, everyone needs to pay the mortgage, I know that. So you make a joke record, another guy works down the filling station, some people even become A&R men. You might make money out of music, that'd be great, but don't let the business rule your life. It makes no difference to the music, man, if you want to play, then play.'

'I'm a writer.'

'Well then, write. Whatever turns you on. Just do it and stop complaining.'

Jules looked at Mike and laughed.

'That was one son-of-a bitchin' entrance, wasn't it?'

Mike laughed back. 'We'll probably sell another million records when the story gets out.'

'How much money have we made on that poxy record?'

'Just short of a million quid.'
'What kind of a plonker makes a million quid out of utter silence?'
'Love this business!'

# 75

## SLIME TO THE RIDICULOUS

Heroic failure Jules Charlie made a bit of a splash at his party last night to celebrate the 1,500,000th sale of That Bloody Awful Record. He showed up late with rock legend Neil Down and several billion gallons of uninvited sludge which he generously donated to the rest of the partygoers in an orgy of sex, mud and rock and roll.

But the rock and roller-coaster rolls on, and sales of his classic anti-hit, 'Utter Silence', have now exceeded two million. The joke may be thinner than Michael Jackson's nose but his bank account just keeps getting fatter. Charlie's personal fortune, now estimated to be in the region of 2.5 million, has accumulated in a little over six weeks and sets a new British record for achieving unspeakable wealth with unseemly haste. There is reported to be much celebration down at the offices of the Inland Revenue.

Charlie, who once referred to yours truly as a talentless bitch from Hell, expressed his sincere regrets in a heart-warming night of kiss-and-make-up down at his Squelcheramic Christmas Groove. He told me confidentially that his plans are to co-write with Neil Down for his next album, get the band back together and to marry buxom Glenna Washington (31) although not necessarily in that order.

Jules and Glenna did not read Bernadette's article. They were asleep and would remain so until at least Monday. They slept the sleep of the just. They slept the sleep of the just had sex.